The
POISON FLOOD

ALSO BY JORDAN FARMER

The Pallbearer

The
POISON FLOOD

JORDAN FARMER

G. P. PUTNAM'S SONS
NEW YORK

PUTNAM
— EST. 1838 —

G. P. PUTNAM'S SONS
Publishers Since 1838
An imprint of Penguin Random House LLC
penguinrandomhouse.com

LIBRARY OF CONGRESS CATALOGING-IN-PUBLICATION DATA

Names: Farmer, Jordan, author.
Title: The poison flood / Jordan Farmer.
Description: New York : G. P. Putnam's Sons, 2020.
Identifiers: LCCN 2019049459 (print) | LCCN 2019049460 (ebook) |
ISBN 9780593085073 (hardcover) | ISBN 9780593085080 (ebook)
Classification: LCC PS3606.A7176 P65 2020 (print) | LCC PS3606.A7176 (ebook) |
DDC 813/.6—dc23
LC record available at https://lccn.loc.gov/2019049459
LC ebook record available at https://lccn.loc.gov/2019049460
p.   cm.

Printed in the United States of America
10 9 8 7 6 5 4 3 2 1

Book design by Nancy Resnick

For all the longshots and the lost causes
Achieve your glory

The
POISON FLOOD

I

TROUBADOURS

THE GHOSTWRITER

Two Days Before the Contamination

'm chasing a song down the neck of my guitar when the pain in my back breaks the spell. The fighting cocks across the creek crow in added interruption, and I know it's pointless to continue. I can work past the pain, but never the racket of the chickens. Just one rooster singing is enough to make the others convene an ill choir, all their voices rising in shrill music that spills through my walls. Sometimes the distraction tempts me to go free the flock from their coops, only I'd never get past Mr. Fredrick. Generations of his birds have fought in the local pits, their spurs adorned with razor blades that gouged through opponents' feathers. In Coopersville County, anything accustomed to that much violence is worth protecting.

My lost melody had repeated in a loop all morning. I thought I'd play until I found a bridge, but songs are fickle. They rarely appear fully formed. Most must be mined slow from the subconscious in fragments. The tune won't drift back, so I light a cigarette and remind myself not to worry. It's just another love song I owe Angela.

Caroline is playing in the other room. I grab my cane and shuffle across the floor littered with dirty clothes. The place smells like an animal den. Beer bottles rest on the bedside table and the ashtray overflows with crushed butts. A few of the filters are marked by Caroline's lipstick. I try to recall last night, but my back protests with each step until I can't remember our evening. Everything will remain foggy until I swallow a few pills.

In the living room, Caroline strums my unplugged hollow body. She still can't quite create proper barre chords. Each note is full of static, but her rhythm is coming along. The guitar presses into the white of her bare thigh as she leans over the instrument. Blond hair dangles against the strings and her lips purse in concentration. Lacquered nails rub the fret board as she shifts to a C chord to play one of the many cowboy tunes I've taught her.

"Sounds like cats fucking," I say.

There is no discernible pattern to Caroline's visits. She comes and goes like a stray, often showing up in the middle of the night. Usually, I can sense her before she arrives. I'm not superstitious, but winter nights feel hotter as if warmed by her approach. The air carries a slight electric charge in her vicinity. These sensations should only be brought on by a lover, but I'm uncertain how to define my relationship with Caroline. I'm something between teacher and curiosity. She came to me a year ago, traveling across the creek no one dares to cross, saying she wanted guitar lessons. I should have sent her away, but something inside me was too lonesome for company. There's a classic archetype in our dynamic. The withered expert and the brash student. In the old parables, the reclusive master doesn't get to turn the cocky apprentice away. I guess I felt teaching her was owed, no matter how much I knew it was a mistake.

"I can't get these chords," she says and demonstrates by forming another poor F. "How long before I can just pick it up and play whatever?"

"Depends," I say. My back hurts too much for conversation. I move around the couch to the end table, where my pills lie spilled from the bottle. Lately, I need more to numb the pain and these larger doses transform me into something formless. A euphoric ghost drifting about the confines of the house, content just to listen to records. This new dependency is half the reason I'm behind schedule on The Troubadours' album. Just a few more songs for Angela, then I'm calling it quits.

"What were you playing in there?" she asks.

"It's a secret." I bite one of the pills. I've taken to chewing them just enough to get the chalk taste in my mouth. There's no reason it should, but the medicinal tang makes me numb quicker.

"It's all muscle memory," I say, pointing to the guitar. "You just gotta keep at it. All day, every day."

"How long if I practice for an hour each day?"

"Years."

I sink into the couch above Caroline and hang down the cigarette to let her steal a puff.

"Piss on that," she says, neck still craned back from the toke. Her wild hair brushes against my knee. "Got one of those pills for me?"

"I thought you were quitting."

She's probably taken a few already. I never keep an exact count, but the bottle rattles half empty and Caroline's eyes carry a wet shine. It isn't anything personal. She enjoys my company and is an adamant student, but some things are about need. If I refused her, she'd just sneak and steal them. We both know that truth. There's no reason to debase ourselves by making it a reality.

"I'm trying," she says.

When I don't hand over a pill, Caroline tosses me the guitar and rises to get a drink of water. I watch as she goes, the backs of her thighs red from sitting on the carpet. She leans under the faucet and slurps up a drink while I tune the guitar.

"Remind me what time you got in last night?" I say.

"Pretty late. I borrowed Jeremy's truck."

Caroline doesn't belong to anyone and she makes it a point to remind men. Some of her lovers must feed off the evolutionary principle that they're in competition for mates and that a woman who makes them compete so fiercely is a sort of thrill. I hate knowing but feel so fortunate to have been occasionally included in her rotation, I don't question motives. I believe it's probably the novelty of my body that's responsible for our few nights together. Each time, she ran hands over the great curve of my back that bends me low like a snow-heavy tree. Her fingertips never examined in that clinical way I've often endured. I read somewhere that certain ancient cultures used to look at the misshapen as touched by the Gods. Once, we revered deformity rather than isolated it. When Caroline touched me on those nights, she seemed to be paying respect to whatever force could twist me so severely.

"I'm going to need a ride into town."

"What for?"

"I need a guitar fixed." I wish she'd just offer the favor without questions. I already feel impotent relying on favors. Delivery boys bringing groceries and medicine, Caroline providing rides on the few occasions I slink into town. Sometimes I want to pretend there's no burden in my requests, to focus less on the blatant charity.

"Can't we just stay here and relax awhile?"

Nothing would make me happier, but I promised myself I'd finish the song today. I've been ghostwriting for Angela over eleven years. In all that time, I'd never felt the desire to compose my own work. I thought it would always be that way, but recently I've been inundated with snippets of tunes. Tones invading any silence until I'm compelled to transcribe the strange songs. I've even heard lyrics. Their singing interrupts my thoughts like some schizophrenic episode. Now Angela's tracks are a hindrance keeping me from this new material. Things were simpler without ambition.

"I've got to go to Murphy's," I say. "I'm way behind, so get dressed. Please."

Caroline adjusts her cut-off denim shorts, throws on a light jacket.

"Too chilly for those shorts," I say, but she just shrugs before stepping outside.

I go down the hall to fetch the broken Telecaster from my music room. Guitars line the far wall, shapely acoustics hang suspended next to electrics with chipped paint, the road-raw and pristine, all preserved in the humidified air. My recording equipment sits in the far corner. It's an older outfit, everything analog since I've never seen the use in upgrading to digital. All I do are mail tapes to Angela. The real treasures are secured in a tall gun safe. Inside, early recordings from my days on the road collect dust. The Gibson that Angela gave me is hidden away here, too. It's older than either of us, a 1927 model that she signed and sent for one of my birthdays. I've memorized the inscription but can't bring myself to consider the words. Lingering here is dangerous.

The memories can overwhelm, so I grab the Telecaster and head outside to meet Caroline.

The sky is gray, the mountains hulking over the valley make noon seem like dusk. Songbirds sing from trees on the hillside and chicken shit wafts heavy on the wind. I own the ten acres on my side of the creek, but like most property in southern West Virginia, the land isn't good for much. Nearly all the acreage is hillside. I have no claim on the minerals or timber. What little flat land does belong to me is too stony for even a fit man to farm. Caroline tried to start a small garden last summer in the soured earth. After she lost interest, crows ate the abandoned crops. Now nothing is left but dead tomato vines tied to wooden stakes with old rags and rows of wormy, rotten cabbage protected by chicken wire. Near the tree line of softwood sycamores and hard oaks are the charred remains of my father's church. Fire took it more than a decade ago, but sometimes when the wind blows just right, I can still smell the burnt planks. It's my favorite scent.

Privacy is a necessity for a man who looks like me, so I'm grateful for small blessings of self-sufficiency like the house and my well. Since I maintain no official writing credits on any of The Troubadours' albums, there are plenty of rumors about where the money came from. Theft of the proceeds from my father's congregation, murder of rich outsiders and trafficking narcotics have all been theories floated to explain my meager wealth. The most endearing I've heard is that Angela bought the house for me after she became famous. It has a kernel of truth to it, I suppose, but Angela would never give so much without receiving something in return. Perhaps she might have done it when we were children. Time has a way of severing charitable tendencies.

I don't mind the rumors. A man like me would amass legend

in such a small community one way or another. I'm glad it isn't only over my appearance.

I avoid town as much as possible, so it still surprises me to see Coopersville is mostly dark windows now that the mines have all closed. Crooked politicians promised a return to work and some voters sold their souls to those unworthy men, but I think we all knew the days of descending into the earth seeking frozen fire were gone. The few surviving stores look defeated. I take stock of what's left: the Goodwill, a used bookstore some well-meaning fool opened that won't last till Christmas, two bakeries in constant rivalry and a jewelry store that's almost certainly a front. Shift bosses no longer have the means to spoil mistresses and coal wives with diamonds. There're few people left to shop anyway. Maybe it should hurt more, but town has never meant anything but ridicule to me. My father thought even less of it. Preached hard about the evils found in pavement and streetlights. If The Reverend had lived to see such decline, he'd have proclaimed it God's punishment.

Caroline turns into Cherry Tree, a stretch known for the ramshackle beer joints and prostitutes who stroll the road looking for rides. Legitimate residents either stay clear or roll through the single stoplight with their windows up. I don't spot any girls prowling this early, but a few unemployed miners and their wives stand on the side of the road waving picket signs. They've been camped out for the last three months protesting the chemical companies that poison our creeks. A few college girls from Marshall or West Virginia University, their skin still bronzed despite an overcast April sky, stand alongside them. Each sign shows mountains with the tops sheared off, banners reading BOYCOTT

WATSON CHEMICAL and PROFIT DOESN'T JUSTIFY POLLUTION. I admire the spirit, but the college kids are never in it for the long haul. They always return to campus after a month or so.

The Blackhawk Pawn Shop sits on the right side of a wide turn, its shuttered windows and gated front door closed. A neon sign flashes OPEN and a plastic banner fluttering in the wind reads WE BUY SCRAP GOLD! The building was a dirty bookstore in the town's more formidable years, but Internet porn and the church crowd caused it to fold. Rumor is the pawnbroker bought out the remaining stock. Most of his revenue comes from a back room of dusty adult novelties sold online. I asked Murphy about it once, but he denied it.

Caroline parks in the lot beside a Pontiac.

"Will you wait here?" I ask. My hands are shaking at the idea of being seen. Some child will point, or an old woman will give me a look. I don't want Caroline to see that. To be honest, I'm afraid she won't bother defending me.

"Like hell," she says.

It's better not to argue with her. The pills are in full effect now. A cool tingling has replaced the dull throb until all my extremities feel loose. I'm hollowed out like a rotten log. It took three doses this time.

An electronic bell announces our entry. The floors inside are concrete. The center of the room is filled with rows of aluminum shelves covered in leaf blowers, chainsaws, DVD players, even a full set of Ping golf clubs. Mounted animals hang on the walls. Pheasants frozen in midflight and deer with dazed marble eyes. I keep my own eyes low, avoiding the patrons who I'm sure are looking at me. Caroline leans on the display case housing the pawned engagement rings. She taps on the glass that's trapped all that tarnished love inside.

"Can I help you, miss?" Murphy, the owner, comes forward and rests his arms on the case. He sucks in his gut to look more robust.

"I hope so." A hint of honey sneaks into Caroline's voice, but she doesn't need to pour it on too thick. Some implication in her stare has always let me forget my body. If those eyes can erase my maladies for even a moment, I can't imagine what they do to the average man.

"Hey, Murphy," I say, stepping forward. "Busted it good this time."

"Let me look," Murphy says. He takes the guitar and turns it in his hands, inspecting the scratched pickguard and checking to see if the pickups wobble inside the frame. He twists a tuning peg and listens for the string to wind tighter.

"At least a week."

I don't have a week. If I'm ever getting back to my own writing, I need to finish these songs I owe Angela. I suppose I could record on an acoustic or the hollow body, but that feels too much like half-assing it. Even this close to the end, the tape should sound the way the song is intended.

"You got any antiques I can borrow? I need that tone."

"I can't believe you don't have anything in that music room of yours," Caroline says. She thinks she's whispering, but the drugs have her talking loud. "You'd think all that old shit would be useful."

My collection isn't any secret in Coopersville; still, I don't like Caroline mentioning it. Poverty has made Coopersville a dangerous place, and fear of my grotesqueness is the only real protection I have against robbers. If some of these men knew the true rarity of my memorabilia, they might come take it.

"Wait here," Murphy says. He retreats into the back of the

store. Business pretends to go on, only I remain the main attraction. Most are polite enough to glance while a few stand slack-jawed. Finally, Murphy returns with a seafoam-green Stratocaster and small amplifier.

"Seventy-three," Murphy says. "Will it work?"

I need the whine of a Tele, but I'm desperate. "I guess."

"Try it out," Murphy says.

He holds the guitar out like a squire offering a sword. I haven't played in public for years. Haven't played with a band since my twenties. All I do is pop my pills and write alone in the house. On a rare occasion, Caroline will get a song out of me. I sweep my eyes over the room. Most patrons have stopped pretending to shop. They stand holding the items they were ready to hock, waiting to see if I'll do it. I'm afraid, but it's not the old fear of the spotlight and it's not fear of failing. If I can do anything, I can play guitar. This is something deeper. A concern that if I let the least bit of oxygen reach whatever embers are still smoldering inside, I'll feel the old pull like before.

"Why not show off a bit?" Caroline says.

Sounds harmless, but it's the same as holding sour mash under an alcoholic's nose.

The amp looks as if it's been banged in and out of a thousand touring vans. The screen protecting the speaker is full of small holes, but I've made do with less. Before The Troubadours, Angela and I begged to use the equipment of bands we opened for. Murphy plugs a cord into the amp.

The guitar won't fit my body while standing, so Caroline pulls a stool over from behind the counter. Once I'm seated, it happens the same as always, my fingers proving they are the only part of my body that hasn't betrayed me. While the rest of my genes are hell-bent on destroying themselves, my hands feel noble grasping the rosewood neck. They slide up and down the frets independent of thought, instinctually aware of the right sound to create in the quiet. Music begins to provide, the way it always does, and for one blessed second, I'm not a hunchback playing in a pawnshop. There is no separation between my imperfect flesh and the sublime sounds emitted from the amplifier that crackles out the notes.

The amp has neither distorted channel, nor the vintage whine of the tube amplifiers that provide such voice on my favorite blues albums, but it manages some twang. I drag it along like I'm spurring a horse nearing collapse, force it to create the transition from melody into a solo. Most young musicians are concerned with playing fast, but Angela taught me the real secret is groove. From an early age, she showed me how to slow the tempo and bend the strings until the guitar weeps out a serenade that might scratch the surface of some emotion buried inside any listener. Because that's all I'm doing when I'm playing or singing a lyric. I'm trying to find the emotional pressure points inside the audience. I'm manipulating you as easily as if I could reach out and caress your skin. That's all art has ever been. Unlike other manipulation I've encountered, there's something pure about it.

I don't need to look up from the floor to know the expressions on the shoppers' faces. It will be the same look of awe that blossoms across Murphy's. I let the notes dissolve, then slide back into the chorus. Suddenly, I realize what I'm playing. The first song I ever wrote with Angela. We worked all day in the basement of her father's music store, her acoustic guitar finding the perfect complement to my electric licks. We had no idea the hit the song would eventually become, or what the band we built would go on to achieve. The memories start to hurt, so I strike the final chord and let the amp crackle feedback.

"I've always loved that one," Murphy says. "You don't write any originals, do you?"

I've written most people's favorites. Of course, I'm contractually obligated to never utter that this song is an original.

Looking at him, I know this will be a story for Murphy. Perhaps not anytime soon, but one day he will be sucking on a beer with friends, swapping tales of strange things they've witnessed in their time, and he'll share about the day a hunchback played guitar in his shop. The listeners wouldn't understand. Just have a few laughs at the bizarre nature of the tale, but the pawnbroker will keep trying to explain the way he felt. In the end, he won't be able to manage. It will remain something that only he understands.

THE FAN

Two Days Before the Contamination

When we step outside, the protest is winding down. Signs sag forgotten as most of the college kids stand quietly conversing with one another. Most look bored yet prepared for a few more hours of tepid resistance. The cadence from their singsong chants is gone, replaced by a light breeze that billows through the dirty streets. They'll drift home soon, proud that they took a stand against corporate greed. Only, the toxic chemicals will still be dumped in vacant mine shafts on the blasted mountains, the groundwater still contaminated by years of sludge pond seepage and other pollutants. This anger was only a gesture to make them feel like they'd done something against the inevitable. That sounds like harsh condemnation, but really, what more could they have done? When you're as powerless as we are, even a gesture is something to be admired.

One figure moves through the mass of wilting kids. A long-legged man wearing a dark denim jacket, a brown felt western hat pulled low over his face. His boot heels clack on the asphalt as he hands out flyers. Though he is likely among allies, there is nothing friendly in his demeanor as he hands over the pamphlets. It seems an obligation, the sort of unpalatable task that makes a man commune with those he despises. The college kids don't seem to notice. Most take the papers with a nod. They read with furrowed brows, eyes lingering on the ground as the man moves on to the next cluster of bodies. The cowboy moves fast through the young ones but slows to chat with an elderly couple. He nods in agreement to something said by an old man wearing reflective orange mining stripes on his workshirt. It's during this conversation that I notice the gun belt slung low on the cowboy's hip. The wooden handle of a revolver juts from underneath his denim jacket. Plenty of men in Coopersville County wear guns. Even more own at least one rifle for hunting or a shotgun to kill varmints. Still, the fact that he displays it, out for all to see, it reminds me of the sort of men who walk the aisles of grocery stores with assault rifles on their backs. Carrying a gun for self-defense in a dangerous town is one thing. Walking around with one on display seems to be waiting for the opportunity to use it.

As I'm climbing into the truck, I notice a piece of paper stuck under the windshield wiper. Caroline plucks it up and is in the process of crinkling it into a ball before I stop her.

"Let me see that," I say.

She hands it over. There's not much text, except a bold typeface on the header that reads STOP THE MARCHES AND MAKE A REAL DIFFERENCE. Below is the URL for a website. I look out the dirty window to check if the cowboy is handing out any more pamphlets, but he's gone. I shove the paper into my pocket while Caroline secures the guitar behind her seat.

It takes us an eternity to reach home. Caroline accelerates

into the curves and is late applying the brake, but the pills have me too high to mind being tossed around the cab. Out the window, trees with trunks white as false teeth pass by. Crows pick a few bites from roadkill splattered across the margins before flying away from our approaching grille. Steve Earle's "Copperhead Road" plays on the radio, but I turn it down. Music only makes the memories of Angela stronger. Better to listen to tires on the busted blacktop, the wind rushing in through the cracked windows. I know she will be in my dreams tonight.

There is no bridge across the creek that separates my house from the lone dirt road leading back toward civilization. It has one shallow bend that can be forded by a vehicle if it rides high enough. The county would build something if I kicked up a fuss, but I view it as a useful deterrent. If anyone wants to find me, they'll have to risk being washed away by a high swell.

My father baptized me in this creek. Broke ice from idle December waters and plunged me under. After my back began to curve, he took me to the creek again. This time a witch woman named Lady Crawford anointed me in oil. She covered every inch of me until I was slick and said that the Lord might provide his salvation. That night I learned two things: I'd never see a doctor and my father would never be sane.

Caroline parks the truck in the driveway and hops out. "Need help?" she asks. She offers a hand, but I just shake my head. Caroline walks toward the house. I watch her go, those long legs cutting through high grass perfect for snakes. Once inside, I check out the website on the flyer, which turns out to be the page for an environmental whistle-blower group called The Watchmen. The site is full of videos of oil spills where animals lie beached and covered in the combustible liquid. Clips where methane gas, only visible through the filter of a special lens, boils from the earth. Fracking operations where Midwesterners can light their tap water on fire. The more I see, the more I begin to wonder just how much the poisoned creek I was baptized in affected my body. Did the pollution change me while I formed in my mother's womb, or was the damage done when my father dunked me? Is there an answer here, or is the reason nothing more than the random shit luck of genetic mutation?

I remind myself that not all the material online has equal merit. The problem with the unlimited information of the Internet is so many fraudulent claims. The ravings of liars, bots and misinformed reactionaries can be easier to find than legitimate journalism. Still, the videos are hard to ignore. What I can't reconcile is the messages of warning on the site versus the man who left the flyer. This seems like the work of a benign progressive group, the sort to push for legislation guaranteeing lower emission rates and recycling programs. The cowboy seemed weary past words.

I should be writing for Angela instead of reading all this, but more and more, all I want is to escape into my secret project. It's a concept album that's been formulating since I began watching the environmental protests happening in my backyard. All the songs are performed by a sick minstrel I've created who travels a wasteland version of America with only his guitar, playing concerts for the beasts along the road or the starving strangers he meets. No narrative existed early on. Just daydreams of the man lost, singing among bleached bones until eventually he found a boy hiding in the graveyard of some city.

As soon as the boy entered the fantasy, I knew I had to finish. I didn't want my own project, but when I picked up the guitar it was like playing old classics instead of writing new material. That's never happened before. I also knew The Troubadours couldn't have these songs. Of course, now that I've made that decision, I'm not sure what to do about it. After I provide Angela with the last few songs I owe her, I've only got enough money squirreled away to sustain a few years of isolation. What I don't have is money for a proper studio to record and master these new tracks, and I can't keep writing for Angela if I want to make my own music again. I'm not that productive.

A bigger issue is whether people will accept the music from me. I decided a long time ago that the world needed my magic but didn't want to hear it coming from such a ruined man. It wasn't just my insecurity. I've watched enough audience reactions to know it's an unpleasant truth. While the grotesque can create, they aren't a welcome vessel for presentation. At least, I used to think this. The moment in the pawnshop has me questioning that belief.

I close my eyes and try to tap into where I left off in the narrative of my last song. The man walking tired and hungry. The boy beginning to lag. The child is ignorant of the old world, so the man instructs his younger companion with history lessons set to music. The lyrics chronicle a world our hubris destroyed, referencing blue skies and lush vegetation the boy will never see. When they rest during the day, the man sings the kid to sleep with songs about places more than ash. The boy hums them when they travel by moonlight. Some nights, I hear these wasteland lullabies when I lie down to rest. Clear and bright, accompanied by the lonesome sound of a harmonica with a busted reed the man has scavenged.

I'm outside on the porch, picking out a verse for Angela when I smell something on the wind. A scent that reminds me of fires from my youth. My father often preached at revival bonfires, the night lit up as if God's power radiated through him. Sometimes the congregation threw books and records they found sinful on the blaze. Those flames always burned the highest. The scent of melting vinyl and old leather bindings lingered in my hair for days afterward.

I see the plume of dust first, then a black hearse materializes in the distance, bouncing hard over potholes in the dirt road. Its windows are tinted a presidential black. Even with mourners at the door, no funeral home ever risked its Cadillac on these trails. When the chicken farmer's wife passed years ago, her coffin was strapped down in the bed of a pickup and brought home to be interred beneath some apple trees. The same with my father. I lean on my cane as the vehicle stops in the middle of the road. The death wagon is an old Lincoln with a grille like a lunatic's smile. Creekwater beads on the polished hood, and I wonder how they ever made it across.

Two men climb out. The passenger is a lanky scarecrow of a man that I recognize immediately. The cowboy from the protest. Closer, I see he's wearing a different western-cut gingham shirt, straight-leg jeans and a rodeo belt buckle that glints in the sun. The brown felt hat sits low on his head as he saunters forward in ostrich-skin boots. The sandalwood grip of a six-shooter juts from the holster on his antiquated gun belt.

The driver resembles no mortician I could've imagined. A young man in dark denim and a sleeveless T-shirt, feet covered in two-tone black-and-white oxfords. Barely an inch of his exposed skin is free of ink. Arms illustrated with arch-backed Halloween cats yowling at zombie lovers who rot in each other's arms. Green-skinned witches drawn like pinups fly across the ham of his bicep, their gartered thighs wrapped around broomsticks as if in copulation. Even the man's neck is tattooed with tiny leaking punctures meant to resemble vampire bites. The only clean patch left is a handsome face. Not the chiseled jaw of an All-American quarterback, but attractive despite chubby cheeks. He fingers the grease-laden pompadour atop his head while the cowboy waits against the car.

"Can I help you?" I ask. I'm a little fearful that they've followed me here. I keep trying not to stare at the gun. The cowboy keeps the same quiet intensity from the march.

"Holy shit," the tattooed one says. His voice is high-pitched like some brat that's never fully matured. Considering his looks, I bet most women must find it a real shame.

Strangers often approach me as if I exist only for their amusement, but this man doesn't have the sideshow glee of someone ready to jeer. No, his face reminds me of the trance my father slipped into when the spirit ran hot and the faithful convulsed with Bibles clutched against their chests. This is the mania of worship. Even before he reaches me, I know this man desires communion.

"I mean, holy shit," the tattooed man says. Closer now, I smell the mint chewing gum smacking between his jaws. The cowboy keeps his distance. He hasn't even acknowledged his partner's excitement.

The illustrated man extends a hand. DEAD tattooed on his left knuckles. LOVE on his right. "My name's Russell Watson. Mr. Bragg, I'm your biggest fan."

"Watson" is a common enough name, but I think of the protests, of the college girls with their picket signs.

"One of *the* Watsons?" I ask.

Russell's face goes red at the mention of his surname. "Don't judge me the same as my daddy," he says. "I despise everything that son of a bitch stands for."

"It's true," the cowboy says. "If he wasn't an ally, I wouldn't ride with him."

The blurted confession explains the tattoos and the odd friendship. Rich kid rebellion, guilt because the silver spoon was acquired at the expense of others. Still, I understand the sentiment. It's the same way I felt about my father.

"I didn't mean anything by it," I say. It's been years since I've felt the grip of a man's handshake. My first reaction is to pull away, but I resist that impulse. Russell jerks my arm hard. He's grinning again, so I start to wonder what he meant by "fan."

"This is surreal," he says. "I hope I'm not intruding."

"How can I help you, gentlemen?" I ask.

"I told you, man. I'm a huge fan. When Victor here saw you down at the protest, I knew we had to come introduce ourselves."

"Big fans," the cowboy says with little enthusiasm. It's clear he's only here because his friend wishes to meet me. He's bored with this errand.

"I think you're mistaken," I say. "I'm not whoever you think I am."

"Come on, man. You grew up playing with Angela Carver. You're an original Troubadour."

I try to control my face and hide the shock. Panic floods in as I construct a million different lies at once. What I need is to remain calm and keep my composure. A lot of people remember I played with Angela as a child. It doesn't mean he's sussed out our current arrangement or knows everything about our history. Still, it's a dangerous precedent. If the truth is ever revealed, it will ruin Angela and steal my anonymity. After all this time, some part of me still wants to protect her.

"You're mistaken," I say.

"No, I'm not," Russell says. "I've seen a bootleg tape of you and Angela Carver playing 'The Poison Flood' from the first Troubadours record. You're in Bowling Green, Kentucky, two years before the album dropped. You guys were called The Ramblers back then, but it's you."

I remember that night. We were onstage in some biker bar, surrounded by hollow-eyed drunks and big-haired women wearing their lover's leather jacket. The microphone smelled of bourbon and my ears rang from the amplifiers until all that remained was feedback. Even then, I knew my hearing would never fully recover, just listened to the swan song of that certain decibel and welcomed it. With the gain cranked loud enough, there was no silence between songs to hear the audience whispering. I could just avoid looking at their lips and pretend all the wide eyes were from the sounds coming out of my guitar.

"I had to meet you," Russell says. "It's amazing that someone from here could make music like that."

We were just dumb hicks killing time, but I recognize the myth building, can see Russell turning a lucky bar band into a bunch of poor kids expressing their resilience through art. Nothing so serious ever crossed my mind. I kept playing because it made Angela need me.

"Listen," Russell says. "Our band, we've been together for a few years. We're all giant Troubadours fans. Murphy down at the pawnshop said you had a lot of music memorabilia. I was wondering if you have anything from Angela Carver or The Troubadours you'd be willing to let us see. Maybe share some of the old war stories?"

I suppose I deserve this for not being more careful. Secrets stay kept by convincing yourself the past never really happened. I should've destroyed all those relics years ago, but I'd just been too nostalgic about past glories. The night I showed Caroline the guitar Angela signed, I'd been drunk with gratitude, looking to impress the beautiful woman who occasionally shared my bed. I needed her to see I'd accomplished something once.

"I played with Angela, but I was never really a member," I say. "I don't really have anything worth showing."

Behind us, Victor rests on the car hood. I'm beginning to discern this relationship. The master and the servant, but I still can't figure how the two hooked up. Even if Russell is in some sort of rebellion against his father, it feels extreme that he'd befriend someone like Victor. It's one thing to resent your family's privilege, it's another thing entirely to actively try to dismantle it.

"Come on," Russell says. "Too big-time to thrill some locals?" Something in his voice sounds truly slighted. I'm not surprised he isn't convinced. My lies never hold water. "I just want to see the stash."

"All right," I say.

Russell smiles, but Victor doesn't budge from his place on the car. "Do you mind if I walk down to the creek while you're visiting?" Victor asks Russell. "I wanna take some water samples."

Russell is visibly deflated. "You'll be missing out on some cool shit."

"You can fill me in," Victor says. "This is important."

"I checked out the website on your flier," I say. "Some pretty awful stuff."

I'm not sure the reaction I was expecting. I blurted it out without really weighing the consequences, so I'm unprepared when Russell offers a solemn nod while Victor perks up for the first time. He pushes off the side of the car, loops his fingers through his gun belt like some kind of matinee cowboy and looks me directly in the eye for the first time.

"What do you think ought to be done about it?" he asks.

24

I'm not prepared for the question. One minute I'm trying to deal with the fresh intrusions of fandom and now I'm being asked what kind of justice is proper. I think about the words on the flyer again, the call against more useless marches.

"I think people should be more motivated than just complaining. Bring about some civil action."

Russell nods again, but it looks like he just wants the conversation to move forward. Victor is disappointed. Head lowered, shoulders weak under the checkered cloth of his shirt.

"The rich are poisoning the rest of us and you think the best course of action is a lawsuit?"

I look to the gun again. The back of Victor's fingers almost brush against the weapon.

"What would you prefer?" I ask. "Guillotines and heads on spikes? I don't think most are ready for armed rebellion."

"You mean self-defense?" Victor says. We let the silence hang between us until Russell clears his throat. He offers me an apologetic smile, something that quietly implies we can all be friends again. Only Victor isn't convinced. His eyes have never left mine, staring as if trying to bore a hole straight through the center of me.

"You're just as useless as the rest of them," Victor says. He doesn't wait for my rebuttal. He turns and walks away, moving down the hillside toward the creek.

"Don't worry about him," Russell says. "Victor's just passionate about the troubles around here."

"Is he that hard on you?" I ask. "You know, being a Watson?"

"No," Russell says. "But he would be if I wasn't proving myself."

I watch Victor go until he fades into the thicket that surrounds the creek on this side of the property.

"How'd you two meet up?" I ask.

"He answered the ad I put out for a bass player. We got to talking about music and bonded quick." Russell smiles at me. "I make a lot of friends that way. All I need is one or two common interests."

"Seems like he must stay busy with the band and the protests. Especially with that Watchmen site."

Russell's eyes go wide at the mention of The Watchmen. "Look, it's better not to mention that stuff anymore around Victor. They booted him out. I guess it's for the best. They weren't getting much done."

"But I saw him passing out their flyers?"

Russell shrugs. "Gotta get people started somewhere, and those guys are a good source of information. Just not willing to do what's necessary."

I see that Russell's grown impatient, so I invite him up on the porch and hold the door as he steps inside. His anticipation is palpable. He nearly vibrates following me down the hall. Caroline is lurking somewhere, but I don't hear her as Russell's footsteps reverberate on the hardwood floor.

"Nice place," he says, but it's an empty pleasantry. My home is impressive compared to most in Coopersville, but Russell is a Watson. This place is a hovel next to where he was raised.

I take the keys from my pocket and unlock the door to the music room. Russell pauses at the threshold to look at my guitars. Eventually, he claps me on the back and lets out a loud wolf whistle.

"Jesus Christ," Russell chuckles. "And you said you didn't have anything." He covers his mouth with his hand, but I'm still feeling the pain from that good-natured slap. Most treat my body like something too fragile to exist. I'm a little pleased Russell could give me a familiar whack before pacing around the room to admire the framed playbills that cover my opposite wall. He's the only person I've met in years who didn't have questions about my appearance.

Russell stops when he spots the safe. "What's in there?" he asks.

"A few guitars. Some autographs."

He plops down in an office chair next to my recording console and crosses his legs. "Can I see?"

We're flirting with danger now. The smart answer would be no, but something about the kid makes me want to share. I punch the code into the safe's keypad and let the door swing open. My scrapbook and recordings are stowed in the bottom compartment, so I remove the guitar without fear of exposing the tapes. I hand the instrument over and watch as Russell orbits his thumb across the tobacco sunburst erupting from the sound hole. He flips it over to read the inscription on its back.

"'To Hollis, my friend and the man the music speaks to, Angela Carver.'" Russell strums a few chords. "So, you were there when those first songs were written?" He begins to pick out the solemn intro of "The Poison Flood." The sound is haunting coming from Angela's old guitar. Even though she always played a bit sloppy, this rendition is the same as the first morning in her father's basement.

"Some," I say. "Not many."

"Did you help write them?"

"No," I lie. "That was all Angela." I can't understand how, but he knows. As sure as people in Hell want water, he sees right through my falseness. I've been careful over the years. Never told anyone about my arrangement with Angela. It's stupid to be found out this way. I let the silence hang to see if he'll push the point.

"But you're 'the man the music speaks to.'" He smiles, releasing me from the need to answer. "You know, what I'm really looking for is something like that bootleg I saw. You have any old recordings?"

I keep my eyes from drifting toward the bottom compartment of the safe. "Nothing like that."

Russell's fingers spiderwalk down the guitar neck. "Well, if you did, I'd pay top dollar. Money wouldn't be a concern."

My first instinct is to tell him to go fuck himself, but I'd be lying if I pretended there wasn't some temptation simmering below the anger. This is an endless supply of cash staring me in the face. A few minutes of tape could be enough to support my own music for years. I could sell him some harmless grainy tracks we threw out. No one would ever have to know I wrote most of the first album. This selfishness evaporates as I remember passing a joint with Angela in her father's basement. If our secret is exposed, all the fallout will land firmly on her. I agreed to our arrangement, so I owe her more protection than just my personal comfort. It might be best to just send Russell on his way.

"I'd even buy this guitar," Russell says.

"I don't think I could part with it," I say and take it from him. I clip the neck on the side of the safe as I'm placing it inside. The hollow ring echoes until I close the door against the sound. I usher Russell out of the room. Any awkwardness disappears once our shoes hit the tall grass outside. He smiles again, the insinuations from earlier now absent. The sudden change is a little unnerving.

"It's just a real honor meeting you," Russell says. "Can I give you something?"

"Okay," I say.

"I'll be right back." Russell runs to the hearse. He opens the tailgate and digs through a mess of cardboard boxes stacked where a casket should lie. "Victor, where's it at?" he calls. The cowboy comes around the car to help.

After a minute of rummaging, Russell returns with an album. The cover is homemade. A black-and-white picture of four men in front of a brick wall. Guitars hang from straps on their shoulders and the drummer sits on a bass drum with THE EXCITABLE BOYS inscribed across it in gothic calligraphy.

"Some name," I say.

"Zevon, man," Russell says. "Give it a listen and come to the show if you like."

"I'll check it out."

We both fall silent, listen to the birds warbling in the trees. The cowboy, Victor, is the first to move. He clears his throat and stands from the hood.

"Well, I'll let you get back to it." Russell shakes my hand again. "Think about what we talked about. The offer stands if you change your mind."

Russell climbs in and the hearse's engine growls to life. The radio blasts a punk track with a screaming, spitfire chorus I can't decipher as the vehicle turns around in my yard. This music seems to linger long after they've disappeared. I look at the record in my hand. Such an effort to avoid attention, then this rock 'n' roll disciple arrives in a car meant to taxi the dead. I suppose you can't send creations out into the world and expect to remain anonymous. I curse Angela for igniting the initial spark so many years ago.

Inside, I make a sandwich before going to lie down in the bedroom. I brush crumbs from the sheets and try to figure out the strange meeting that just transpired. Was Russell threatening me with his knowledge? If I don't sell him what he wants, will he expose me? I consider the angles until Caroline enters the room.

"Where've you been?" I ask.

"In the bathroom," she says. "Who was that jackass?"

"A fan, if you can believe it."

"A fan. That sounds bad."

My clothes stick against my skin with sweat. I'm worried the reek will permeate the bedsheets, but I'm too lazy to undress. At the foot of the bed, Caroline begins to peel her clothes off. There's a profound beauty to her body that anyone would notice, but I'm envious of the glory present in the mundanely normal. When your spine bends, any straight back contains grace. I consider it now, watching her stretch as the T-shirt comes over her head, raises her hair aloft and lets it fall against even shoulders. Their perfect symmetry is only broken by a small raspberry birthmark.

I grow hard watching her, but my mind is racing with other thoughts, wondering why a woman like her could possibly desire a broken man like me. Just like the few other times a woman has touched me, I'm mired in a state of disbelief. Every coupling of my life has been consummated in a fever dream of confusion. An awareness that my brittle body is too malformed for the task. I wonder if I'll ever be able to just enjoy the act, or will I always be scared, programmed with society's disgust at the idea I could ever be an adequate lover.

"We shouldn't do this anymore," I say. "I'm too old. I'm your teacher."

"So, teach me," she says.

The other fear is that I'll be unable to keep this in perspective. Caroline is interested in the pleasure of the moment. I know I'll want more. A woman to wake beside each morning. A partner instead of this temporary respite from my loneliness. Caroline climbs under the sheets. I pull her close, spoon my body around her as best I can, but my poor posture keeps our wet skins from sealing together.

"Don't quite fit, do we?" I say.

"Of course we do." She begins to work on my belt buckle. "Let me show you."

I wait until Caroline is snoring and try to go about my day, but eventually put the album on my turntable. Guitars drowning in distortion, feedback that threatens to burst the speakers. The drummer beats a jack-off rhythm on the snare and high hat. Not much skill to it. Fast four-chord verses followed by a faster three-chord chorus. The soul is right. Seething anger and all the attitude amputated from radio rock.

Two more songs play before I turn it off. If they have a real flaw, it's in repetition of subject matter. Lyrics about werewolves, vampires and other B-movie drive-in horrors. I understand the hearse now. Another part of their brand identity, like Russell's tattoos. Bastard punk children of Alice Cooper and The Misfits, full of Roky Erickson copied madness. Nothing original but dedicated in their ethos. If there is one positive, the kid can write a solid song. One of the best tracks is a piece of Fifties-style prom rock. The song sounds a little like "Earth Angel" if it were written by the monster hiding under your bed.

I'm still trying to process how it feels knowing I'm someone's idol, wondering why he jumped straight to questions about the old recordings. It reminds me of my father's sermons. The night after the old man was buried, I set fire to the church. Stood outside in the pale moonlight and watched the flames climb across the rooftop. The living element grew, devouring the holy planks as the past perished, but the flames hadn't fixed anything. Destruction, I learned, was as impotent as anything else. That feeling has stayed for years.

Maybe I should go and watch these kids, see if listening to their music makes me feel anything. I'm afraid that whatever organ allowed my investment years ago has fallen as ill as the rest of me. I'm afraid that these new songs may simply rot on the vine before I complete them.

Caroline would ask what I was going to do about that fear. I do the same thing she does to silence whatever hounds her and swallow another pill.

THE CHOICE

Day One of the Contamination

Caroline is gone for two days, then arrives late one night in a stupor. I watch out the window through parted blinds, wondering just how bad it will be this time. Her borrowed truck nearly clips a chestnut tree on the edge of my field, but she maneuvers around it, grinding the gears while throwing the truck into park. When she doesn't emerge, I shrug into a robe and go outside to check on her.

"Strip the transmission driving like that," I say.

She slumps behind the wheel as rivers of sweat run down her neck. I reach out to touch her, but she brushes by, pulling at her tank top and baring her midriff to the night air as she complains about some oppressive heat I don't feel. Black bruises that remind me of the spots on a dog's tongue line her stomach. I want to inspect them, but she's too far ahead.

"Are you finished?" I ask when she stumbles on the porch steps. We do this dance every time she goes on a bender. Each new episode is harder than the last, and looking at her crumpled on the bottom step, I'm losing faith in our ability to change it.

Eventually, she lets me lead her into the living room and cover her with a blanket on the couch. I stand watch for a minute. Each breath comes easy, her chest rising and a tiny ragged snore emitting as she exhales.

"I really believed you this time," I say, knowing she'll never hear.

Once I'm convinced she isn't going to vomit, I go back to bed. We won't discuss this later. No questions about where she's been, what she was on or why her stomach was covered with bruises. It'll remain one more thing unsaid between us. I think about all the things I've never bothered trying to articulate. So many of those true moments were put into music. My own way to say the unsayable. I don't know why lyrical metaphor became a substitute for communication, but I don't want Caroline to become just another song.

The next morning, I sulk while she fries eggs. The sight of her in the kitchen makes a bit of the anger ebb away. The scene is normal enough for us to pretend the last night didn't happen. Were it not for the lingering smell of vomit on her breath and the pills beginning their slow journey through my blood, we might seem like normal people. I'm just happy to see her alive, and even though I know my care should override my selfishness and force me to explain how hard these binges are becoming, the truth is I benefit from them. If Caroline were healthy, would she be here? Dependence, I'm realizing with advancing age, is more potent to some men than love. Love can leave. Love can tarnish with time or implode for unknown reasons. I've known better men than myself whose love ended not by one disastrous event, but a slow bleed. Death by a thousand cuts the lovers inflicted on each other. Maybe that's what happened with Angela.

Grease pops in the skillet, speckling the backsplash while we talk about Russell Watson.

"Sounds like a creep," Caroline says. She splashes Tabasco in the skillet and sprinkles cayenne pepper on the bubbling yolk. Caroline likes breakfast so spicy it becomes an act of attrition. "You've gotta be flattered though. It's harder for rich people to get excited. He must really care."

My storytelling technique isn't eloquent enough to make her understand without revealing my secrets.

"You had to be there," I say.

Caroline joins me at the small booth near the kitchenette's island. It forces our knees together. We could sit in the dining room at the banquet table, but I like the intimacy of this breakfast nook. Caroline shakes even more pepper over her eggs. I'm still wondering where those bruises on her stomach came from and what the rest of her body looks like. Watching her eat, I remind myself that her time alone isn't my business.

"Will you play it for me?" she asks while breaking a yolk and sopping up the yellow leak with the corner of her toast.

"Okay, but I don't think it'll be your style."

The vinyl is still on the stereo. I lower the volume, stand close by in case she begs me to turn it off. Caroline just goes on eating, says nothing as the first track ends and the second is half finished. Each song is so brief the album might conclude before she has cleared the table. After the second song, she raises her hand.

"I've heard enough."

I kill the volume, wait for her opinion as if I've written the music.

"It's not very good," she says.

"We established that before I played it."

There is a slip of paper inside the case with recent tour dates. Most are mountaintop honky-tonks where even the police don't venture. Tonight, they are playing in Cherry Tree at a bar called Ace's High. I know the place. The owners change every few years and have struggled to keep a liquor license due to the violence that erupts each night. Recently, a patron was bludgeoned into intensive care with a pool cue.

I don't want to venture out into public, especially not to some bucket-of-blood, but Angela keeps coming to mind. If I don't offer something, maybe Russell will reveal me? Maybe I want to be revealed? It would certainly allow the new songs to get some attention. Perhaps even lead to the recognition I've never had, but that would mean being in the public eye. People will never accept me. I can live with that, but I do want them to accept the music. What I must decide is whether it's enough to see it celebrated through some conduit. A part of me feels like Angela's had her time. Maybe I'm supposed to offer this last bit of protection, but how much do you sacrifice for someone who stopped caring for you a long time ago? There's also the money. How much would he offer for a single piece of Troubadours memorabilia? I need the money if I'm going to record my own album, and Caroline is broke, too. Maybe I could even convince her to use the money for some kind of treatment. A few more months like this and I'm afraid what will happen to her.

Whenever my conscience is divided, it always helps to have my guitar. Just feeling the wood in my hands calms me, so I go into the studio and play for a few minutes. Not any original work, just a few outlaw love songs from my youth. Songs often act as nostalgia. A lyric can put you in the backseat of the Chevy where you lost your virginity. A chord progression can remind you of your grandfather hoeing the garden or bring a certain girl's smile back across time. Music taps right into your subconscious even if the song has no thematic resonance to that moment. Just another application of those emotional pressure points I'm always searching for.

Caroline comes in and kneels next to me. She runs her hands over the scarred wood of my guitar, traces the scrapes around the sound hole from a thousand errant strikes of my pick.

"So old," she says. "Is this your first guitar?"

"I told you, Mr. Freemont's guitar was my first one."

"What happened to it?"

The guitar has been missing for years now, but I can't remember how I finally misplaced it. Now, I'm only thinking of the day I laid hands on it. Those steel strings biting deep into the pads of my fingers, letting me know for the first time that beauty has a cost.

"What was the first thing you learned to play?" she asks.

"Gospel songs."

Her eyes look up at me, letting me know she doesn't want me to stop strumming.

"'Cause your daddy was a preacher?"

"'Cause it was all I had," I say.

She nods like she knows something about that.

TITHES

I received my first guitar after a church meeting I wasn't allowed to attend. I'd been banned from the sanctuary after Lady Crawford's anointing failed to heal me. The book of Leviticus says no man with a defect can approach the altar, so I was made to stand outside and listen to the services. While other local sanctuaries had a steeple and white siding, our church was constructed with rough, split logs the congregation helped fell from the other side of the creek. The amalgamation of untreated oak, sycamore and locust stayed covered in bark. Knots like puckered scars were plentiful and the stubs of sawed branches stuck out from our cabin walls like the nubs of amputated limbs. The fist-sized holes between logs were filled with a mortar made of mud that washed away bit by bit with each storm. I spent that morning peeking through one of these holes.

When my father got what he referred to as "the call from the Lord," he knew no church in town would suit him. His doctrine was too archaic, the demands too pious. His rituals of worship carried a similar strangeness: An opening benediction in my father's rough voice, followed by a brief reading from one of the angriest sections of the Bible. Always Old Testament reminders of the cost of disobedience, never any emphasis on mercy. Jonah swallowed by the great fish, not delivered from it.

Our parishioners were all outcasts. Strange hill folk whom the starched-shirt preachers in town wouldn't want to touch long enough to baptize in the creek. They seemed genuine about the Lord but were full of the worst aspects of superstition. My father's darker sermons appealed to that. Most considered me marked like Cain. Touched by something even the witch lady's holiness couldn't counteract. That morning, they walked past me holding Bibles against their chests like shields.

I mention all this because the fever ran especially heavy on the day I received my guitar. The worshipers came outside after the service still stunned from their trances where they babbled in tongues. They brushed the church's dirt floor from their clothing, unconcerned that the mud they wallowed in was the same ground where wild animals came inside to piss and rut. Lady Crawford exited first. A middle-aged woman with her body hidden in a white dress, her eyes scanning the tree line rather than look at me. Looking back, there was something beautiful about her long dark hair and the sallow paleness of her long neck. Of course, I didn't see any of this back then. She frightened me so much that my eyes could only concentrate on her fingers. The way the yellowed, brittle nails were always caked with earth and how they'd felt rubbing the holy oils onto my concave chest.

Weeks earlier, I had caught her fucking my father. The two of them hidden in the brush by the creek, The Reverend (the title with which I thought of my father) in a continuing state of undress that passion wouldn't allow him to complete. He still wore his coat, pants slid down below white shins as his black wingtips worked for purchase in the dead leaves. Lady Crawford lay underneath him, writhing the same way she did when entered by the Holy Spirit. I still don't know if she refused to look at me because she knew I'd witnessed their sin, or because she failed to heal me.

Annabel Freemont, the daughter of the portly guitarist who played our hymns, followed on Lady Crawford's heels. I loved Annabel. She was one of the only girls my age I ever interacted with and was probably single-handedly responsible for my puberty. Still, I knew she was afraid of me and kept her distance.

Inside, I could hear my father speaking with Mr. Freemont, but their voices were too hushed to discern. I retreated around the building and put an ear against the best listening spot in the wood.

"This is my church," The Reverend said. "I built it with my own hands. I won't harbor those who do not contribute."

"I just don't have it," Freemont said. His voice cracked whenever he raised it. Now I realize this is one of the reasons my father thought of him as a suitable deacon. He needed a quiet man who would offer praise and never challenge his authority.

"For the Lord's house to flourish, we all must sacrifice," my father said. "He requires we all tithe."

"I just don't have it," Freemont said. A whine stifled in his throat.

"Do you believe I would extort you?" The Reverend asked. "Do you think I'm some swindler?"

"Of course not," Freemont said.

"Then why this refusal?" The Reverend asked. "Have you forgotten your scripture? 'One gives freely, yet grows all the richer. Another withholds what he should give, and only suffers want.' Proverbs, Chapter Eleven, Verse Twenty-Four. Do you still say you have nothing to give?"

I heard something passed from one man to another. I sprinted from my hiding place, cautious to be nowhere near the spy hole when they emerged. As I rounded the corner of the church, I almost crashed into Annabel. She kept her head down until blond hair covered her face, strands catching light as if she wore a golden mask. I thought she might tell them I'd been snooping, but she stayed quiet when Mr. Freemont stumbled out and took her by the hand. They disappeared into the tree line as The Reverend came out carrying Mr. Freemont's guitar. I remember how weathered it was even in those early days. Covered in nicks and scratches, strings played so thin they threatened to snap with the next vibration. He handed it to me.

"Carry this up to the house," he said.

In those days, we lived in a three-room camper without running water and only a generator for electricity. Instead of spending time in that hotbox, I took the guitar down to the creek. I sat on a fallen log, pantomiming the finger placements I witnessed Mr. Freemont make. When I strummed, the thinnest string broke, lashing my palm as if in retaliation. I kept at it anyway. Tried to make the odd shapes on the neck that allowed Freemont to perform his plainsong gospel. I knew those formations were the key to unlocking something more. I never made music that day, but it was the start of something.

The following weeks belonged to the guitar. As soon as my eyes sprang open, I had the instrument in hand. I carried it out into the woods and played a racket that frightened anything feral. Eventually, my presence became so normal even the squirrels ceased barking and fled into the leaf-packed globes of their nests. The guitar never fell silent until late into the night.

By the third week, I began to wonder why my father wanted the guitar in the first place. He hadn't sold it to help the church. Looking back, I suppose it was something to keep me occupied. It allowed him to slip away with Lady Crawford.

My fingers had surpassed the malingering pace of dark country ballads, discovering joyous speed. It was during one of those faster sessions that the uppermost string snapped. I tried to repair it, but the severed coil was too short to thread through the eye of the tuning key. I knew my father wouldn't replace it, but I took it home anyway.

I found The Reverend standing in our field, Bible open in his right hand as if about to prophesy to all creation.

"Where have you been?" my father asked.

"Down by the creek."

"With Mr. Freemont's guitar?"

"Yes."

The Reverend's disapproval always read like apathy. It made me wonder why we bothered speaking at all.

"Has the Lord given you skill?"

Even then, I knew any ability had been acquired through diligence. The belief of inherent talent is false. My earliest attempts were an offense to the ear. Any improvement in art comes the same as in masonry. Building weak walls until the apprentice hones their trade. That's the great lie that no artist will ever tell you. They need the myth of talent to make them feel chosen and to weed out competition. Teaching myself without even rudimentary materials helped chip away that conceit with every new sound I discovered. Not that The Reverend wanted to hear that. He needed to know if the Lord finally granted me a gift.

"I don't believe so," I said.

"I've wondered why God has seen fit to give you so little. I've prayed on it. I would never question his will, but I long to have understanding. Or lacking that understanding, some sort of peace."

It's the most my father ever said on the subject, but by then I didn't need to hear it. I understood life was largely just a roll of the dice. Lightning must strike somewhere. Waves must break against rocks until they are eroded down, and with enough rain the creek must rise. Some days this randomness is still a comfort. Other times, I wish there was a force I could lash out against. A God to curse instead of whatever internal mechanism inside my body failed to perform. In certain moods, celestial tyranny is still more comforting than poor luck.

"Make yourself presentable," The Reverend said. He pointed to the mud caked on my boots. "We're going to town."

The downtown we saw that day didn't last. In those early years, the main thoroughfare was a constant throb of people, men and women exiting shops with parcels under their arms, wallets lighter than on arrival. Children roved in mischievous packs, laughing and nearly ungovernable now that they finally had concrete underfoot. Lights shone from every storefront and cars belched exhaust on every corner.

Most of those downtown buildings are gone. The department store at the corner of Main burned when I was twenty-five, a mystery blamed on insurance fraud, its remnants looted for copper by vagrants. The Methodist church was eventually abandoned, the windows busted by kids and the pews filled by drifters needing a night with a roof overhead. Other structures endured the sharp decline, but eventually the sort of decay my father liked to preach about seeped in. It wasn't divine punishment that crippled my home, just the cold economics of a state where energy companies have a monopoly on jobs and a society that has little need for men to toil underground extracting coal anymore. After outside money gutted this place, the mines closed. As I look back on how it was, now Coopersville is only the memory of a town. The streets littered with solemn reminders of what once occupied each corner.

That morning, I watched families shop while The Reverend drove. Mothers in their best dresses, fathers smoking or shoving wads of tobacco into their jaws. Teenagers in stone-washed denim. A few of the rich kids walked with headphones in their cars as if worry were a foreign concept. I sweated at the prospect of exiting the truck. I didn't want people looking at me.

We made a left turn at the end of Folsom Street and parked in the lot behind Perkins Hardware. The marquee above Carver Music greeted us with its tall, black letters. Even before The Reverend rounded the truck, I knew we were selling the guitar.

"Come on," he said.

Inside, the display floor was filled with blinding fluorescent lights. Scents of wood polish and wax filled the air. Dented brass instruments hung on the walls as decoration. The shop was laid out in sections. The pianos, both the upright and baby grand variety, positioned near the entrance. Giant music boxes with pools of black wood and elegant ivory keys. I'd never seen anything like them before, and if I concentrate hard enough, I can still feel that distant awe at so much space devoted to tools of creation.

A small man, his shirt pocket overflowing with loose cigarettes, came past the drum kits where cymbals hovered like midnight movie UFOs. Something about seeing him made me realize my true purpose in the interaction. I was a bargaining tool. A sad sight to elicit enough pity that the owner might fork over real money.

"I'm looking to sell this," The Reverend said. He held out the guitar as if it were something unclean.

"What were you looking to get for it?"

"Whatever it's worth," The Reverend said. "We're putting the money towards my church. Repairs and the like."

The church comment was also meant to soften the man, but the owner remained unimpressed.

"I ain't the expert on guitars," the man said. "Best check downstairs with Eddy." He pointed to a staircase descending into the basement of the shop.

"Let's go, son," The Reverend said.

The carpeting hadn't been fully installed downstairs. Just cut in long strips and tossed over the concrete. It might have been cream-colored before stains darkened the shade. Guitars hung around us on every wall. Seafoam-green Fenders and sunburst Les Pauls. A blood-red Gibson SG, its body resembling some sort of sleeping bat. I'd never seen instruments like that in person. We had no television or Internet, but I heard plenty of rock on the radio despite The Reverend's attempt to shelter me from such evil. A man can't battle all the invisible waves coursing through the air. I remember a profound sadness knowing he wouldn't let me touch one.

An amplifier hummed at the end of the row, feedback whining as a mustached man sitting on another amp toggled the switches on his guitar. A girl with deep-red hair sat beside him. Freckles dusted her nose and mascara branched from her eyes like some Egyptian princess. Her solid black clothing was covered in patches of various rock bands I'd never heard of. Everything about her felt sharp-edged and violent. Even her boots ended in a long stiletto heel that tapped in time with the music emitting from her fire-red Stratocaster.

Watching, I noticed her fingernails were the color of overripe blackberries. Her plump lips smeared with the same shade. The only women I saw on the mountain were modest girls from my father's congregation who feared painting their faces and wore dresses that hung shapeless over their bodies. Even if the young runaway look was a staple for rock chicks wishing to be Joan Jett, I couldn't have imagined a girl like Angela Carver before seeing her.

The man let his fingers hammer on the strings before bending them high. He only stopped playing because my father cleared his throat.

"Sorry," the man said, brushing the wrinkles from his dark trousers. "I got to fiddling around down here and didn't even hear you come in."

"I was hoping to sell this," The Reverend said, holding out the guitar. "We need the profits for our church."

"Is that so?" the man said. He smiled, but I understood these people hadn't darkened a church door in ages. The girl kept playing, palm muting the strings at the bridge as she strummed power chords.

The salesman led my father across the showroom, and suddenly I was alone with her, trying not to stare as the guitar's groove cupped the underside of her breast.

"What stuff are you into?" Angela asked.

No one ever asked about my interests, and to be honest, I hadn't been given the freedom to foster any. My entire life was situated around what the church dictated. With everything I experienced policed by my father, my only real outlet was the guitar. I was jealous of Angela's freedom. Her ability to sit in the basement and play music all day, to wear the patches of bands on her clothing and paint smoky eyeliner on her lids. She had some level of control over her identity.

"Music?" Angela said when I didn't answer. "What kind of music do you play?"

When she looked at me, her dark irises neither contracted in confusion nor dilated with fear. I knew she had to have questions about my appearance, but I'd become so used to naked disgust I didn't know how to respond to her small talk.

"I don't know."

"How can you not know what you like to play?"

"I've only been playing a few weeks."

"Dad was a music man, so he started me early."

A lock of red hair fell into her open mouth. I watched her chew the strand, her fingers absently making chords on the quiet guitar. "You play electric?"

"No," I said.

"You want to?"

"I better not."

"Don't worry about them," Angela said. She began a slow blues arrangement, her boot tapping in time. "I know who you are, you know?"

I understood how infamous we were in the town. Locals' gossip abounded about The Reverend's cult, whispers about the monstrous child he kept hidden in the hills. Normally, I didn't mind the assumptions, but I hated that it preceded me in this meeting. It hurt thinking she'd never get past the rumors.

"It's kind of strange meeting you," Angela said. "I mean, not bad, just different."

I waited for the questions. Any time things progressed past awe or revulsion at my body, the questions came.

"Why do you guys live out there by yourself? Why don't you go to school or anything?"

"I'm homeschooled," I lied. The only teaching I received

were readings from the Bible and drills on how to lie to outsiders. What little bit of culture I found came from books my mother had left behind when she escaped my father. Everything from murder mysteries set in strange cities to romance paperbacks. Both showed me what I was missing in isolation, and how different I was from the masses.

"Must get lonely living out there," Angela said. "You like it?"

"People don't bother me," I said.

Angela nodded. "That's what I like about the basement. I can come down here and just jam."

Angela stepped closer. Her body smelled like peppermint.

"Here, show me something." She offered the guitar.

"I'm not very good," I said, but it was an excuse. I knew what would happen if my father saw me playing with this girl. There would be swift punishment for the rebellion, but despite that I didn't want to refuse her. This was my first invitation to normalcy, and I wanted to feel just a little bit closer to her by holding the things she'd held.

"I give lessons down here after school. I've heard the worst of the worst, believe me."

I took the guitar and strummed a simple three-chord arrangement. Some G, C, D configuration invented down by the creek. Angela retrieved a hollow body outfitted in golden hardware from the wall and plugged into another amp.

Three notes echoed as she played them over and over. I had never heard the song before, but somehow the tune felt familiar. Later, I would learn that's the secret power of music. The true songs, the ones that implant themselves deepest inside us, are the ones that we feel like we've always known. Each one is different yet offers instinctual comfort like a mother's voice.

"*Crimson and clover*," Angela sang. "*Over and over.*"

I watched her fingers and began to take up the rhythm. Once I established the backbone of the song, Angela was free to embellish quick licks on her guitar. Soon we were harmonizing, the sound reverberating through the store so loudly that I didn't hear my father approach.

"Sorry we couldn't come to a deal," the mustached man said, "but it's better this way, I think. Your boy is pretty good."

"We're leaving," The Reverend said.

"Cool jamming with you," Angela called as he dragged me away. I've never wanted more to turn and offer thanks, but I kept reminding myself of the story of Lot's wife and the consequences of longing.

When we reached the car, my father struck me across the jaw. A quick slap with the back of his hand that busted my bottom lip and clacked my teeth together. The blow didn't knock me unconscious, but I had a moment of confusion until the tang of blood brought me back. By then, he had his hands around my throat, pulling and pushing me until I thought he might wring my neck like a chicken.

"You said the Lord gave you no talent," The Reverend said. "Do you want to explain that?"

"I don't," I said. "I'm not any good."

"Good enough to get that jezebel's attention," The Reverend said. "Good enough to play blasphemous music."

I waited for another strike, but my father released me. We drove on in silence with the guitar knocking against my knee. I was scared, so I just looked out the window and thought about Angela Carver. Her fingers with their blackberry-stained nails. What they might feel like prickling up my chest to cover my heart. And in my head the melody was still playing, over and over, just like the lyrics.

THE SHOW

Day One of the Contamination

The signs from the bar cast their neon glow through our truck's windows, rendering the dashboard an iridescent green. An ace of spades and an ace of hearts have been emblazoned on the bar's metal door. Just underneath this, another sign proclaims CHEAP BEER & LIVE MUSIC NIGHTLY. Caroline and I watch the couples arrive and climb down from the tall cabs of their pickups. The women are wispy, their men thick around the middle in western shirts with straining snap buttons. Bodies so normal their imperfections make me jealous. The longer we sit, the more I start to grow nauseous at the thought of going inside.

I always felt sick before a show. Needed to sit alone for a few minutes and just meditate on my breath. Try to exorcise all the fear so that my hands could steady and play. I'm not sure what exactly brings on the upset stomach tonight. Maybe it's Angela's signed guitar, secured in the hard-shell case and resting at my

51

feet. Hidden underneath the instrument in a secret pouch is a 45 record of Angela and me playing "The Poison Flood." The guitar is Russell's if he wants it. I can still deny my involvement in the band if he shows it off, just say it was a kind present from a childhood friend. The record is different. It feels more like a full betrayal, one where I'm still contemplating whether or not the money is worth it.

The plan is to blend into the crowd as best I can and sell the memorabilia afterward. Caroline, however, is dressed for attention. Tight jeans and a dark halter top. Wedge heels and scarlet lipstick. She checks her reflection in the side mirror, and I know I'll be noticed just standing near her. As we climb out, some high school boys exit the bar. Country music washes out on their heels and fades as the door swings shut behind them. They lean against the banisters that hold up the rusted metal awning, share cigarettes and swig from longnecks.

The pack notices Caroline right away, but she keeps moving forward through the catcalls, dodging the deep puddles in the road as she carries my guitar case. Russell's black hearse is parked by the front door where a man struggles to unload a drum kit from its rear. He deposits the bass drum next to the alley entrance and returns to retrieve the snare. After all the drums are accounted for, I watch as he strains lifting a Vox amplifier. Caroline and I step to the side while a bouncer holds the door open for the staggering roadie.

"Wouldn't a van be easier?" Caroline asks.

The bouncer shrugs. "These are some strange cats. Five-dollar cover charge." His eyes move over her body, down to the guitar. "Unless you're with the band."

Caroline hands him two crumpled fives. The bouncer never looks at me, just keeps his eyes buried in Caroline's cleavage.

Inside, the dead blue haze of cigarette smoke swirls as butts burn in outlaw satisfaction at the broken no smoking laws. Men sit upon unsteady Naugahyde stools that sway as they shift. Bar lizards with leathered skin and unlit smokes bend toward offered flames. Glasses clink in the quiet. On a small stage raised only a few feet higher than the dance floor, a man begins tuning a Telecaster while another bends behind the drum kit, his beer belly hanging pendulously over his rodeo belt buckle.

Caroline orders a Jack and Coke at the bar while I climb up onto the stool beside her. I notice no one tips the gaunt, pigtailed blonde who digs low into the cooler, pulling deep in the ice to get regulars the coldest High Life possible. All around is the sense of a community. Acceptance through forced camaraderie like soldiers in foxholes, love at the knowledge one has no other tribe. I wish I was a part of it. I haven't felt included in something since the band, and that was all Angela.

Onstage, The Copper Thieves, the opening act of the evening, begin a low-pitched rendition of Dwight Yoakam's "Guitars, Cadillacs" that sends a few couples swaying to the beat, boot heels stomping a rhythm. I steal a sip from Caroline's cocktail and feel the whiskey burn its way down. She lays a fat tip on the bar despite the obvious breach in etiquette. The blonde's smile looks eerie through the tobacco cloud brightened by red stage lights. The patrons have yet to notice my ugliness. Maybe the haze works as a shroud. If so, I'm thankful for it.

"What's with the hearse outside?" Caroline asks the bartender.

"The Excitable Boys tour with it." The bartender shouts to be heard over the music. "You heard of them?"

"Yeah," Caroline replies. "I'm looking for a certain singer."

"Ain't we all?" The bartender gives her a conspirator's grin.

"His name is Russell Watson," Caroline says. "You know him?"

The blonde shakes her head hard enough to send her pigtails lashing. One wraps around her neck like a constricting serpent. "Don't know them personally, but they put on a hell of a show."

The band plays a southern rock tune that gets the women out on the dance floor. The men slide close and grind. Even though the music is all wrong, the same sort of hoodoo that used to pump from Angela's guitar is in the air. I can feel the power of it infecting the audience, whittling away the hard work week, the cousin in jail and the hollow pain inside all of us poor rednecks that whispers you're nothing but country trash, that if there is such a thing as a soul, yours is made of dog shit. Music was the only thing I ever found that could mute those voices for even an hour, but since I left the band, songs bring on memories of Angela. I wonder if anything good will ever be free of her.

After the Garth Brooks and George Strait covers end, the bearded man with the Telecaster strapped shotgun high across his chest tells the audience to stick around for something different. He leaves the stage to a plump roadie who begins exchanging the equipment for the next set. Couples wander outside or return to the bar for refills. I watch as the crowd begins a slow metamorphosis. Cowboys slink out, as men without a stitch of clothing a brighter hue than gray stalk in. Both males and females are raccoon-eyed with mascara, their faces full of piercings. The Excitable Boys' fan base.

The band comes onstage to the ominous sound of an organ. A fog machine belches across the crowd, catches the purple and blue stage lights as Russell hobbles his way to the microphone on a silver-capped cane. He wears a black suit smeared with dirt, the white tuxedo shirt so soiled it looks as if he's been buried in it for centuries. The shoulders and lapels of his jacket writhe under the lights as live night crawlers hang from his clothing. The slimy bodies drop atop his shoes to writhe blind across the floor. Behind him, the rest of the band stand caked in makeup to resemble ghouls. Ashen faces with bits of drying gore at the corners of their mouths. Bloody wounds drawn on foreheads or throats. Victor plays bass and is the only member not in the black suit of a pallbearer. He wears a new cream-colored Stetson hat and dark boots with rusted spurs. His gun belt is strapped low on his hip. The peacemaker still rides in the holster.

"These are The Excitable Boys," Russell says, pointing at the band.

No further introduction. The drummer and guitar player blast into a deafening barrage that shakes the small space. The crowd surges, slamming into one another and the stage. Maybe fifty kids in all, but the cramped dance floor makes it seem like a swarm beyond comprehension. Russell leans down, occasionally offering the microphone to a fan screaming lyrics. I can't make out all the words through the buzz and distortion, but the kids eat it up. They sing back the chorus. Scream as the guitar player leads the band into a solo.

Even as I watch Russell vomit fake blood on the front row, the music incites a pang of nostalgia. It carries echoes of my own adolescence fueled by hate of The Reverend. Worse, I envy the stage presence. Russell prowls, twirls the microphone or falls to his knees crushing worms into the floorboards. I was always stationary. A man cemented to a barstool or a chair, my body unable to carry the guitar if I stood. Sitting so rooted in place made me feel vulnerable before the audience. Russell controls them.

The Excitable Boys play a full hour. Mostly originals from the album Russell gave me, but a few covers like T.S.O.L.'s "Silent Scream" and The Cramps' "I Walked All Night." They conclude with Jim Carroll's "People Who Died." After the final feedback dissipates, the members drop their instruments on the stage and step behind the curtain without a word. Applause follows for nearly a full minute after.

"You think I could meet them?" Caroline asks the bartender.

The blonde wipes the bar clean with a moist rag. "I guess. On through the back."

Caroline lifts the guitar case, pulls me off the stool and we navigate through the people clamoring for drinks. I squeeze between leather-clad shoulders studded with spikes, women who smell of skunked beer and marijuana. Caroline opens the back door, pushes me inside and closes it behind us. We swim through total darkness, hands searching until I discern the margins of a narrow hallway. We follow the sound of voices down the path.

After a moment of blindness, the room materializes. Strangers mingle around a row of liquor bottles, laughing as they toss back shots or stand in a circle passing blunts. Cigarettes are dropped to the concrete floor and left to smolder out. I search the crowd and find the band members lounging on plush couches augmented with duct tape. The guitarist is smiling at a girl who's picking fake blood from the hair of his goatee. She stops plucking at the coagulation as Caroline approaches, but the band members all keep their seats. Only Russell stands from the chair he's been straddling.

"Are you lost?" he asks.

Streaks of mud run down the lapels of his dinner jacket. He's much taller than Caroline and uses his size to loom over her, teeth exposed in a grin that shows incisors capped with long fangs. He wasn't wearing the teeth when he came calling at my house. I wonder how he can sing with them in his mouth.

"I brought Hollis to the show," she says.

"That's awful sweet of you," Russell replies, but his focus has already shifted to me, eyes brightened by the same hero worship as before. He lays a hand wearing a dirty white dress glove on my shoulder. "I'm really honored you came."

Behind us, two girls lie atop a table. Two men sprinkle their taut stomachs with salt, then lick the exposed abdomens before sucking tequila from the hollows of the girls' navels. Tongues trace their way up toward eager mouths. A vacuum-hard snort through a rolled bill echoes from the far corner of the party and another girl is swept off her feet by the potbellied drummer, swung over his shoulder like a bindle as he performs a swaying dance. Her giggles turn to a cackle that pierces the murmured conversation. She might be nineteen. The same sort of safety pins in her earlobes and black-nail-polished punk as Angela growing up.

"That for me?" Russell asks and points to the guitar case.

"Once we agree on a price," I say.

He nods. "I'm thrilled you changed your mind. Can I offer you a drink?"

"No, thank you," I say. "Just wanna talk business."

"We got plenty of time for that. I'll have to swing by the house for the cash anyhow."

Russell gestures for me to sit. Across the room, Victor sparks a fresh joint and passes it to the guitarist. Remnants of fake blood stain the paper. Everything about the man makes me uneasy. The way he stands off to the side of the party, not engaging with this group of misfits, feels wrong.

I sit and listen to Russell hold court on music. The partygoers lean into his talk, but after about five minutes of his diatribe on X, Caroline asks if they have anything to drink. Victor escorts her to the keg. Russell keeps me cornered, talking so fast about

The Stooges that spittle flies from his lips. Occasionally during his lecture, Russell pulls an iPhone from his pocket and texts someone.

"So, you're a musician?" the guitarist asks me. He's a large man with neatly trimmed, purposeful stubble that I'm tempted to call a "city beard."

I don't know how to respond. I don't want to give up any more information, and I've lost track of Caroline in the crowd. Russell pulls his dress gloves off with his teeth. Lets one of them hang limp from his mouth as he talks. His eyes are covered in enough eye shadow to resemble black holes. "Hollis used to jam with Angela Carver before The Troubadours."

The guitarist gives an amphetamine-induced titter.

"No shit," Russell says and sucks on the passing joint. "He's the best musician in the room." No one challenges the statement.

When Caroline returns, she's clinging to Victor so that half the snaps on his shirt have popped open. Her cheeks are flushed, all the muscles in her face slack. I'm not sure what she's taken, but her eyes have the wet slickness from a fresh line. It's been something strong. Caroline can typically handle enough drugs to stun a mule.

"What's with all the makeup?" Caroline asks. She slurs, tongue too medicated to enunciate.

"Don't we look pretty?" Russell asks.

Caroline laughs and falls against Victor's chest. She straightens up as Russell leans toward her.

"Appalachia is the right place for the grotesque. Don't you think?"

"It's nothing new to me," Caroline says. "I lived here my whole life."

"Then you understand how people see it," Russell says. "A

fatalistic, feudist country. Half the town has a man who's died in a mine somewhere. Some relative who stood in the picket line during strikes. As far as the rest of America is concerned, we're different. Have you seen the protesters?"

We passed the protesters along the highway again this evening. Men, women and children all holding signs attributing atrocity to Watson Chemical. Sludge ponds of mud left behind where the company used to wash its coal, now quagmires rumored to swallow up small animals too foolish to avoid them. One day, when the companies are finished with this place and the strip-mined mountains are free of people, those preserved skeletons will be all that is left. I wonder how Russell really feels about these people. Sure, he runs with Victor and spouts his rhetoric. Even now the lecture he's laying on Caroline is more reciting the things Victor has likely taught him. Still, I'm not sure one could totally turn against their family. It took years for me to dispel my father's influence and even now, on the right sort of night, I can awake with the certainty that The Reverend's preaching was true. That I've lived a false life and eternal Hellfire awaits. If gospel ghosts can linger like that, why wouldn't the influence of something as tangible as money hold Russell's allegiance?

"But what does any of that have to do with corpse paint?" Caroline askes.

"A local girl should have read Anthony Harkins's *Hillbilly*," Russell says. "Heard of it?"

"No," Caroline says. She's wearing a smirk now. The last thing I'd have expected from a man dressed as a corpse is a book recommendation, but I can see Russell is serious. All the swagger is gone. He isn't purring out the information like before. Victor is watching his protégé lecture, a pleased grin on his face.

"Harkins traces the whole history of the Hillbilly as a cultural icon. Used as noble pioneer when Americans are weary of urbanization, other times as something he calls 'the last acceptable ethnic fool.' Something the white middle class can publicly vilify."

I don't think America ever limited itself to one fool or villain. Looking back at our history, no atrocity has ever been off limits.

"You always try to impress girls with this stuff?" Caroline asks.

The fangs appear again as Russell grins. "Is it working?"

Caroline shrugs, collapses into Victor's chest again. I'm beginning to get angry watching this display. Not rage, but a simmering indignation that makes it harder not to say something. I know she isn't mine and I have no right to dictate how she behaves, but I thought she'd have the decency not to do this in front of me. I tell myself it's just the pills, that Caroline would never hurt my feelings intentionally. This does little to soothe the fact her hands are all over Victor, fingers snaking inside the popped buttons to rub his chest as I sit next to them pretending not to notice. Victor seems almost bored with the attention. Accepting, but his mind elsewhere as her fingers caress his chest. I can tell he wants to join the conversation but is too proud of Russell to interrupt.

"The people who truly feel grotesque want to blend in," I say to Russell.

"Maybe that's their problem," Victor interjects. "Maybe they should just embrace who they are. If more people stood up, we'd have control of this country instead of all these corrupt corporations."

Words that could only be spoken by the painfully average. I wonder if my definition of *corrupt* would be the same as Victor's.

I'm about to ask him to elaborate, but am distracted by a woman stepping away from the keg. My first thought is how she reminds me of Angela. There is no physical resemblance; this woman's skin is darker than the translucent pale that let me see Angela's veins, and her hair is fashioned into a pixie cut where a silver butterfly barrette a child might choose secures the few longest locks. Still, her style is all Angela. Faded brown leather jacket, black skinny jeans and a T-shirt bearing the album cover from Blondie's *Parallel Lines*. Each step she takes cools the nearby men's conversations, a funeral-parlor quiet echoing with the click of high-heeled Doc Marten boots. I notice the camera bag that hangs against her cocked hip and immediately understand she is Press.

"You boring these nice folks?" she asks Russell.

"Of course," he says. "Rosita Martinez, meet Hollis Bragg and Miss Caroline."

Rosita takes the seat beside me. She crosses her legs, her heavy boot nearly touching my knee. She's the kind of woman who makes men like me realize how stunted we are. Flawless caramel skin, large brown eyes and a beauty that comes without effort.

"Let me guess," I say. "An artist?"

Rosita smiles. "Is it that obvious?"

"I'm psychic," I say. It's as close to flirting as I'll allow myself. Rosita doesn't even raise an eyebrow, but Caroline spews beer and doubles over into a laughing fit.

"What sort of photography do you do?" I ask, pointing to the camera bag.

"I work for a magazine called *Strange Sounds*. I'm here to write a piece on The Excitable Boys."

Strange Sounds is the younger, hipper version of *Rolling Stone*.

Most hungry journalists would probably prefer it. The sort of place that isn't going to run an article on some band playing Madison Square Garden for the hundredth time, but up-and-comers getting millions of streams or selling exclusively in vinyl. It's the cool gig even if it holds less prestige. I knew she was more than the guitarist's wife or a groupie with an expensive camera, but sitting next to an actual music critic makes my mouth feel dry. Russell may have already talked to her about me. He's certainly made it no secret that I used to play with Angela Carver. A smart reporter would take mental note of that and try to find out just how much involvement I've had with Angela. The night is turning into a trap.

Rosita takes a slug of beer. "You're a musician?"

Before I can respond, the blond bartender runs in with her pigtails flapping. The apron is still tied around her waist, shirt-front wet with spilled drinks.

"Turn on the TV," she shouts.

"We're chatting," Russell says.

"It's important," the bartender says. "Some serious shit is going on."

Russell retrieves the television remote from the end of the couch and turns on the flat screen mounted to the far wall. As he cycles through the stations, every channel displays the same image. A woman in a blue raincoat stands at the edge of the Guyandotte River, wind blowing the dandelion-white strands of her hair across her face. On the far shore behind her, several hulking storage tanks rise behind a fence topped with razor wire. One of the tanks has a deep gash in the bottom corner that pours out a frothing chemical. A wall of sandbags has been laid out in a weak attempt at containment. Overhead, each smokestack expels a continuous cloud that billows and grows, spreading out across the sky until I wonder how the plumes don't blot out the moon.

"We're being told that the spill occurred sometime earlier this evening," the reporter says. "Residents alerted American Water to a strange scent they described as similar to licorice whenever they turned on their tap." She gestures toward the chemical plant. "Others living close to the river claimed they could smell a similar odor in the air. Not much is known about the chemical other than it's used to process coal. It's considered dangerous and can be absorbed through the skin."

Islands of white foam float by on the water's current. Some clumps beach themselves against the weeds near the bank and break up before continuing downstream. Others collide, converging into larger masses. I search for dead fish or animals coated in the froth, but the camera pulls back to the reporter. The screen is split now, a man in the newsroom on the left side, the woman in the field on the right.

"Jessica, do we have any information as to the danger this might pose to residents?" the man asks.

"We don't have any specific information at this time, but the governor has issued an order restricting water use in several counties."

A scroll of names covers the bottom of the screen as the anchor recites the list. The room fills with a prickling energy of panic. I feel it spreading just below the surface, the surge passing from person to person. Victor tosses an unopened beer can at the television as Coopersville County appears on the bottom scroll. It bursts and sprays across the room.

"Motherfucker," Russell says. He points his finger to the dripping screen. "You see how big that tank is?"

Victor removes his hat and rubs fingers through his hair, scratches the stubble on his jaw. "I tell you one thing," he says. "It's everybody's problem now."

"What do you mean?" Russell asks.

"Pretty soon all that tainted water flows to Louisville."

"It'll dilute by then," Russell says.

"Something needs to be done," Victor says. "This is the opportunity we needed."

All my concern over Rosita and jealousy regarding Caroline are gone. I'm thinking of the wasteland lullabies I've written. Is this how it starts? A sudden catastrophe that makes it impossible for men to imbibe the water, mutates the fish and withers the crops? Am I a prophet and is today the first day of the scripture I've been writing? My father would certainly be on his knees, praying for the strength to endure these newest trials.

"Thousands of gallons," Victor says. "National media will be here before tomorrow morning. We have to use this. Otherwise, we won't have another chance. Are you ready?" he asks Russell, but Russell is glued to the television.

"Focus," Victor yells to get Russell's attention. He turns from the television, locks eyes on Victor, who has removed his hat and sits turning it in his hands. "If we really want to make a difference, now is the time."

The screen cycles through the same images: the river, the storage tanks, an ominous shot of a kitchen sink with a dripping faucet. There is a photo of a woman who'd been washing dishes without knowledge of the spill. Her fingers are swollen twice the normal size, the pads of her hands lobster red and skin peeling. The worst are her fingernails. They've begun to turn black, as blood wells underneath them and oozes from the end of each digit. The news anchor informs us the woman is being treated in the hospital's intensive care wing.

Russell raises his arms for the group's attention. "We need to make a run for some bottled water."

This isn't what Victor wants to hear. His brow creases in frustration and he leans forward like he's ready to say something, then considers his audience. He sinks back down into the couch, ready to wait for a better time. There's something that strikes me as dangerous in this waiting. Victor doesn't recline and relax, but seems to be settling into his position like a coiled snake. As soon as he has Russell alone, he'll say his piece.

"Does the bar have any bottled water?" Victor asks the bartender.

The bartender shakes her head. "Just a soda gun hooked up to the tap. We got some ice, but not much."

"We could hit Shaheen's," Russell says. "Grab some provisions before things get wild."

"Who?" Caroline doesn't speak to anyone directly. Her half-lidded eyes blink slow and she slides down into the plush couch as if hoping to recede into the cushions.

"You okay, sugar?" Rosita asks her.

Caroline nods, but her eyes stay closed a bit longer with every minute that passes.

I want to retreat home where we can safely drink from the well, but that's not going to happen. I've gotta stick with Russell if I want to get paid. Besides, I have no driver. Caroline is barely conscious, still draped across Victor's chest, head dangling on a bobbing neck and then jerking erect.

"I need some air," I say.

The group is still debating, so I head into the hall before Russell can follow. My eyes suddenly feel hot and wet. My throat raw. I can't recall if I've drunk any water since leaving the house but decide it's just paranoia. If I had, my face would look like the dishwasher's hands.

Outside, the lot is empty aside from the hearse and Caroline's truck. Down the street, a few vans from the local news stations already idle by the curb. I can't make out their logos in the darkness, just the newsmen milling around, snaking cables out the back of the panel doors. In minutes, the street will glow from all the lights. I want to disappear before one of the cameras finds me vulnerable under the buzzing neon of the bar sign.

I hear the door open behind me. When I turn, Rosita holds it while Russell and Victor come nearly dragging Caroline. She staggers with the guitar case clutched like an oversized infant.

"What the fuck did she take?" I ask.

Victor shrugs. "Whatever was cut up on the table."

I should be more worried, but the images on the television have inspired my internal conductor to strike up the band. A guitar plays against the steady throb of an improvised drum. Rusty scrap metal utilized for percussion. I can hear the weary chords. A tune that personifies the schools of bobbing fish and the islands of toxic white foam. I need an instrument and a pen, but my driver is too stoned to be left alone. If I'm ever going to make it across my creek—a dangerous proposition considering the quality of the water—I'll need help.

Russell unlocks the hearse. Rosita and Caroline climb in back where a casket should lie. Victor sits on the floor between the girls, his back to the driver and long legs extended until his spurred boots rest against the closed back doors. I take the passenger seat as Russell pulls onto the main road.

Once safe inside the car, Victor can't contain himself. He turns forward so that Russell can see his eyes in the rearview.

"Those were your family's tanks," he says. "I need to know you understand that."

"I do," Russell says, but I don't hear the same conviction in his voice.

"You can see the truth now, right? You see that they are killing us. Can I depend on you? Do you have the resolve to see this thing through?"

"Of course," Russell says.

I'm about to interject when we reach the roadblock. The protesters stand across the yellow line with their hands linked into a human chain. The spectacle has drawn some rubberneckers, who are kept behind sawhorses by a small group of state police. The cops stand beside their cruisers, muscles tense under the green sleeves of their uniforms as they wait for things to escalate. One officer, short and mustached, is shouting for the protesters to clear the road. They only tighten their links, coil inward and look to one another for assurances no one will desert if the hickory batons come out of the cops' trunks.

Watching them, I feel ashamed of how many times Caroline and I have driven by. I wish I'd done something to show solidarity. I'm considering how it's too late when a man breaks from the chain and staggers into the median.

"He ain't gonna move," Victor says.

"Yes, he will," Russell replies, but I'm not convinced. The man looks transfixed by our approaching headlights, ready to let his body meet the hearse's grille. Russell stands on the brake. I see his eyes close in the illumination from the dashboard lights.

Behind the man, the human chain begins to cheer. Russell rolls down the window to shoo him away, but it's taken as an invitation. As the loner approaches, I think he'll reach through the window and grasp the crooner. Instead, the man slams his fist against the hood.

"The road's closed," he screams. "No one passes."

Russell nods in agreement, reassures him by saying, "I'm on your side, man."

The man has finally noticed Russell's ghoul paint. His upper lip pulls back in disgust. "You Goddamned freaks," he shouts.

"Step away from the car," an officer calls. He draws his gun as he steps forward. Rosita screams from the backseat and places her palms flat on the glass. I'm suddenly taken over by survival tactics my father taught me. Anytime I was approached by some authority figure from town, I was told to run through the same internal list. Be polite. Cooperate. Assume you are in violation of something. Do not bring unwanted attention down on the church. I follow Rosita's example and place my palms on the windshield. Her shallow breathing seems obscenely loud in the quiet.

"Step away from the car," the officer says. I can't tell if he's noticed the man isn't armed. The gun stays on target.

"Fuck you, pig," the man screams. He swings a haymaker reminiscent of something from a John Wayne western. The trooper tackles him to the ground and slaps the bracelets on his wrists while another officer approaches my window. The protesters hiss and shout insults as the cop wrestles with the man. A random bottle sails through the air and smashes against a nearby cruiser. Another officer points his firearm at the crowd in warning. This is answered with lobbed rocks and more bottles that shatter in front of the man's feet.

"Road's closed," the officer says to me. He shines his Maglite on Russell. If the ghoul makeup shocks him, he suppresses it well. "I'm going to have to ask you to go back the way you came."

The cop smells like sweat-drenched polyester and morning breath. I guess no one has showered this evening. Caroline leans toward the front like she wants to ask a question, but Victor pulls her back. Russell whips the car around and drives away. A flash erupts from the backseat as Rosita takes a picture through the tinted glass. Inside the confines of the car, the light is blinding as a supernova. My retinas are imprinted with spheres of red long after the bulb is extinguished.

"Wrong lenses for this dark," Rosita says to herself.

"Put it away," Russell yells.

Several protesters break from the chain. Bottles and rocks continue to rain down on the police. Most seem aware that this rage is misdirected and refuse to unhinge from their link. These bodies hold fast, leaving the group divided. I watch in the rearview as the police move in with clubs held high. Before the two lines converge, the groups become dark shapes indistinguishable from one another.

RESUPPLY

Day One of the Contamination

When we pull up in front of Shaheen's Grocery, I realize all the cops are in the wrong place. Frantic shoppers extend out the open doors in a line that's crushing the weak and elderly against the door frame. Through the storefront windows, I watch men and women run down the aisles grabbing cases of bottled water. One couple stands in the frozen food section, the man heaving items into a shopping cart held by his wife. They've amassed perhaps twenty dripping bags of ice, but the man keeps loading until the buggy sags under the weight. A woman in a bathrobe holds five 2-liter bottles of soda to her chest. Each one is a different flavor. In the produce section, a man fills his coat with heads of cabbage that become leafy cleavage. The orange shaft of a carrot protrudes through his coat buttons as if he's been impaled by an organic arrow. The cashiers are under siege, conveyor belts and scan guns unable to operate fast enough. Eventually, people begin to slap money down next to the register and leave.

In a few moments, the situation will escalate into looting. I'm about to tell Russell to just drive on, but he turns toward the backseat.

"You girls stay here."

Russell jumps out of the car, dirty spats smacking the pavement as he runs for the door. I look in the back and see Caroline leaning her forehead against the window. Each of her shallow breaths fogs the glass.

"You okay?" I ask. "Because we need to get home."

It's probably already too late. I don't think we can get past the protesters again to retrieve the truck. That leaves Russell's hearse the only available vehicle. Rosita must recognize some desperation in my voice. She leans forward and puts a hand on my shoulder. Even through the fabric of my shirt, her palm is warm and sweaty, somehow more alive than any skin I've recently felt.

"She'll be okay," she tells me. "She's just a little fucked up."

Out the window, I see Russell push against the crowd to get inside. I consider climbing behind the wheel and driving on to find a less populated store, but the bastard took the keys with him. A smile spreads across Victor's face as he watches the chaos inside.

"I guess this is what it takes for people to wake up," Victor says. "Years of mines caving in, the mountains blasted away till it floods with every hard rain, cancerous chemicals in the groundwater, and now this. We gotta do something to make it stick this time. People can't just ride it out and forget."

"What are you talking about?" Rosita asks.

"I'm talking about rich boy in there," Victor says. "He's the key. We need him to deny his birthright. If he don't get his head crushed in aisle eight."

"You should go help him," I say, but Victor doesn't move. One of his arms is wrapped around Caroline's waist. His eyes travel from this trapped appendage back to me.

"Somebody's gotta stay here with the girls," he says. "Keep them safe."

Rosita rolls her eyes at this, but I'm not bothered. It's just more of the same condescension I've always known. An average man burying my face in the dirt to make himself feel stronger. If he wants to humiliate me, who is going to stop him? The world's reverted to survival of the fittest.

I look out the window again and see Russell has made it inside the store. Rosita will protect Caroline if I leave, but I'm worried about the guitar case. Victor isn't the sort above sneaking a look inside. What if he finds the record while I'm fighting over supplies? Maybe it doesn't matter. It's not like he could listen to it now, but there'd be questions later.

"Will you be okay if I go help him?" I ask Rosita.

She nods, so I climb out on my cane.

Inside the store, a woman drags a chubby little boy past me as they sprint for the coolers in back. A father points to shelves as he shouts to young sons who move like soldiers receiving orders. Dropped cans of Coke and packages of shrink-wrapped meat lie in the aisles. The floor is sticky with spilled soda, so I move slow, depending on my cane. My back aches again, but I push through it. I don't have any pills with me, so relief won't come anytime soon. I can suffer through the pain. I'm more worried about losing the new song. It's still there, playing low just under the surface of this commotion.

I pass the man loading bags from the ice chest. Up close, the ice hoarder's neck and face shine red from the exertion. He looks ready to drop, but his wife screams for him to hurry as a pond expands beneath their cart. The man wipes his forehead with the back of a wet arm and leans down to pull another bag from the chest.

I grab two jugs of water from the nearby cooler. Behind me, a small man in a hooded jacket and basketball shorts edges his way between the couple. He's almost squirmed close enough to take a bag when the big man turns and pushes him away. Just a single stiff-armed shove, but the smaller man slips in the accumulating puddle and tumbles backward.

"Back off," the ice hoarder says. He tosses another bag onto his pile. I can see he is unhinged, the sort who has probably been waiting for a day like this one. Canned food covered in dust in his basement, a doomsday bunker of some kind buried in the soil of his backyard. He's prayed on the inevitable approach of days like today, seen himself as above the help suggested at least once by a brave friend or relative. The wife looks like a believer, too. She watches as her husband loads the cart, her face twisted into the sort of violent contempt that might look appropriate on a comic book villain. Neither turn from their task to see if the smaller man is injured.

The cashiers are watching now, but with so many shoppers tossing money in their faces, they seem reluctant to abandon their post. The man in the hooded jacket climbs up off the floor. The back of his white basketball shorts drip and cling until I see the pale hocks of his ass through the material.

"What do you need with thirty bags of ice?" he asks as he gets in the hoarder's face. "Ever heard of sharing?"

The ice hoarder hits him in the stomach. All breath leaves the smaller man in a gust and he crumples forward as if his waist were a well-oiled hinge. I think someone will step forward now and stop this, but the tiny man rises again, this time armed with a can of peas that have tumbled from a nearby shelf. He clocks the ice hoarder just behind the ear with the dented can, delivers another blow as the big man staggers, trips and collides into one of the cooler doors. The ice hoarder doesn't go through the glass, just shakes the frame and slides down it. The smaller man tosses the peas aside and turns to grab his own bag. He's hefting it over his shoulder as a gunshot rings out in the silence.

For one deafening moment, I know I've been shot. Pain surges in my back until I decide that must be where the bullet entered. In a moment, I'll feel the warm leak of blood. Screams pierce the echo. I turn and see the ice hoarder brandishing a snub-nosed revolver from his prone position by the freezer. Glass shatters and frozen pizzas disintegrate like clay pigeons as he fires another shot. Everyone seeks cover, hiding behind display cases of beer and saltine crackers. One cashier covers her mouth with a wad of bills meant for the drawer, but the denominations do little to muffle her cry.

The shot man looks more surprised than harmed. He sits down in the water, his hand clutching the wound as he sinks back until his eyes lock on the lights overhead.

"Son of a bitch brained me with a can of corn," the ice hoarder says. The gun hangs limp in his hand as he pleads his case. "What was I supposed to do?"

I dash for the exit. My back agonizes in protest, but I just keep moving, my jugs of water dropped and forgotten at the sound of the first gunshot. Russell clears the door with a gallon under each arm. Out in the parking lot, a man stands on the open tailgate of his pickup and haggles with a group about prices.

"Twenty dollars a case," the man calls. "Best get it while you can. They're all sold out inside."

We jump into the hearse and lock the doors. The radio comes

on at high volume as Russell turns the key. The announcer reports that the governor has declared a state of emergency. The National Guard is being deployed to offer relief.

"Things are only going to get worse," I say. "The best thing to do is drive straight for the interstate. Hit the Kentucky line and get a hotel somewhere."

The idea of a dingy Super Eight has never seemed so close to salvation. I can put Caroline to bed and take a shower. When she wakes, we'll sit with our feet dipped into a chlorinated pool. Perhaps the girls will convince the other men to wade out in their underwear. I won't participate, just be happy to watch those better-made bodies prickle with gooseflesh and grow high from the smell of pool chemicals instead of fearing the sweet scent from my creek. Only problem is, I'm still at the mercy of those with wheels, and I still covet the money Russell will pay for Angela's signature.

"Or just take me home," I say. "Please."

Even the gunshot hasn't managed to drown out my internal music. When I close my eyes, the musician I've invented walks with the boy, both in rotting garb that doesn't manage to keep the sand from their crevices. The guitar's strings are growing thin. The man knows the music will not last much longer. He needs to ration the art, play only the essential pieces from the old world for the boy. I feel that same urgency. I need to transcribe before this revelation leaves.

"Take me home?" I ask again, but Russell shakes his head. "Where are we going then?"

"We need to go to your father's house," Victor tell Russell. He's leaned forward into the front of the cab until he's inches away from Russell's ear. I expect the conversation to proceed in whispers, but Victor continues loudly enough for all to hear. "We need to discuss this with him."

"It won't do any good. You know that."

Victor shakes his head. "It's time he was held accountable. If you tell him about all you've seen, I'm sure he'll listen. After all, you're his son."

There is a preaching quality in Victor's voice I recognize from The Reverend's sermons. Seduction clothed in the false garments of pride and concern. This is all fork-tongued lies, but Russell seems captivated by it.

"What if it's just like every time before? What if he won't listen?"

"Then we make him see what he's done," Victor says.

Russell looks at his reflection in the rearview. Smiles wide until his fangs sparkle under the interior lamps. Rosita glances in my direction, but I know it's best not to protest now. No sane conversation is going to end this. We're going to confront Russell's father.

In the back, Victor has the revolver in his hand. The cylinder hangs open as he loads it with fat cartridges. "I knew you wouldn't disappoint," he says. The brass gives a dull shine before Victor spins the wheel and snaps it closed.

SANCTUARY

Day One of the Contamination

The Watsons have been dug into Bradshaw for generations, the only family of note among the cluster of trailers
and one-story shacks in the deep hollow. Their clan
owned most of the timber leases in Coopersville at the turn of
the century. This near monopoly on resources allowed the earliest Watsons to invest in coal and its related endeavors. Once they
amassed enough wealth from underground, Watson Chemical
and Watson Trucking provided even the most distant relations
with a fortune. It stands to reason anyone who became so successful would have fled, abandoned our mountains for the thrill
and luxury of a nearby city. For some reason, the Watsons decided to stick close to their roots, building a mansion at the head
of Bradshaw Hollow.

The stories I'd heard about the house don't do it justice. The
large bay windows and high steeple roof loom down from the top
of the hill we ascend. The brownstone façade looks like no basic

brick I've seen, but a more vibrant red stone as if blood were mixed into the mortar. It's the closest this redneck hell will ever come to seeing a medieval castle, and I can't help thinking it's cruel to build something like this so close to squalor. Maybe that's the point. A brick-and-mortar reminder of familial power.

Russell drives up to the wrought-iron fence that surrounds the compound, presses a button on the control panel next to the gate and waits as it rolls away on the mechanical track. As the hearse creeps up the hill, I look out the passenger window at thousands of dollars in ruined landscaping. The sprinkler system has been on, dousing the flora with the tainted water. I'm surprised the chemicals could work so fast. Only a few hours and already dead wildflowers spread out in rows as the stench of fresh mulch enters our cab. A mosaic of multicolored stones weaves a path through these wilted gardens. In the center, tall shoots of elephant grass circle a fountain. The sweet scent of the water overpowers the manure and mulch, putting the taste of spun sugar on my tongue.

I've seen opulence in my few travels, but all those adventures have been voyeuristic glimpses over the fence. Inside these surroundings, I'm uneasy. It doesn't help that this feels less like a homecoming than a raid. Victor is still spinning the cylinder of his revolver. Russell driving sullen and working himself up for some subversive act. I'm not too worried about Russell. This place still belongs to him. He might march angry down its halls, but the insidious haunt of home will win out. As much as he may want to act out for Victor, I doubt he can fully cast off such an essential part of himself. No, for Russell the anger is closer to a tantrum. Victor is the one to watch. Something has changed in his posture since we crossed the gate. The usual languid way he's slumped in the seat is gone. He sits forward now, muscles tensed beneath his denim.

Caroline's eyes open for the first time in nearly an hour. She's beginning to sober as her gaze scales the outside terrace. All her lovers live in trailers or apartments overtop the Cherry Tree bars. She's never seen anything like this either. It must seem like the end of a narcotic dream.

"Where is everyone?" I ask.

"I suppose my father is off doing damage control," Russell says.

My back spasms as we park, so I wait for someone to help me rise. Russell comes around the car to assist me. The demons on his forearms lurch as his sleeves slide up. There is a mushroom cloud on his left bicep, mutated green men glowing in the fallout on his wrist.

"Should we be here?" I whisper as he helps me climb out.

"It's all mine," Russell says. "I'm going to do what I like with it."

Once I'm standing on my own, Russell lifts a rock from the path and bashes it against the front door's glass as if to punctuate this point. A spiderweb pattern begins in the center and bridges out toward each wooden border.

"It's all just shit anyway," he says, striking the door again before tossing the stone out into the elephant grass. It disappears in the foliage. After this violent outburst concludes, Russell looks toward Victor for approval, but Victor doesn't say anything. He just waits for Russell to unlock the door by typing another code into a keypad, then helps the girls climb out and takes my guitar case.

Russell ushers us into a foyer so grand it feels like a parody. A high-domed entryway replaces the typical popcorn ceilings I'm accustomed to, as a crystal chandelier dangles low to greet us.

Warm oak covers the walls rather than drywall. The furniture, all plush red velvet, looks as if it's never been sat on. I follow Russell past a staircase where a grandfather clock ticks. Victor brings up the rear, his boots sullying the polish on the parquet floors. Caroline is more mobile. She drags her feet over the Persian rugs, staggers while staring at the marble fireplace.

There is a studio at the end of the long hall. The door is open, so I can see the walls inside are outfitted in acoustic foam. Two different drum kits, a stand with an electronic keyboard and a large console rest in the far corner next to a sectional couch. An array of guitars hangs on the wall. It's the sort of setup I've always dreamed about in my house, but it felt like tempting fate. Almost a cruel joke to give so much equipment to a man who was never going to compose anything but tracks for others. Russell sees me looking inside and claps me on the back. It hurts, but I manage not to wince.

"Make yourself at home," he tells me.

I've never written outside of my studio, but the song still plays in my head. If I don't allow the thing to breathe a little, I'm going to lose it.

"What about our deal?" I ask and nod toward my guitar case Victor is carrying.

"We've got all night to negotiate price," Russell says. "We're going to have a drink. Can I get you one?"

I shake my head. I don't understand where his interest has gone. Before, he'd been thrilled just to touch the strings. Now, he seems ambivalent, more concerned with Victor's approval. It's strange how often I've seen this quality in other men. A hungry need to be accepted. I never shared it. Perhaps because I knew I'd never be able to achieve it from most. Seeing how it's made Russell act, I'm grateful to be spared the impulse.

The group retires to the kitchen to raid the liquor cabinet and watch more news coverage. I stand in front of the rows of guitars and feel a hot needling in my back. I need the pills. If I'm not going anywhere tonight, at least there's music to take my mind off the pain. A nagging voice inside tells me I shouldn't play with Rosita nearby. Not until I learn what she already knows, but I'm not going to follow that precaution. Without the music as a distraction, this pain will never cease.

Victor has left Angela's guitar sitting by the door, but I decide against playing it. Instead, I take a Takamine acoustic from the rack and sit on the stool behind the drum kit. With the door open, I hear the others ravaging things. The crash of china breaking, glass shattering and the shrill burst of drunken laughter. A slam and jarring of gears as I assume the grandfather clock by the stairs is pushed over. Even the loud TV can't drown out the sounds of Russell rampaging against his birthright.

I push the door closed with the toe of my shoe and let my fingers take over, sweep down the neck to play a soft melody. In my mind's eye, the man is playing the same song for the boy that he used to sing to a woman when the trees still budded in the spring, a time when seasons like spring still existed and there were green pastures to lie in. Sunlight and flannel blankets, bees buzzing and birds squawking instead of the relentless winds that carry only acidic topsoil.

I'm not sure how long I play. The song feels complete, so I consider using some of Russell's recording equipment, but I'm superstitious about such things. Bad enough I'm writing with someone else's guitar. I can't say when but at some point, I decided that instruments are imprinted with the experiences of their owners. I'm a little embarrassed by this belief. After avoiding my father's religious tendencies, I feel like it's a failure to put faith in anything intangible. I don't follow other superstitions. Don't even believe in an afterlife.

Still, some of Mr. Freemont's personality stayed trapped inside his guitar after I inherited it. The wood seemed incapable of offering a bright tune. Everything I wrote with that guitar was solemn and bittersweet. Of course, that could have just been purging the pain of my childhood. I'd believe that explanation if I hadn't written a few happy songs during those years on Angela's guitar. That instrument felt as kind and generous as her whenever I touched it.

I don't feel anything in the Takamine on my lap. I suspect it's been too pent up. Unloved and unexperienced. Never seen the road or a barroom gig. Just a pretty thing without use, like everything else in this house. I hang it back on the wall thinking the guitar must be disappointed our session is over, wishing to prolong the moment like a homely man experiencing a night with a beautiful woman. I remind myself it's only a guitar and go see about Caroline.

As soon as I step into the hall, I notice the disarray. The grandfather clock has indeed been turned over. It lies on its side, glass door shattered and the exposed face motionless. The hands are frozen on eleven fifteen. The far wall of the dining room is full of deep holes in the drywall, the wooden supports visible. Some openings are the size of cannonballs, others made by fists or boot heels. Beer cans are scattered across the floor. Cigarette butts extinguished on the hardwood.

I find them in the kitchen. Someone thought it would be amusing to discharge the fire extinguisher under the sink. Now the floor is coated in white chemical snow. Caroline holds a bowling ball overhead while Russell stands behind her watching. I can see she's sober now. Clear-eyed and aware, which makes me wonder just how long I've been upstairs playing. I'm relieved to see she's better, but disturbed to see she's taken part in the mayhem. I almost wish she was still high. At least then she'd have an excuse. Caroline throws the ball at the far wall, where it cracks the tile over the sink and clatters into the steel basin.

"No, no, no," Russell says. "You gotta throw it with your chest."

He plucks the ball from the sink and throws it hard with one arm. More tiles shatter. Rosita and Victor watch from the small kitchen table. Four places are set, but the dishes and platters are all broken, the silver candelabra on its side with the white candles snapped into thirds. Victor is spinning his pistol, performing tricks for the others' pleasure. Tossing the gun high in the air and catching it behind his back, twirling the polished steel until it's a gleaming blur.

The destruction doesn't surprise me, but I can't help wondering why primitive appetites always win out in times of strife. What sends me to the guitar, seeking escape in a fabricated world when others are busy tearing reality down? Does it feel that much better to watch a bowl shatter and know you've kept it from ever being whole again? To look at a broken wall and feel reassured your fist can achieve that result? If that's the greatest pleasure a healthy body can bring, maybe I'm better off.

"We're vandals now?" I ask.

"My father's the vandal," Russell says. He waves his arms around the mess. "This is just some payback."

"I doubt the law will see it that way," I say.

Victor never stops twirling the gun. It rolls over his finger, rotating like an extension of his body.

"Isn't that thing loaded?" I say.

"Wouldn't be impressive if it wasn't," he says. He aims the gun at me, then spins on his heel, the entire room locked in his sights as he revolves around and around. When he finally stops, he gives a dizzy giggle and goes back to his tricks. Caroline applauds these antics, but I can see she's finally sober enough to reason with.

"You stay if you like, but I need to get home," I tell her. The money isn't worth it. I'll take the guitar and walk if necessary. "I'm not taking the fall for all this."

"What we need is something real," Victor says. "A confession." The gun is finally motionless in his hand.

"How so?" Russell asks.

"I mean making your father renounce what he's done. Exposing him for what he is."

"And how would we do that?"

"We put a camera on him and make him admit everything."

Russell smiles at the idea, but I can see he's confused. "How do you make someone confess when they don't think they've done anything wrong?"

"You make them feel remorse."

Russell chuckles. "He's incapable of feeling remorse. This shit is all he's ever cared about." Russell picks up the silver candelabra and throws it at the far wall.

"If they can't feel remorse," Victor says, "make them feel pain."

I understand this logic. As a child, I waited for some equalizer, something that would square the books and force fairness into existence. The same is true for all the poor hillbillies I've known. Most outsiders who bother to consider us think we want equality, a chance to remove the unfair stereotypes and degradation, but we've never been that optimistic. We just want a sucker punch worthy of payback. A chance to make those who've laughed at us feel an inkling of our desperation. Despite all the speeches and zealot's rhetoric, Victor doesn't want to put Russell's father under the gun to instruct him. He just wants revenge. I'm afraid if I listen long enough, I'll want it, too. I can see it's working on Russell. This carnage shows he's already fallen in line more than I expected.

I turn to walk for the door, but Russell grabs my arm.

"Hear him out," he says. "The man poisoned a whole state."

"You'd be wise to shut this down," I say. "Or just leave."

"It's my home," Russell says.

"And that's why it's the perfect place to make him admit it," Victor says. "We can cause some real change. So long as you've got the courage to go through with it."

I shrug off Russell's hand and move to the foyer. Behind me, the men are still sparking a revolution, but all I want is a bed. If this isn't something I can escape, I'll sleep through it.

Russell offers us a few different rooms for the night. Among them is the master bedroom that no one feels comfortable accepting, several spares and one filled with posters and rock memorabilia that obviously belonged to Russell in his youth. I bunk in one of the spare rooms where the walls are made entirely of mirrored panels. Even though I'm tempted, I don't offer to share my bed with Caroline. By now, I believe she knows the invitation is open. I've almost convinced myself it's better to be apart when she takes the room across the hall from Victor. Does such a strategic position mean she's decided to spend the night with him? I close myself up in the mirrored room and try to dispel my worry with action.

As soon as I'm alone, I pick up the phone and dial 911. I've never been one to rat, but the conversation in the kitchen and the damage to the house have me scared. No answer. There is only a strange tone. Something loud and not unlike a busy signal. I try two more times before giving up. The thought occurs to grab my guitar case and walk out the gate, but I wouldn't make it far. If I can't even reach a dispatcher, the whole county might be burning.

I roll over onto my side, back still aching as I stare at my reflection in the mirrored wall. I've always found my face handsome. A strong jawline, good hair and a heavy brow that is a touch villainous. If only I could be as satisfied with the rest. I wonder if I'm the only man with an empty bed tonight. Women have shared themselves with me, but one who will stay seems out of the question. That's why it hurts seeing Caroline lust after Victor. I'd deluded myself into thinking she could be content with just my body. Perhaps some woman could accept fidelity with a man shaped like me, but I've known since the early days that my life is not that kind of story. Intimacy is always going to be hard to come by. I used to accept that with some grace, but my time with Caroline has reminded me how much I missed women. If I'm being honest, how much I missed Angela.

Someone knocks on the door. I climb out of bed thinking Caroline has come to apologize, but find Rosita standing in the hall. She clutches her bag, eyes downcast as if already regretting this decision. It must be about Angela Carver. Russell has told her everything and she's here to pry the details out of me. In some way, I'm relieved. After days of fear, it's a mercy to be found out. Like a murderer finally secure inside a cell, maybe I'll even sleep afterward.

"Come in," I say.

My reflections surround her as we pass the mirrored walls. I stand in every corner, omnipresent, as I pull a chair away from the vanity. The furniture is not suited to my posture. When I sit, my body pitches forward and threatens to fold into itself like a shrimp broiling in a skillet. Rosita perches on the edge of the bed. I notice her watching one of my reflections. Her eyes measure the curve of my spine like an architect wondering how to mend a bridge's flawed foundation. I let her look. The sooner she sees her fill, the easier this will be.

"What's up?" I ask.

"I wanted a moment to talk with you."

The tentative way she speaks frustrates me. I'm trapped under her thumb and she can't muster the courage to just say it.

"Well, unless you're offering a ride out of here, I'd like to get some sleep."

"It's too dangerous out there," Rosita says. "You remember the grocery store."

"Too dangerous out there? You really believe that after that scene in the kitchen?"

"That's just drunk bullshit," she says, but I hear her trying to convince herself. "We shouldn't leave till morning."

"We? I thought you agreed with Russell? I didn't hear you protesting his plan."

"I don't bother arguing when I can't win," Rosita says.

I look at her legs and wonder about the shape of her calves under the tight denim. Her thighs are thick, rubbing together in a caress I admire when she walks around the room. I imagine her kissing me, pushing me down on the bed as I slide my hand between those naked thighs, feeling the muscles clamp tight on my wrist in excitement. I'm ashamed having such a fantasy in front of her, but something about our closeness in the shadows makes it hard to cast the thoughts aside. Lust always feels like a double-edged sword. I'm glad I haven't given up that part of myself after Angela, but I can't help knowing most women would be disgusted by my desire for them. When your body is different, the world wants to strip you of all those human impulses. To render the sick or malformed sterile. Sometimes life would be easier without those urges. I tried to tell Caroline that once. She took me to bed, pulled me between her bare breasts and stared into my eyes. "So, you'd rather not have this?" she'd asked, while I plunged inside. I loved her for that brief moment of reassurance.

"What are you doing here?" I ask. "With Russell, I mean?"

"I'm writing an article about imagery and persona in shock rock. You know, Alice Cooper guillotines and Kiss makeup? I found their website and flew to town."

"For a shitty bar band?"

"Don't let Russell hear you say that," Rosita says. "He tells me you're an influence. Is that true?"

"First I've heard," I say. We're moving into it now. One or two more bits of small talk, then she'll be asking all about The Troubadours. Maybe even my ghostwriting.

"Why'd you quit playing?"

The question could have a thousand answers, so I choose a lie. "I wasn't any good."

"I don't believe that. I had my ear to the door when you were in the studio."

When I don't reply, she smiles and leans close enough to whisper in my ear.

"I haven't been entirely honest about things. I hope you'll forgive me, but I didn't want to talk about it in front of the others."

I imagine her hand caressing the stubble sprouting from my jaw. I try to clear my head of these longings, but since Angela, no woman has spoken to me in the dark. No one looks at my eyes because they feel the need to gawk at the rest of me. All the hope I've spent years purging is beginning to grow.

"Russell told me about how you played with Angela Carver," Rosita admits. "But that's not why I'm here. I'm hoping you'll participate in a project. I curate an art website that specializes in bodies."

Here is the inevitable exploitation. A chance for cash or other promises if I will just be debased. It's the dream offered to all the alienated. Desires fulfilled if you will only sell yourself. While the average man might incur only minor degradation, men like me are asked to endure open ridicule. What sort of pictures could she be dressing up with words like *curate*? Daguerreotypes of dwarves in their tiny vests fill my mind. Shadowed images of the Elephant Man struggling to hold his tumor-heavy head aloft. And I thought the mountains would guard me from these examples of carnival lust.

"What sort of bodies?" I ask. Anger edges into my voice, but Rosita looks ready for this. Her intentions have been questioned before.

"Bodies that are overlooked by society. Bodies that are misrepresented."

"Bodies like mine."

She takes a small laptop from the bag on her shoulder. "Can I show you some pictures?"

She turns the screen toward me and pulls up an image of a blond woman. The work is a rough draft. The red eye still present, the light filters need altering to fix the shadows climbing across the woman's hips, but I can still see enough to understand.

In the first picture, the woman sits topless in front of a fireplace. The tone is almost boudoir photography, the woman's head slightly cocked, braided hair dangling like a golden tassel between breasts that have been burned so long ago they couldn't develop naturally. I trace the texture of the scars, the way each pore of the skin has let the burn form in a different shade and severity. Flesh rendered elderly and wrinkled in one spot yet maintaining an incredulous pink in others as if insistent on keeping a modicum of youth. Over 70 percent of her body must have been covered in flame.

Rosita presses a button. The woman is fully nude now, her crossed legs hiding her vulva. My eyes linger on those flesh columns. No part of my body is as strong and complete as these legs with their striations of muscle. They are untouched. The only other part of her so preserved is her neck. The beginning of a borderland with freckled ivory on her face, webbed scar tissue below her clavicle. An arm must have been tossed up to block the fire, a holy appendage sacrificed to save her face and create this quilt of different skin.

Certain chambers inside myself come alive looking at the girl. There is a pang of empathy that feels like camaraderie. We've shared something others couldn't understand. For instance, I know this woman has looked at her body in the mirror and wondered what caused such an injustice. Knowing someone else has felt that exact emotion, regardless of how impossible it is to describe or how they chose to cope with it, that makes them less of a stranger. Still, I can't understand what she must have thought while the camera captured her scars. The answer must be in the legs. They are so long and glorious she must have wanted to honor them in some form of preservation before age robbed the only part of herself she loves. Maybe it's a substitute for never wrapping them around a boy's waist. Then again, maybe she's straddled many beautiful boys. No one ever thought I'd have a woman either. I look at two more models, an amputee and a man

with a congenital condition that makes his limbs disproportion-
ately small, before I decide I've seen enough.

I close the laptop and hand it back to Rosita. "What makes
you entitled to this project?"

"Do I need an entitlement to create art?" Rosita replies.

"It's someone's body," I say. "They aren't oil on a canvas."

"I'm sorry it upset you," Rosita says.

Upset isn't the right word. The woman in the photo is free to
show herself however she chooses, but I'm thinking of all those
anonymous trolls who will scorn her. Men like that will never
appreciate the courage they're seeing.

"So, you want me to do this?" I ask. "You stuck this shit out
to add me to the project?"

"Sounds creepy when you say it that way," she says.

"Maybe it is." In the search for rare bodies, I am a worthy
quest. Still, I don't recant. I let her sit with it a minute.

"Will you pose for me?" she asks.

"No."

The silence between us is as final as a soldier's white flag. I
walk Rosita to the door.

"If you really want to help people," I tell her, "take more pictures of what's happening around here."

After she leaves, I sit up considering if I misspoke. I could
always write a beautiful line, but my tongue remains clumsy in
the heat of the moment. I did my best to be measured, just speak
the truth as I saw it, but after gazing at the burned blonde, I'm
afraid too much of the past bled in. The worst is realizing how
astounding my paranoia has become. I believed I was important
enough to draw the attention of a New York music journalist. Of
course, she was only here for the freak show. My body is the only
truly unique thing about me.

I strip and appraise myself in the mirrored wall. While every other man is interested in his paunch or growing love handles, I've always wondered about my skeleton. It grieves me that I'll never see it. There are the phantasm blue X-rays the first doctors took after my father's death. Captured ghosts that make my bones look like alien relics, but they're poor substitutes. I want the bones outside of the flesh and in my hands where I can touch their porous surface. I want to gaze into the sockets of my own skull. Carry the empty vessel like Hamlet with the remains of Yorick. I know how insane the idea is, but it doesn't change the wish.

I came close to a decent substitute once. Back when Richard the Third was exhumed from under that parking lot. Those royal bones gave me solace. Seeing his remains was like looking in this mirror.

According to most historians, the king's deformity was slight. A skilled tailor and armorer could have hidden the affliction so that most soldiers at the Battle of Bosworth Field would only think their fallen ruler a small man. At least, until someone removed the armor to examine the wound. The skeleton in the photos didn't look like a man with mild deformities. The vertebra bent like a strung longbow, the lower jaw hung open as if the skull were frozen in eternal laughter over the indignities. A true form of infinite jest.

The first time I looked at the pictures, I wept. It was like seeing my own open grave after the creatures that resided in the dirt finished their work. I saved the images on my computer, spent time tracing that track of spine until I could mark its margins perfectly in the air. At night, I'd lie in bed and form the shape on my ceiling like a prisoner imagining the constellations in a free sky. The more I remember those bones as my reflection watches me, the more Rosita's pictures begin to make sense. Bodies that just wish to be seen while they are here.

I believe Angela loved my body. I know she took pleasure in it and provided the only love it has ever known. Considering this, I begin to feel very guilty about my contemplated betrayal. I sit on the edge of the bed, open the guitar case and play a single soft ballad. The wood feels warm and inviting against my bare thighs. The sheets are cold underneath me. At the end of the song, I take the record out of the hidden pouch and snap it into four equal pieces. I stick them back into the case, toss the guitar on top of them and lie back down. Things should feel easier with the temptation gone, but I can't help chuckling thinking of that king's skull. The way it seemed to be laughing at some final joke keeps me awake all night.

THE WITCH

I lost my guitar a second time. One morning, the sound of The Reverend's truck departing woke me and by the time I reached the window, the taillights were disappearing in the early darkness. The first thing I did was check under the bed. The guitar was gone. I decided my father took it to sell somewhere, or perhaps just smashed it against some railroad ties to keep me away from the danger of girls like Angela Carver. Either way, I tried to make my peace with the loss.

I didn't cry over the guitar. Part of me wanted to, but my mind was too pleased by dreams of Angela. She'd been filling my sleep, playing inside a dream so real I expected to wake and find her singing at the foot of the bed. I'd never felt that way about a girl before. Even the infatuation for Annabel Freemont was abandoned in a new sort of devotion. I only wept when I realized we'd never play together again.

The saddest part about tragedy is how the world continues despite it. Outside, the woods were still waking. Nocturnal animals moved home through the brush. Birds sang out from the high branches. Frogs croaked from the distant creek. Everything in nature reminded me of the insignificance of my pain. Up at the church, a glow emitted through the spaces in the logs. It seemed impossible that The Reverend would leave a burning candle unsupervised. While I was trying to figure out who might be inside, the light vanished as something eclipsed the source. I knew my father would punish me for violating the sanctuary, but he'd kill me if I let it burn.

The church door's rusted hinges creaked as I let myself inside. A single candle melted down into a pool on the altar. Lady Crawford lay curled in the corner. She'd constructed a small pallet out of straw and piled a few quilts atop her body to stave off any chill. A tin bucket of wash water rested near her, another one empty and awaiting the needs of a full bladder. I considered turning for the door, but she let out a moan. I tried to silence my breathing. I'd never been alone in the presence of the witch and worried that if I startled her, an unspeakable retaliation would occur. Some backwoods magic employed to twist me further, or perhaps she would simply drop me down the well, fabricate some story about my disappearance.

The candle gutted out. In the new darkness, Lady Crawford turned and opened her eyes. She sat forward, pushed the layers of blankets away until I saw her legs dirty and white as bones wild dogs might scavenge. The puckered flesh of her knees resembled the faces of mournful infants, but her calves and thighs were firm. Her long hair was still silken, skin still unmarked by splotches or freckles.

"What are you doing here?" she asked.

"I saw the light. From the candle."

Lady Crawford stood to her full height. Her body was straight despite cheekbones hollowed out by a harsh life, but I noticed for the first time that her hips were full and her breasts plump in the loose garment of her dress. I blamed Angela for that new awareness. Never before would I have considered Lady Crawford anything but terrifying, but that morning I could see a bit of the beauty my father must have unearthed when he looked at her.

"Do you sleep here every night?" I asked.

Lady Crawford dipped her hands into the wash water, rubbed a damp finger across her cracked lips.

"Some nights," she said. "I come to pray and if sleep takes me, then I sleep."

The bed was too worn, the buckets too premeditated. I knew she'd been in the church every night but needed to keep it private.

"Your father tells me the Lord has given you some gifts."

It surprised me to be a topic of conversation. I wondered what my father said about me when he was with this woman. Had she tried to talk him into letting me keep the guitar? Did I have an advocate, or was she just someone my father could unburden himself to?

"I suppose," I said.

Lady Crawford shook her head. "Don't suppose. The Lord has his mercies. Did you think he would bestow you such a poor hand in life? You may not have your body, but he has given you something else. Something to enrich the souls of others. This is a precious thing."

I remember thinking if God wanted to bestow something on me, he could give me the right words to impress Angela. No music would accomplish that.

Lady Crawford laid a palm atop my head. She cupped the circumference of my skull until her fingers felt like a massive spider nested in my hair.

"The Lord has great plans for you," she said. "You will lift up our congregation."

She released me, took up both buckets and stepped to the back of the church.

I crossed the field feeling as if the fingers still gripped me. The sensation lingered so long, I traveled to the creek and dunked my head in the water.

My father arrived hours later with Mr. Freemont's guitar. It was restrung and outfitted with a strap that wouldn't fit my body when I tried it on later. The Reverend waved me over, bent low in the tall grass so that he'd be eye level with me. The guitar strings glinted in the sun, throwing shafts of light out from the sound hole instead of music.

"You've finally been rewarded. We will not squander this."

The Reverend placed the instrument in my hands. An almost subliminal connection existed between us in that moment. Even though he didn't say it, I knew what he meant. Any easy break, unchecked avenue or con had to be exploited by men like me. The guitar was my only chance.

"Thank you," I said.

"Thank the Lord," The Reverend said.

He gave me a brown paper bag with two books inside. *Guitar Method for Beginners* and *The Gospel Guitar Book*. I cracked them open, looked at the lines that tracked across the page. It was covered with numbers, the top of the page full of elaborate grids that were labeled by letters.

"The man called it 'tablature,'" The Reverend said. "The book explains it all."

Living out in the woods, I was lucky to be able to read and

perform simple arithmetic. The Reverend's schooling never went further than Bible lessons. I knew I'd never figure it out.

"Angela told me she gives lessons after school," I said. The mention of her was dangerous, but I couldn't resist the chance to see her again.

"You will understand it if God wills it to be so. You will practice every day."

My father plucked a string. A simple, plain sound that concluded the conversation.

I wish the memory ended there, but it doesn't. Later that night, I sneaked to the church. I kept my feet bare to better suit prowling, and every sharp rock in the field impaled their soles until I regretted the decision. At the time, I wasn't sure why I needed to spy. Now I know I needed a chance to hear what my father said about the guitar.

I heard them before I reached the church. Soft grunts and moans, the hot exhalation of ragged breaths. I bent lower as I approached, rounded the side of the church to the usual spot and placed my ear to the wall. Their fucking was amplified through the wood until I thought I could hear Lady Crawford's nails raking my father's back. Her teeth taking small mounds of the man's flesh in tender bites that made his breath catch. I found a small gap between the logs and peered inside.

The darkness hid most of their bodies in shadows, a tangle of arms and legs like a single monstrous insect. My father kissed Lady Crawford's mouth and traveled down her body with his tongue before mounting her from behind. I watched their bodies crash into each other. Flabby flesh rippling in spastic motions. I remember thinking I'd never possess a woman like that. Whether lust or love, I knew my body would be too mangled to merge with another.

"He came in here this morning," Lady Crawford said afterward as my father held her. "He caught me sleeping."

"It'll be fine." My father rubbed her arm to reassure her. "I brought the guitar back. That will keep him occupied."

I blinked dirt from my eye. I needed to see every moment. This was the true man under the parson's shroud. A man who handed out distractions to continue feeding his own vices. In a way, it was a relief. I preferred to think of him as a hypocrite instead of a zealot.

"Maybe," Lady Crawford said. Her long hair entangled my father's wrist as he stroked her cheek. The Reverend looked shackled by soft manacles. "I'm just afraid the congregation will find out."

The Reverend shook his head. "We'll be fine. Let's just enjoy the night."

"Is he any good?" Lady Crawford asked.

My father scoffed. "He can play a few tunes. It's a miracle the boy can do anything. Or maybe it's a tragedy. The Lord does in fact work in mysterious ways."

I traveled across the field, bare feet no longer harmed by cold ground or brittle rocks. By the time I reached the camper, a sort of scab had formed inside me. Over the years, I've picked it into a scar, created an internal armor against all insurgents.

THE SACRIFICE

Day Two of the Contamination

'm in front of Rosita's door at first light, ready to apologize when squeaking hinges cause me to turn. Caroline doesn't sneak past as she emerges from Victor's room. She walks out juggling her jeans, a tube of Colgate, a bottle of water and a toothbrush I assume belongs to Victor on her way to the bathroom. We lock eyes and I almost speak, but what would I say? I just watch her go until the closed door is another barrier between us. A familiar pain rises in my chest that I swallow down. It's not like I didn't know the limitations of our arrangement.

When I turn, Rosita shrinks back inside her room, trying to help me save face during this cuckold.

"I wasn't snooping," she says.

Below us, hushed voices ride the high-ceilinged acoustics up the staircase. One voice belongs to Russell, but I can't understand what he's saying from so far away. The tone and inflection tell me it's nothing pleasant.

"How about a ride out of here?" I ask Rosita.

"I'll see what I can do."

I linger at the top of the stairs while she collects her things. When she comes back out of the room, the straps of several camera bags hang from her narrow shoulders. Her face has already been washed clean. I wonder how long she's been awake, waiting for this feuding to end.

"What's going on downstairs?" I ask.

She gives a weak shrug, her body weighed down with all the gear. I collect my guitar case and lead the way with easy footsteps. I've always been slow, but surprisingly good at stealth. Our descent would be soundless if it weren't for my cane tapping against the wood.

A man in an unseasonable black overcoat stands in the foyer. His back is turned toward me, untamed white hair spilling out onto his collar. Wrinkled hands adorned with too many rings hang by his pockets. Russell and Victor sit together on the silk love seat while the man paces. Russell has slept in his soiled tuxedo. Sitting so sullen in the dirty garb, he resembles a punished child on Halloween.

"Look at this," the man shouts, pointing toward the broken mirrors, fallen family photos and bits of plasterboard sprinkled on the floor. The way he's taking stock, I decide he must be Russell's father. "Look what you've reduced it to."

Mr. Watson plucks up a piece of broken mirror from the shattered pane over the mantel. His elderly blue eyes shine in the elongated sliver before he throws it against the floorboards, fracturing it into smaller pieces. Something in the old man's posture reminds me of The Reverend. There is the same hot demeanor, a stomp and lurch to his gait my father often adopted behind the pulpit. I'm ready for him to gaze up the staircase, find me crouched and bellow out that I'm a sinner. Despite the similarities, comparing the two men isn't fair. The Reverend never built anything but a congregation of lies. Mr. Watson has amassed something substantial here. I understand his anger at seeing it disrespected.

"This was all going to be yours," Mr. Watson says. "But I can see you've stayed the same indignant little shit as always."

Russell stands with his fists clenched, but there's no real conviction in it. He looks more like a boy than a man ready to defend himself. Waiting for Mr. Watson's words to whittle his son down to nothing, I'll admit to some mixed feelings about the exchange. Echoes of The Reverend fill the room, but unlike the punishments I received, I know Russell deserves condemnation. I just wish his father wasn't enjoying it so much.

"Turn on the TV and look how we got it all," Russell says. "You've poisoned the entire state."

Mr. Watson dismisses this with a wave. "You can't blame me for the accident."

"The tanks haven't been inspected in a decade," Russell says. "Are you gonna stand here and tell me that you're blameless? That you didn't know how damaged they were?"

Mr. Watson backhands Russell. The packing sound of flesh against flesh is so loud I almost miss the lighter percussion of those diamond rings clacking teeth. Victor stands, but Mr. Watson points a crooked finger at him.

"Keep your seat, trash," he says.

Watson's eyes move over the dirty flannel, the rusted spurs and gray face paint that stains Victor's collar. The Stetson hat lies forgotten on the nearby coffee table beside the gun belt. The revolver is missing. The last time I saw it, Victor was performing gun tricks in the kitchen. Right before he advocated torturing a confession from the home's patriarch.

Mr. Watson picks up the hat, turns it in his hands.

"Singing your stupid songs about Halloween ghouls and pumpkin patches. Look at yourself. More opportunity than anyone else and you stand here preaching at me with greasepaint all over your neck."

"Well, I'd wash it off," Russell says as he spits between his feet, "but the water is poison." He smiles, blood filling the gaps in his teeth.

As Mr. Watson watches his son bleed, Victor launches a quick rabbit punch that catches the old man in the stomach. The arm seems to have shot forward independent of thought, leaving Victor looking at the unruly appendage as Watson staggers backward, trips on the rug and falls atop broken glass. Trying to sit forward, he cuts his palms on the tiny shards. Victor kicks him in the chest to keep him down. Two more stomps follow. The boot heels sink deep into Watson's chest until I imagine I can hear his ribs snapping. I'm not brave, don't even have a plan, but I've started down the stairs when Rosita grabs my arm.

Russell falls on his father, takes him by the lapels of the cashmere coat and shakes him. He batters the side of the man's head into the broken glass on the floor. I try to pull free, but Rosita's grip is too tight around my wrist. We both know I'm too weak to help the man, but I can't just watch.

Russell is crying now, babbling unintelligible words, spittle raining down from his mouth. He strikes his father's bloodied face. Each time he pulls a fist back, more skin is scraped away from his knuckles by the old man's dentures. Russell mutters, but the words are lost underneath sobs. Victor takes him by the shoulders and pulls him close until the crying ceases. He strokes Russell's back in a gesture that seems proud. I want to retreat upstairs but am too afraid of making noise. Even my breath sounds audible in the silence. Rosita still has my wrist in her grasp. She squeezes it tighter and whispers a prayer.

Victor selects a jagged piece of mirror from the floor and drags it across Mr. Watson's neck. Blood sprays the far wall. Russell doesn't speak, just watches it drip and run, the arc of the flow bringing him out of his rage. Just a few tics and twitches from the body, then the muscles sag. I turn away, smothered by the sudden absence. The truth that's all we are.

The entire room is suddenly illuminated in pristine light. For a moment, I think my father was right about the Rapture and we're all about to receive God's judgment while standing over a corpse, then another flash erupts. I hear the snicker of a shutter closing as my eyes try to adjust. The men downstairs look up, and for the first time I realize no one is holding my hand. Rosita leans over the banister with her camera trained on them. The lens telescopes outward as she takes another photo. Now the shutter sounds like the cocking of a gun.

"Give me that," Russell shouts. He begins to climb the stairs with a bloody hand extended. Victor is more deliberate. He places his hat on his head, wraps his hand in a red bandana from his pocket and takes up another shard of mirror to gut us with before following. I back up the stairs with my cane raised like a sword.

"I want that camera," Russell says.

I throw the guitar case. It sails over Russell's shoulder and hits the far wall. The latches pop open and the guitar falls out with a musical crash. The pieces of broken record scatter across the hardwood. When he's in range, I clip Russell on the shoulder with my cane. He tumbles down the stairs, cracks his head at the foot of the flight and lies holding the back of his neck. Victor doesn't stop, just steps over his wounded friend to begin his ascent. He takes the stairs two at a time, the piece of mirror flashing as he chases us back toward the hall. When we reach Victor's room, Rosita pulls me inside, locks the door and puts her back against it.

"Is he dead?" she asks. I don't know if she means Russell or his father. Each thought passes through my mind too slippery with fear to grasp. The panic won't let me concentrate and I don't know how to stop it. I've never felt anything like this before. Not even frozen under the bright lights on a stage, or with The Reverend's hands on my throat. The closest was when I still believed in the Hellfire and brimstone version of God who would judge me after death. Thinking about it now, I'm more frightened of the eternal nothing that is coming as soon as Victor gets through the door.

"I don't know," I say.

Rosita gathers up the bedsheets that still smell of Victor and Caroline's sex. I wonder where Caroline is hiding but can't go back into the hall to find her. Outside the door, boot heels click on the stairs. Rosita tosses the sheets aside and dumps the contents of the nightstand drawers onto the mattress.

"What are you doing?" I ask.

"Looking for that Goddamned gun."

She finds a letter opener among the bits of paper, pens and other assorted junk, and slips it into her back pocket while she rifles through Victor's denim jacket hanging on the bedpost. Something collides with the door hard enough to shake the frame. The wood splinters around the hinges, threatening to buckle with the next blow.

"Block it," she shouts.

I put my back against it, but my misshapen hump keeps me from applying even pressure. Another strike knocks me away, so

Rosita braces herself against the door and tosses me the jacket. I'm unsure what to do with the balled fabric.

"Find the car keys," Rosita says.

Another kick, then silence before Russell's voice comes through the wood.

"Everything's okay," Russell says. "We can figure this out."

My trembling hands make it hard to grope inside the pockets. I finally manage to slip one inside where keys poke my palm. I hold them up, the metal tinkling as I shake them for Rosita's attention.

"Can you walk without that?" Rosita asks, pointing at my cane.

"Sort of," I say.

"Give it here."

She takes on something like a samurai's stance. The cane held high overhead in her right hand, the letter opener a dagger in her left. The camera bags still dangle from her shoulder.

"Straight downstairs," she says. "Don't stop for anything."

I want to tell her that I can't do it. My legs feel too weak to carry the rest of me down the hall, but I think of that arterial spray from Watson's neck and understand we don't have any choice.

"What about Caroline?" I ask.

"I haven't seen her come out of the bathroom. Look, we've got to get out of here."

Rosita throws the door open before I can protest. Russell barrels forward as she brings the cane down. The first swing strikes his neck, the second drives him back as she jabs into his stomach and groin. He flails, trying to deflect the blows, but the cane cuts the air with a sound reminiscent of a grandmother's switch. Every exposed patch of skin Rosita hits throbs red until Russell is forced back.

"Goddamn," he says, but Rosita doesn't relent. She swipes at his chin with the letter opener. Victor watches from the top of the stairs, still holding the long piece of mirror. Russell comes forward again. As he ducks to dodge the next stab with the letter opener, Rosita snaps the cane across his lower back. After a final gouge at his stomach with the splintered end, Rosita tosses it away.

"I'll stab your eyes out," she says, raising the letter opener. "I mean it, fucker."

"I just want the camera," Russell says. He's finished, panting as he rests against the wall.

Rosita pulls me forward. My legs do their best to keep up as her powerful stride closes the distance toward Victor. It looks like she is going to tackle him down the stairs like a runner rushing home plate, but Rosita slows and brandishes the letter opener at Victor's face. I wait for the gun, sure that he'll draw it from the back of his pants and shoot us down. Instead, Victor raises his hands in surrender and steps aside. I grab the handrail as we stagger down the stairs. At the bottom, I trip over my guitar case and turn hoping for a final glimpse of Caroline, but Rosita takes me by the collar.

"Don't stop," she says.

I toss her the car keys as soon as we hit sunlight. She scratches the paint fumbling with the hearse's lock. I know I can't go back after Caroline, that Russell and Victor would only beat me while Rosita escaped, but the guilt of leaving her presses down until my lungs refuse to fill.

"Get in," Rosita calls. When I hesitate, she shifts the car into drive as a final warning. "Get in, Goddamn it."

I fall into the passenger seat. The gate is still open, so Rosita never slows. We hit the main road hard, fishtailing as she tries to straighten the hearse. The silence inside the car is only inter-rupted when low-hanging tree branches scrape the roof as we race out of the hollow.

"What are we going to do?" Rosita asks.

I'm still thinking of Caroline locked inside the bathroom. No doubt they're breaking the door down, dragging her out and ei-ther adding her to the bodies in need of disposal or forcing her to comply with whatever story they fabricate. I shouldn't have left her. I should have stayed no matter what.

"Do you have a phone?" Rosita asks. "I can't find my cell."

I look in the rearview to see if anyone is pursuing us. "No," I say. "Did you get a picture?"

"Several." She points a thumb to the camera bags in the backseat.

The confines of the hearse are boiling, so Rosita cracks a window. I expect the licorice scent of the chemicals. Instead, the sweet rot of honeysuckle floods in until Rosita shakes a cigarette from her pack. She lights it with the car lighter and offers me a drag. The smoke opens my lungs until I feel as if I'm coughing out all the morning's terror. I start to cry, not sure if it's nerves, worry for Caroline or the delayed heartbreak of seeing her with another man. That final reason is foolish next to what's hap-pened, but I can't deny I'm still wounded by it.

"Take me home," I say, passing the cigarette and wiping my eyes.

"What about the police?" Rosita flicks ash out the window. "What about the water?"

"I've got a phone and a well on the property. It's the safest place."

I tell Rosita to take the next left and bypass downtown. Even-tually, the road narrows, poorly managed pavement giving way to gravel and later to dirt. We drive a long spell before coming to the edge of the creek. The expanse at my crossing isn't much, maybe twenty feet through the shallows to the far bank. The current is weak, but I can see the chemical foam sailing on the little rapids. The frothy clumps break apart downstream against the miniature summit of rocks jutting from the water. Invisible particles float on to taint other pools.

I reach for the door handle, but Rosita grabs me.

"What are you doing?" she asks.

"I'm gonna wade across and use the phone." I wasn't aware of my intentions until I said it out loud. "You wait here."

Rosita shakes her head. "You can't get that shit on you."

Images from last night's news flash across my mind. The dishwasher's lobster-red hands and boils the size of nickels oozing on the skin of children. If I wade alone, no one can help me in these woods. Still, we shouldn't risk the car. Russell made it across once in the hearse, but the tailpipe is low, sure to be submerged. After that, the cab will fill, and we'll be stranded in the center. Part of me still wants to risk it. I don't want Rosita to leave and go get help. Maybe it's the way she protected me or maybe it's a lingering curiosity about the project she showed me last night? All those bodies and their scars have become a mosaic in my mind. A swirling that blends mutilations until all the amputations, shrunken limbs and twisted bones feel whole. I still have trouble believing the coincidence that a music journalist only wants to add my body to some strange collage, but that doesn't matter like before. Something inside says Rosita has more to share. I need to get her across the creek to find out what that is.

Maybe we can make it. After all, Russell did just days ago.

Rosita guns the engine. I unbuckle the seatbelt and put my

feet up on the dash in preparation for when the water seeps inside. We hit the creek hard, the frame rattling and a torrent splashing high on the windows. A tire blows out as we roll over the uneven bedrock. The headlights submerge in the deepest pool. I watch a wave crest over the grille and drain inside through the slits in the hood. A hiss emits as water cascades onto the hot engine. Steam roils out until I think I hear the radiator crack. If the chemicals are flammable, the surface of the water will ignite and burn down the twisting stream like a serpent made of flame. I wait for fire as the exhaust gurgles and the tailpipe drowns.

"Don't let off the gas," I say. "Push it."

If the motor stalls, we'll have to wade. I think about my skin peeling off in long strips, but no imagination can conceive of the agony created by such a chemical flaying. If the car stalls, it might be better to sink with it.

Water begins to seep up through the carpet in the floorboards. Rosita stomps the pedal. The hearse doesn't have much of an engine. As we lurch forward, I hear rocks scraping the frame, the flattened tire thumping and sediment clacking against the grille. Rosita is praying again. I consider whether I should join her. Will the old celestial tyrant finally hear if we offer enough voices? Somewhere along the way, I've become too angry to pray.

The hearse makes it to the other side. We coast for about a hundred feet before stalling. Rosita pushes the throttle, but the engine only whines. Eventually, I smell gasoline instead of the sweet creekwater.

"We've killed it," I say. My feet are still up in the seat. I'm pleased to find them dry.

"Fuck it," Rosita says. "It's stolen." She smiles, a bit giddy from the reckless behavior.

Crossing the creek has awakened the pain in my back. The

jostling feels as if it loosened something between my uneven shoulders. I try to stretch my arm and the shock is so sudden all other concerns recede. I stop worrying about Rosita stranded or how long we can hold out on the provisions in the house. Stop worrying about everything until I can swallow a few pills.

I open the door and try to stand, but the pain forces me back down. I bite my bottom lip to stifle a scream.

"Let me help," Rosita says.

She takes hold underneath my arms and heaves. My back protests with another spasm, but she gets me on my feet. The pain won't let me stand alone, so I cling to her for support. This close, I can feel the curves of her body the way I used to feel Angela. I always feel alien pressed against another person. So many others in the world have grown straight and true.

"You okay?" she asks.

"I'll be fine," I say. "I just need my pills."

"Should I run and get them?" she asks.

"No," I tell her. "I can make it. It's not that far."

I rest against Rosita's shoulder as we travel across the overgrown field. It feels like crossing the wasteland from one of my songs, each step forcing me lower until I'm tempted to crawl. When we reach the porch, I sit on the steps and rest for a moment. It's a mistake. As soon as my ass hits the planks, it's clear I'm not rising anytime soon.

In the last ten years, no one aside from Russell or Caroline have seen my home. I watch as Rosita looks over the pergola in need of paint, the wraparound porch with rocking chairs nobody but me ever sits in. The windows haven't been washed in years. A thick coat of green mildew has taken up residence in the corners of each pane. I can't find any judgment in her eyes, but I feel ashamed.

"Where are those pills?" she asks.

"In the music room," I say. There are things inside I don't want her to see. "I can make it."

Rosita puts a hand on my shoulder to keep me from trying.

"You rest," she says and takes my keys.

When Rosita comes outside with the bottle, it's nearly empty. I drop two of the last seven pills into my palm, chew one and dry-swallow the other. Instant relief surges through me, but it's just false comfort at the familiar taste on my tongue.

"You need help up?" Rosita asks.

"Just let me sit a minute."

She rests on the stoop next to me. The wind blows hard, pulling a few leaves off the nearby trees. They sail by, a few stragglers floating down from higher branches to rest at our feet.

"It's beautiful here," Rosita says, "but kind of lonely."

Caroline used to say the same thing. Both must imagine men like me are better off in a city, walking busy streets, standing in line at a coffee shop and sitting in a corner café. Most of Rosita's interviewees probably make that sort of life work. Some might manage to be happy. No different than the average person with more conventional hardships. Would that life be easier? Her voice seems to suggest yes, but I'm not so sure. I think I'd be denied anonymity anywhere.

I stand with a grunt. My knees are still weak, so I grip the handrail of the steps. I barely feel the weathered wood through the calluses on my fingertips. So much damage done to skin with only steel strings and time. I'm not sure what to do now. It could be days before the creek is safe to cross. Even longer before someone comes to look in on us. Perhaps no one will come at all.

"I think you could use some rest," Rosita says. "Help you to bed?"

The offer sounds like exactly what I need. Rest awhile, let the pills do their work and examine the situation with fresh eyes. Only I worry about sleeping while a stranger shares my house. I don't trust her not to examine my music room. The things inside would offer her an unbelievable story.

"What about the police?" I ask.

"I'll handle it," she says.

We go to the bedroom where I collapse atop the comforter. Rosita stands at the foot of the bed, her back turned as she looks at the picture of Angela Carver. It's a subject she'll broach eventually, but I'm not about to offer anything. The first time Caroline shared my bed, the picture seemed to watch us as she rode atop my lap. Afterward, she lay wrapped up in the sheets, observing the photo while we shared one of her joints.

"Old girlfriend?" she'd asked with just a hint of surprise. As if a man like me could ever have someone in his past. It was an old picture, but I was shocked she didn't recognize Angela.

I remember Caroline just days before, nude except for her socks, stroking the concaved recess of my chest. If I truly cared for her, I wouldn't have abandoned her to murderers. If I ever really loved Angela, I wouldn't have considered selling her recordings.

"I left her," I say, but it wasn't meant to be said aloud.

"There was nothing else we could do," Rosita offers.

It's a poor comfort. I roll over, wait until Rosita departs before closing my eyes.

THE REQUEST

Day Two of the Contamination

When I wake, the pills are percolating through my extremities, spreading a euphoric emptiness I both love and fear. I'm thankful for the absence of pain, but the numbness pricking my fingertips will keep me from playing for at least an hour. I use it as an excuse to stay in bed, wrapped up in the familiar comfort of my narcotic blanket. The truth is, this is the best I ever feel. I'd probably trade the rest of my life for a few years of its permanence. When I consider this, I think of Caroline. It's the last thing I want my mind to linger on, so I climb out of bed.

The lights are on in the hallway and voices drift down the corridor. I follow the sound and find Rosita sitting at my breakfast table. The television on the counter cycles through footage from outside Shaheen's grocery store, shots of the polluted river and interviews with protesters.

"You see this?" Rosita asks. Her eyes are shielded by square glasses with tortoiseshell frames. The cheap plastic has a certain geek appeal, but the lenses are too thick to be a fashion state-ment. They magnify her eyes, allow me to see specks of black inside the hazel rings of her irises.

"You have to respect their resolve," she says, pointing to the protesters who march on-screen.

When I join her in the booth, our knees brush underneath the table. I can smell the greasy, fried-chicken odor of fear sweat still clinging to me. Feel the dried saliva collected in the corner of my mouth. The drugs always make me drool when I pass out. My appearance is always a concern, but it's especially embarrassing looking so disheveled in front of a woman like Rosita. I worry that my breath will be rank when I speak.

"How long was I out? Where are the police?"

"Not too long," she says. "The phones are acting weird, but I think I got through. Someone will be on the way."

Her laptop rests on the table between us. On-screen, a young man with no arms sits on the sort of dingy beige carpet that can only be found in a rented apartment. He's shirtless, allowing the camera to see his hairless chest, dime-sized nipples and the half-formed flesh orbs of his shoulders. A calligrapher's pen is clutched between his toes, writing what I assume are Chinese characters on a sheaf of paper. I don't want to seem like I'm pry-ing but can't pretend not to notice the image.

"What are you working on?" I ask.

"Things you wouldn't want to see."

I know my shortcomings, so I can admit I've never been the best at articulating my thoughts. Years alone have left me too brusque and with so little interaction, the raw anger inside bub-bles up sometimes. I was hurting for the pills last night when I sent her away and worried over Caroline, but it isn't an excuse. The truth is I felt objectified in the same old way as always.

Studied, not desired. That's not Rosita's fault. Feelings and in-securities will always be an unwelcomed presence I'll have to contend with. We don't get to choose our emotions, but I should be able to control my actions despite them.

"I'm sorry about last night," I say. "I was too harsh."

"I don't know," she says. "Maybe you've got a reason to be upset. I don't pretend to understand everything about these peo-ple I photograph. I just wanted to help them feel special."

Special is my least favorite word. Too many insidious mean-ings hidden within the term. A word carted out so often and for so many different purposes it has lost all relevance. Who'd want to be special, anyway? I've always longed to be normal.

Perhaps isolation has made me a paranoid cynic, but I wonder if she's fishing by accepting my apology. Opening up so that I'll unload my own sorrows about Angela Carver. I glance to the laptop screen, then stare at her like a kid initiating a contest. She smiles, a little puzzled by the way I've locked eyes. I smile back, wishing I were the sort of man who always received shy grins from beautiful women.

"What's he writing?" I ask, pointing to the armless man on the computer screen.

"He's just practicing his Chinese in this shot, or is it Manda-rin? Are they the same thing?" She laughs. "He's been writing his memoirs, too. The whole manuscript is in this elaborate calligra-phy. He said that the words should be as unique as his body."

"He's writing his memoirs in Mandarin?"

"Of course not!" She laughs again. "In English. He's still learning Mandarin."

"He said all this in the interview?" I ask. I point to the screen. "Can we read it?"

"Not here," she says, her voice bright as she begins to explain the project. "This feature of the website works as a slideshow." She turns the computer toward me and scrolls to the next image. "Just images of the interviewees. It's my favorite feature. No words. Only bodies as text."

Bodies as text. The phrase has a philosophical ring that I enjoy. I look at the armless man's elegant writing. If my body is a text, what does that say for its diction? The run-on sentence of a humped back, the broken and inarticulate divot in my chest. If I'm a text, is the meaning indecipherable because of the fallibility of my language?

"Turn it a little more?" I ask.

I'm not just being polite because she's in my home. The burned blonde invaded my thoughts in a way I thought only songs could. Lying in bed on the edge of sleep with the pills coursing through me, I imagined her body dipping into a steaming pool. The clear water running down goose-pimpled flesh in tiny rivulets. There was a desire to track those imagined rivers down the different varieties of scar. Follow each drop and see where it lingered. I need to see if other bodies will have a similar effect.

"Push this to scroll through," Rosita says. "You can look at the whole series or shuffle randomly."

I push the button, and the man who appears has half a face. His lower jaw is absent, leaving the whole of his throat open and exposed. I wonder if there is some apparatus that allows him to eat and drink. If so, he's removed it from the photo shoot. Now it is only a ragged maw leading into darkness. In the next photo, the camera is pulled back. The man sits with his legs apart, limp penis and scrotum sagging between his thighs. Somehow these hairy legs and shrunken prick look perfect compared to the rest of him.

"Why do they need to be naked?" I ask. There are secret parts of me that only Angela and Caroline have seen. Usually, I feel separated from myself. Not a body, but a brain trapped inside a broken vessel. I wonder if I could let strangers see those parts of me. Rosita opens her mouth and looks ready to launch into a speech prepared for critics who've considered her work pornographic or the acts of a provocateur, but she just shrugs instead of unscrolling the diatribe.

"Because they're beautiful," Rosita says. "Don't you think they're beautiful?"

Something shines through in the isolated areas. The man with no jaw has a sculpted stomach, the burned blonde from last night the toned legs of an Olympian. These pieces of the whole have the fickle spark of conventional beauty, but I know that isn't what Rosita meant. She's referring to something else we can't quite name. Something in the fact that such malformed things persist. A man continuing to breath even if the oxygen must travel through a gaping hole. Skin still warm with life despite being scorched dead by a long-extinguished fire.

"How do you convince them to undress?" I ask.

"I do it with them. That way things are equal."

Looking at Rosita next to any picture in this collection proves nothing in life is ever equal. I imagine her setting the camera aside and sliding out of her shirt. Her body looks delicate lounging in my booth, but without clothes I think she would be all muscle, like a skinned squirrel. If I agreed to the photo shoot, would she undress for me and would I be able to keep the act in perspective?

We're interrupted by the sound of tires crunching gravel. As Rosita pulls back the window blinds, a green Jeep Cherokee with a light bar mounted on the roof pulls into the drive. COOPERS-VILLE COUNTY SHERIFF is painted down the vehicle's side in gold lettering. I exhale slowly through my nose as the driver steps out and try to swallow down the fear that always accompanies meeting outsiders.

Sheriff Elizabeth Saunders is a small black woman, barely five-foot-three in her low-heeled boots. Her uniform is poorly tailored, puffy at the sleeves and chest—she looks like a child playing dress-up. Only the hat, a wide-brimmed drill sergeant lid favored by the state police, rests on her head with the proper air of authority. The angle covers her eyes, but I see her face is clean of any makeup. Sheriff Saunders takes off her hat and rests it on the handle of the collapsible baton on her utility belt. Rosita opens the door.

"Mr. Bragg," Sheriff Saunders says. "May I come in? I'd like a word with you."

I can tell she's prepared herself before arrival. There is only a moment of shock when she looks at me. If I wasn't used to it, the microscopic furrow of brow wouldn't even register. I wave her inside, and the sheriff follows us into the kitchen. I sit in the booth beside Rosita, but Sheriff Saunders remains standing. She looks surprised that my kitchen is so domestic. The cherrywood cabinets and new appliances don't fit with the mountain hermit narrative.

I've heard plenty of stories about the sheriff. She took over after Sheriff Thompson was murdered, then she won reelection by a landslide despite being a woman in a county where the most important qualification for a lawman is his dick. She shot an armed robber who tried to knife a teller at Coopersville Bank and Trust last November. Some called her quick with the gun, but I think that's just the kind of criticism country men are likely to level at a woman with authority.

Sheriff Saunders turns to Rosita. "You must be the young lady that called," she says. "I sent a patrol car to the Watson residence. It's currently a crime scene."

"What about Caroline?" I ask. "Caroline Stephens?"

"We located one body. A male. Aside from that, the house was empty."

The sheriff pulls out a chair, straddles it and removes a notepad and small digital recorder.

"I need you both to run through it all again. Tell me exactly what happened."

I let Rosita talk. Sheriff Saunders never interrupts, never asks for Rosita to elaborate until she's finished her point. I nod along, only interjecting occasionally to keep from being entirely silent. Caroline's absence scares me. I should be glad she isn't dead, but I keep thinking of terrible scenarios. Her body submerged in some poisoned pool or ravaged by nocturnal scavengers in the brush of the thicket. She could be bound and gagged, suffocating in the trunk of a car. The possibilities play endlessly as I watch the glowing red eye on Sheriff Saunders's recorder.

"I'll need to see these photos," Sheriff Saunders says when we finish.

Rosita takes out her camera. "I couldn't get to the digital in time."

The sheriff sets the camera on the table. "What am I going to see when these are developed?"

"Russell Watson and Victor Lawton committing murder."

A spark of recognition flashes across the sheriff's face when Rosita mentions Victor.

"You recognize the name?" I say.

"Everyone knows the Watsons," she says, but I won't let her deflect that easily.

"No, the other one. You already knew it was the Watsons' house, so it's the other name that surprised you."

Sheriff Saunders seems annoyed but leans forward and turns

off her tape recorder. "We've run into him a few times. He was caught vandalizing some coal trucks at a depot when he was a minor. Cut some brake lines hoping the drivers might crash. Luckily, the sabotage was discovered before anyone got hurt. He spent some time at the Tiger Morton Juvenile Center."

I think about Victor's rant the first time he and Russell crossed the creek. I'd tried to convince myself my feelings of dread were too extreme. Now I wish I'd have trusted my gut and never gone near him.

"You're not supposed to know any of that. Juvenile records are sealed. Repeat any of this, or what I'm about to tell you, and I'll deny it. I can't prove it, but I also think he took a couple shots at some chemical trucks on the interstate. Two different drivers arrived at their destination with .38 slugs in their grilles, spiderweb cracks in the windshields."

"That's Victor," I tell her. "He was talking wild shit all night. Saying he wanted Russell to prove himself. I think he may have hooked up with him just to get close to Russell's father."

"So, Mr. Watson was dead when you fled the residence?" the sheriff asks.

"Yes," Rosita says.

"And in what condition was the body?"

I picture Mr. Watson lying on the floor, the glass shards orbiting his head as the pool of blood spreads.

"Why?" I ask.

The sheriff sighs. "We haven't released this information to the public, but we found the body duct-taped to a chair in the kitchen. It looked like he might have been tortured, but if what you're saying is true, the wounds must be post-mortem."

I remember Victor twirling his gun, saying that we should make him confess.

"There was a note pinned to his chest," Sheriff Saunders says. "Just one word. 'Traitor.' That fits with Victor's history. The things he said in the interview, too."

"What do you mean?" I ask. I don't know what interview she's talking about.

The sheriff takes out her iPhone and plays a video of Victor marching with the protesters. His face is still ashen with gray paint, dusty flannel covered in crimson that may be either from Mr. Watson or fake blood from the concert. A tiny anchorwoman stands on tiptoes even in her heels, stretching to raise the microphone to his lips.

"Can you tell us why you've dressed this way?" she asks.

"The corporations that poisoned our water view our lives as worthless. I dress like a corpse to illustrate the damage they've done in this region."

On the small screen, Victor incites the crowd. He waves his arms like a conductor as the chanting voices rise.

"Quite the opportunist," Sheriff Saunders says. "I can't believe he's got the balls to be in public after something like this, but we'll find him. What about you two? How are you people holding up?"

"We're okay," I say. I'm still worried about Caroline, but there's nothing more the sheriff can do about that.

"Well, you certainly seem better off than most. We got three hundred thousand residents without drinking water in this state." Sheriff Saunders turns her attention to Rosita. "What brings you to Coopersville, Miss Martinez?"

"I came to interview Hollis."

If it's a lie, she's the best I've seen at it. I wonder why she doesn't mention The Excitable Boys but keep quiet.

"Interview him regarding what?"

"An art project of mine. *The Body Book*."

The title is enough for Sheriff Saunders to give a dismissive nod.

"I understand you've got a well on this property," she says. "I'd like permission to extract some of your water. We got a lot of thirsty people."

I imagine a line of parched refugees standing in my field, passing overflowing buckets. Some might find a sort of savior's pride at the thought, but I feel invaded. Rosita is already more than I'm used to handling. When I hesitate, the sheriff rests her elbows on her knees and leans forward into the silence.

"I'd leave you be if I could, but we got people in trouble out there."

"When would they be here?" I ask.

"I couldn't get the trucks here for a few days, but I'd have some people here tonight. Civilian volunteers, a few nearby families willing to tote water."

I know Rosita wants to watch the locals arrive. Maybe snap a few photos. If I won't pose for her, maybe I owe her that. Even if all they've done is ridicule me, I certainly owe the people of Coopersville something as simple as a drink of water, but I only agree because Rosita is watching. I'm too afraid of what she might think if I refuse.

"Go get them," I say.

Sheriff Saunders dons her hat and stands. "Thank you, Mr. Bragg. Do you need a ride, miss?"

Rosita looks to me for an answer. "It's up to you," I say, but hear the loneliness in my voice. Not quite pleading, yet I'm certain she recognizes it, too.

"I'm fine," Rosita says. "Thank you, Sheriff."

"I appreciate this, Mr. Bragg," Sheriff Saunders says. "You

don't know how many people you're helping." I follow the sheriff to the door. "Oh, one last thing. We have your guitar at the station. Wouldn't want to lose something that special."

I nod, glance back to see what Rosita thinks about this, but she shows no sign of having overheard. I watch as the Jeep drives away and am back in the kitchen, lighting a cigarette on the stovetop before Rosita speaks again.

"Thank you for letting me stay," she says.

"I'm not sure why you'd want to."

"I'm enjoying the company."

Fantasy will take over if I allow it. I remind myself that while Rosita finds beauty in broken bodies, that doesn't mean she wants mine. At least not outside the pages of her project.

"Can we finish looking at those photos?" I ask.

It's clear my newfound interest perplexes her, but Rosita opens the laptop, clicks some keys and hands over the computer.

"This is a man I interviewed in Delaware," she says.

The man's face has melted. Nose reduced to nothing but a mound with surgical bore holes. Lips absent, eyes boiled away and covered by grafted flaps of skin harvested from volunteers or other parts of his body. This donor flesh looks smooth and fresh. It begs to be touched. The man sits on a plaid couch in his living room, nude and perfect from the nipples down. In several of the following shots, Rosita focuses on his feet. Long-toed and wide-arched, covered in hair like a hobbit.

"He likes to rub them together since the accident," she says, pointing at the furry feet. "It makes him calm to feel the hair, but he said it also makes him nostalgic about the hair on his head. That's the word he used, *nostalgic*. Like he was talking about an old job and not missing part of himself. His wife used to love his curls."

I pick up on the phrase "used to love." It makes me wonder if any of that love was salvaged. If his wife's admiration has been transplanted to the wiry hair atop those feet. Perhaps, when they're lying in bed together, she rubs her smooth calves against the coarse strands. Perhaps the man's bed is empty. His wife sleeping curled around a new man whose sight won't allow her features to be lost in the fog of memory.

"Most people cringe when they see him," Rosita says.

"What happened to him?"

"Chemical burn in a factory accident."

I consider the toxins floating down my own stream. "Tell me some more of these stories."

"What do you mean?"

"I mean, the history of the people is here, some of their own words, but that isn't the same. Tell me about meeting them."

I watch Rosita try to transport herself back to that distant morning when she rang the faceless man's doorbell. She looks at the tiny details in the margins of the photo. The brick wall behind the couch. The mug of tea on the coffee table and the invisible ghost of steam that couldn't be captured by the camera. Hours pass while Rosita narrates the lives behind each picture. She shares the jokes the men made, the women who laughed or cried, the spouses who stayed and the spouses who left and those who've never had another who loved them. Explaining the moments of silence is hardest. Like the steam from that coffee cup, there are things the camera can't capture, things words can't make clear.

THE LOCALS

Day Two of the Contamination

We've gone through six different interviews when the first of the locals arrive. They cross the creek like a defeated army, a sad procession of old men and women migrating slow from the far shore, ferried in the back of pickups that surge through the water. With so few trucks, the drivers are forced into return trips to collect fresh groups. One man wears waterproof waders that come up to his chest and wades across with a little girl riding piggyback atop his shoulders, her stuffed bear clutched tight over her mouth. I watch out the window, concerned the girl may drop the teddy, but both she and the bear make it unharmed.

Rosita squats on the porch snapping pictures. When she notices me, she holds up the camera. "If this makes you the least bit uncomfortable, I'll put it away," she says.

Both of us know the moment deserves documenting. Rosita focuses on the children. None of them laugh or play. Either they've been strictly warned of the dangers or realize whose house they're approaching. They must know the rumors. Local horror stories about the twisted mountain man who lives in these woods. The adults will be whispering worse to one another. I wonder how many of Coopersville's residents will be too afraid to show up on my doorstep.

Sheriff Saunders isn't present, but two of her deputies keep things orderly. They herd the men and women across the field, guide them to the well where a line has formed to fill improvised receptacles. Two-liter bottles of Coca-Cola with wrappers still attached. Empty jugs still containing the white film from milk since it is unsafe to rinse them clean. A few even have funnels to assure every drop is collected. Some of the kids whine as they wait, but the parents stroke their hair, tell them to be thankful and polite. One man strikes his unruly child, but the deputies put an end to it before the disgruntled crowd can turn on him.

Rosita moves closer for better angles. I know she sees my two fingers holding the wooden blinds open to look out on this bizarre assembly. She gives a little tilt of her head meant to coax me outside, so I close the blinds. There are too many. Just like those nights onstage. They need nourishment, but that doesn't mean they want to see me. Charity is hard enough on country people. Receiving it from someone like myself would only be added insult. There are also the children to consider. Those I didn't frighten would be full of questions their parents won't know how to answer. I'll be even more frightening to the children now that the sun is down.

I peek again against my better judgment. Rosita gives another wave before going back to her pictures, but that isn't the end of it. After a few more minutes, she opens the door as predicted, stands in the kitchenette where I sit looking at her photos of the mutilated man from Delaware.

"How long you gonna peer out the window like this?" Rosita asks.

"All Goddamned night if I want," I say.

"You need to come outside and make these people feel welcome."

"You're mistaken if you think I can make them feel welcome. Just let them drink in peace."

Rosita snaps the laptop closed so fast the screen almost catches my fingers. "You know what's amazing about these pictures?" she asks.

"What?"

"All those people like you, or worse off, and none of them were so ashamed."

With her scolding finished, Rosita holds the door and I step out onto the porch. The night air is cool, the field illuminated by the high beams of pickups and a few torches some cops thought to stake in the yard. By the torchlight, the scene looks almost primeval. Muddied men and women slogging toward the well with their buckets. They've yet to notice me standing in the shadows.

"Just a few words," Rosita says.

After Angela, I promised myself I'd never change for another woman. After we ended, the drive to improve and all my new-found valor slipped away without me even realizing its absence. One day it was there, the next I had regressed toward all the same old flaws. If the changes were only a temporary augmentation, I knew I'd have to accept myself for the vulgar man I was. Anything else would be an unfair con on whatever woman I was trying to impress. Still, the need for Rosita's approval makes me want to harness a bravery I don't have. I want to be the sort of man who can stand in the torchlight, unafraid of all those eyes on my broken body, and say something to make the moment easier. When I open my mouth, my tongue is frozen. Air emits around my teeth. I swallow and try again.

"Can I have your attention?" I call.

No one turns. Most cannot hear since the intended shout was no more than a baby's breath. Others seem unsure the muttering wasn't from a private conversation. One of the deputies raises her hand. The crowd stills, turns toward where I stand in the firelight. Rosita has moved away from the pulpit of the porch and stands in the field watching through her camera. Framed in the lens, I feel like I'm onstage again. Washed in the same sweat and nausea that used to come with the bright lights.

"My name's Hollis Bragg," I say. The eyes on me are a strange mix of curiosity and sadness. Not even whispers pass through the crowd. I close my eyes to continue, but feel the stares bore into me like I'm a specimen underneath a microscope.

"I just wanted to say I'm pleased to have you all. Thank you for braving the creek and coming out. I ain't got much, but I hope what little I've got helps. I'm happy to share it."

Light applause, a few nods from those embarrassed to be taking anything from a stranger. I sit down on the stoop and let them return to it. It feels foolish letting Rosita drag me out expecting some grand speech, but she walks over with her digital camera and shows me the images in the small screen. Without my awkward words, the true quality of the moment is captured.

I'm standing with a single hand raised high in greeting, the small fires throwing shadows on the strange contours of my body. The picture is beautiful in a bleak way, but the real truth is in the next photo. Just me sitting on the top step, quiet and unmolested, while the men and women march by to quench their children's thirst.

After the residents of Coopersville depart, we sit up with the television muted in the background. I cradle my guitar just to feel the comfort of it, but Rosita asks me to play snippets of random tunes. It becomes a little game. I strum a few chords while Rosita tries to guess the song, or she calls out a title and I attempt it from memory. She's moved close on the couch, her bare foot absently touching my knee. When her skin first brushed the denim of my jeans, I expected her to pull away like a hand scalded on a hot stove. She seems not to notice as her toes tap in time with my guitar.

"Do you want me to turn it off?" Rosita asks, pointing to the muted TV. On-screen, the protesters are marching in silence.

"I'm fine either way. At least the place is getting some press."

"They should have been here tonight," Rosita says. "Those pictures are the most important I've taken since the early days of *The Body Book*."

She tried to show them to me earlier, but I didn't want to see any more. Better to just pick the strings, let their vibrations ring until it hones my concentration. I'm waiting for her to ask about Angela's signed guitar.

"I've spent all night telling you about these photos," Rosita says. "It's your turn to tell me some stories."

"You're not getting me out of my clothes," I say.

Playful moments of flirtation have emerged. Fleeting glances, secret evaluations with bashful eyes. I almost never get any signals from women, and if such a thing does happen, I'm too oblivious to realize. I still don't understand why Caroline ever wanted me. Maybe it's just our circumstances, the close call with death making us both feel too alive, but even my lack of confidence isn't strong enough to mask what's happening.

"I'm not trying to get you to do an interview," Rosita says. "I'll never get a better picture of you than I did today."

I strum the solemn intro to an old love song. One of those tunes you've heard before, but just can't place.

"Will you tell me about Angela Carver?" she asks.

I sigh. "Why would you wanna hear about that?"

"Because of that picture in the bedroom."

I understand the curiosity. No woman remains on a man's wall without a story. I like Rosita, but the ingrained distrust of outsiders reminds me her motives are not completely altruistic. She wants good photos and stories to go with them. Unless I want the whole world to know the truth, telling her things I've never uttered before would be a mistake.

"Did you love her?" she asks.

I perform a quick run down the guitar's neck that makes Rosita crack a smile. If only I could do that to her with a touch.

"It's a long story," I say and shake my head. The truth is, I'm too happy to descend into those memories. "Not tonight."

"Lame," she tells me and opens her laptop. There is a sudden gulf between us as her foot pulls from my knee. I set the guitar aside and start to bed when I hear Rosita's breath catch in her throat.

"Hollis," she says. "Look at this."

Every major news network is running the photos of Watson duct-taped to one of the dining room chairs, his head lolling to the side and the wound on his neck blurred out. A sheet of white paper is stapled to his chest. The word TRAITOR written in fat black letters.

"The article says there was a video online," Rosita tells me. "They've already taken it down, of course."

I can imagine the footage. Victor preaching the same things he shouts from the picket line, standing with the Colt in his hand as he makes a declaration of war against all the traitors.

"We should have done more," Rosita says.

II

TWISTED LITTLE MAN

THE DUGOUT

I spent my days in the woods with the music books, reading and practicing until the mysterious graphs made sense. The Reverend never checked on my progress. His absence made me wonder if I'd done something to offend him. Maybe he knew I'd been spying on him with Lady Crawford only nights before. Perhaps I'd been walking around with the accusations of false prophet chiseled across my face. It would be nice to believe some guilt ate at his conscience, but I suspect he just didn't have time for me. Whatever it was, we avoided each other like sore-tailed cats until one morning when I came up from the creekbank to find him waiting for me. He was dressed in his black suit, shoes polished for a house call.

"The Lord is calling Brother Maynard home," he said. "We need to pray together. Bring your guitar."

Before he joined our church, Brother Maynard belonged to the same snake-handling and mountain-magic congregation as

Lady Crawford. I saw him once without his corduroy jacket, shirtsleeves rolled up to expose the knotted scar tissue from several bites. He terrified me. If copperheads and timber rattlers couldn't kill him, I doubted any illness would manage to finish the job. I didn't want to go but knew I couldn't refuse my father.

Brother Maynard lived behind the baseball field near Bradshaw Elementary. The diamond wasn't quite regulation size. The distance from the pitcher's mound to home plate was noticeably shorter than standard requirements and center field wasn't wide enough to warrant its third outfielder. Despite these shortcomings, it entertained kids and adults a few nights each week. Since it was a rare source of distraction, the school paid Brother Maynard a small sum to work as groundskeeper. He did a decent job with the upkeep, paying special attention to the grass, but the diamond looked rough that day. Right field was a barren patch. The remaining crabgrass blighted until the ground was mostly mud. Rain had washed away the chalk lines. Even the signs that covered the outfield fence and advertised for local businesses peeled paint. Only CARVER MUSIC, with the new addition of a golden saxophone spilling musical notes from its mouth, looked fresh.

The Reverend parked the truck in front of the one-story house and climbed out carrying my guitar. I followed down the concrete walkway, past a broken dog chain that wrapped around the trunk of an elm. Its rusted links lay coiled atop the tree's surfacing roots. I thought I heard an animal howling in the distance, but once the smells of sickness met us at the front door, I realized the sounds were coming from Brother Maynard.

Lady Crawford stood in the hall with her mouth hidden behind a painter's mask. She pulled it down under her chin and offered a smile.

"How is he?" The Reverend asked.

"Worse. I think the Lord will call him soon."

During the ride, The Reverend explained that Brother Maynard had been suffering from agonizing headaches. He finally took himself to the hospital after weeks of praying, but by that time the mass was already the size of a boiled egg. Other small specks surrounded the margins of the X-ray like gnats in a swarm. Since then, Brother Maynard had refused all medical intervention including painkillers. Occasionally, he spoke in a madman's yattering. Fantasy mixed with half-remembered moments of his youth. He begged for water, but Lady Crawford said even a drop made him gag.

I covered my face with a mask as she ushered us inside. The congregation surrounded the sickbed like sentries. Every member wore white clothing that seemed to glow in the dark room.

"Play him something," The Reverend said, as he handed me the guitar. "Something to ease his suffering."

I watched Brother Maynard tremble and sweat until his pillow was saturated. I worried the bright sound of a guitar might feel like hot needles in his brain. Nothing I could offer would make his passage easier. What he needed was a morphine drip and eternal sleep, but I obeyed my father and made the first chord. I don't remember the song, just that I tried to play a soft progression. Brother Maynard didn't dive into convulsions, but his eyes opened wide before going distant. I've thought about that over the years. At the time, I believed it was the look that accompanied any death. Now I wonder if my music hurt the dying man so severely he couldn't even scream. I tried to stop after the first song, but my father made me play "Amazing Grace" while Lady Crawford took up the vocals.

My palms moistened until I almost dropped the guitar.

Everything inside wanted to bolt as the congregation joined in the crooning. I held firm, finished the song and stood aside while they began another hymn. My father expected me to keep playing, but I stumbled outside with The Reverend calling after me.

The chain-link fence surrounding the ballfield was unlocked, so I crossed the faded chalk line into the visitors dugout. Inside, a bench had been formed by a slab of concrete poured against the back wall. I stretched out across it with the guitar forgotten at my feet. I knew my father would beat me when he finished with Brother Maynard. A good strapping to ensure that next time I'd be too afraid to run, but the coming punishment didn't bother me. I just didn't want to lend my music to the Lord. He'd already taken up so much of my life, I'd decided that this one thing would be mine.

It started to rain. I closed my eyes and listened as the fat drops pelted the roof. I wanted to play along to the rhythm but was afraid my father would be searching for me. I'd just gained the nerve to form a chord when Angela Carver appeared at the entrance of the dugout. Her red hair lay matted to her neck in wet curls. The elaborate eyeliner and mascara she wore the first time I saw her were gone. Absent any makeup, I could see the constellation of freckles that covered her cheeks. I remember thinking she looked more like a woman that day. Less a child painted with false maturity.

"I didn't expect to see you again," she said, approaching like the dugout might be booby-trapped. Her canvas sneakers squished with each step.

I had no clue what to say. What would a girl like her want to hear? As much as I desired having her close, the proximity only reminded me how twisted I looked lying on the cold slab. In another time, young women would've been kept from the presence of boys like me. Their husbands would've paid to see my deformities through the safety of a freak show cage, and they'd come home describing the shock of such a horror, assuring curious wives that even a glance at something so sinister could atrophy unborn children in the womb.

"What are you doing here?" I asked. It came out sounding like she was a trespasser. Angela just shrugged.

"I walk the diamond sometimes to clear my head. So, are you going to tell me what's up?" she asked.

"My father brought me to play for Brother Maynard."

"I hear he's a pretty weird guy."

"He's a member of our congregation."

"Yeah, sorry," she said. "I didn't mean anything by it."

"It's all right. We're all weird." It was self-deprecation I hoped she would argue against, but she didn't say anything.

"Do you like your church?" she asked.

I'd been instructed to tell outsiders our congregation was the same as any other. Some of the parishioners might have even considered themselves normal, but a normal congregation doesn't need to train its young members to lie. Maybe it was the recent flight from the sickbed, but I wanted to finally tell somebody the truth.

"I hate the church," I said. "Sometimes I think I'm beginning to hate everything. Except playing."

Angela picked up the guitar and laid it across her lap.

"You played really well," she said. "Especially to just be learning. I know your dad bought some books. How's it coming?"

I shrugged. "I don't know. There are things I want to do, but just can't." I wasn't talking exclusively about music. I didn't elaborate or try to explain, but I knew she understood. Even that early on, we could communicate that way.

"I could show you some things," she said. "I mean, if you want."

Angela slid the guitar onto my lap. As the wooden curves brushed over my thighs, I imagined her fingers trailing across the denim. She took my left hand, raised it to the guitar neck and shaped my fingers into some new chord. Angela strummed as she explained the construction, only I couldn't concentrate. For the first time in months, I wanted something more than the music. I took her hand and held it away from the strings. She let me claim the fingers, so I sat holding them while she ignored my awkward grip.

When she didn't speak, I knew I'd misinterpreted the moment. Excitement caused me to grope for something more than a simple act of kindness. I let go of her hand, and might have fled into the rain, but my legs wouldn't let me stand.

"Sorry," I said.

"It's okay."

Even after all these years, I can still feel the desire to burrow under the pitcher's mound in shame. Sink into the nearest river and let the minnows devour my eyes. I felt too embarrassed to breathe.

"I play in my father's shop after school some days," she said. "He's got a little studio down in the basement. Why don't you join me?"

I didn't believe it was a real offer. Just something to dull the sting of rejection.

"Do you drive?" Angela asked. "I could pick you up."

"No," I told her. The last thing I wanted was someone to see where we lived.

My father's truck rumbled in the distance, tires sloshing

through fresh puddles. In that moment, I preferred the coming beating to another second beside her.

"I have to go," I said. "Thanks for showing me some things."

"You don't have to take off," Angela said. But I'd already started out of the dugout. Angela called after me, but her words were lost in the rain. The Reverend didn't say anything as I climbed in the truck. On the drive home, I kept remembering the warmth of Angela's hand. The feeling of her calloused fingertips rubbed raw from the guitar strings. Something we shared. That day, it felt like the only characteristic still linking me to humanity.

In the weeks that followed, The Reverend's policy on tithes began to change. He balked at any paltry sum, tossed coins from the offering plate and demanded folding cash at the end of each service. I always waited outside until the congregation required me to strum a few hymns. Afterward, they'd kick me back out until prayers concluded, but I no longer needed to spy. My father's preaching echoed through the thin wooden walls like Gabriel's trumpet. If the message could previously be considered one of Hellfire and brimstone, the newer version was apocalyptic. All sermons reduced to speeches where The Reverend frothed and screamed about sin in the camp. He repeated the same commands, told the congregation the best way to save themselves was to abandon all worldly possessions. He became a backwoods version of the televangelists I occasionally heard on the radio. Prophesizing exclusively on how the Lord needed cash.

None of this newfound wealth went to repairs. The roof still leaked and the dirt floor transformed to mud every rainy night. My father hoarded the cash in a wooden cigar box under his bed. I didn't know how much he managed to squirrel away until later, but I'd lie awake at night imagining how far I could get with the money. In these proposed escapes, I'd cross the creek to the blacktop and pay someone to haul me to the nearest town. From there, I'd hitchhike to a city. Lexington, Philadelphia, Atlanta, New York.

It was a pipe dream, but it felt good pretending I could make it alone. I knew a man like me would never even cross the state line. Some redneck would see the cash, bash me in the head and leave my body in a ditch. Fantasizing I had the same chance as others helped me survive the routine of church service, practice and sleep.

Angela returned just as I began to forget about her. She drove up to the camper in her father's F-150, a vehicle that rode too low to risk crossing the creek, but she braved it anyway. The Reverend was away somewhere with Lady Crawford, but I stayed in the camper and peered out the window as Angela paced in the yard. I didn't want to be seen after botching our last encounter. Hope felt too dangerous at that age.

Angela didn't leave. She just leaned against the hood, lit a cigarette and folded her arms across her chest. She'd removed her leather jacket despite the chill, and I could see her forearms covered in freckles as if her whole body had been dusted with cinnamon.

"I can wait all day," she called and slid up onto the hood. Her shoes dangled in front of the grille as she flicked ash.

I took the guitar from under the bed and stepped out to meet her. Every inch of my body hummed until I felt like the most malformed features were trying to capture her eyes. Every man or woman I've ever met allows themselves a moment to take in my flaws. Angela had that same human inclination, but there was a different tone to her observation, more curiosity than disgust. She saw me in a way I never hoped anyone, much less a woman, would.

"How did you find me?" I asked.

"Everyone knows where you live, Hollis." It was a stupid question. In those days, it was a rite of passage for young men to cross the creek and dare each other to walk near the church.

"Let's go for a ride," she said.

"I have to be here when my father gets back," I lied. The Reverend was too enamored with Lady Crawford and his hoarded money to notice my absence. I was just trying to sabotage things. I'd spent weeks telling myself I didn't want her because it seemed impossible to have her.

She picked me up nearly every day to compose music in the basement of her father's shop. Just fragments at first. Everything from distorted rock riffs to acoustic pieces that sounded like prayers and played in my head long after I returned home. I hummed them alone at night, sneaked out of bed to practice the chords outside among the crickets and owl calls. The music wasn't a secret, but I understood it was just for us. No one ever listened, and we never discussed the notion of additional players or an audience. Sometimes I wondered if Angela felt embarrassed to be seen with me. If I were like other boys, would she have encouraged public performances? I struggled with that uncertainty, went back and forth between thinking she just wanted us to be ready, or that I only served as a distraction until someone better came along. Slowly, the music changed me. My stoicism melted away, and I realized all the songs were admissions that I loved her.

Things might have continued this way forever, but The Reverend was sitting outside one evening when Angela dropped me off. My father looked naked in his shirtsleeves, his body lying across the camper's stoop like a man who just completed some incalculable burden. Each breath swelled his belly until his shirt tented and remained aloft even as he exhaled. When I reached him, I smelled the sour mash seeping from his pores.

Angela asked if I needed help, but I waved her on. I poked my father's ribs with a finger. He didn't respond, so I jabbed harder until his eyes rolled and he lifted his neck enough to speak.

"Leave me be," he mumbled.

"What are you doing out here? Come inside."

He wouldn't let me touch him, swung violent slaps whenever I tried to help him rise. I'd never known my father to drink. The Reverend always preached about the wicked nature of spirits, but that evening was a vintage blackout, the sort of bender that looked like farce drunkenness in a poorly acted movie.

"Won't talk to me," The Reverend said to no one. "Won't even explain."

I left him raving and traveled across the field to see if Lady Crawford was in the church. *Let her play caretaker*, I thought. The windows were dark, the normal candlelight that shone through the cracks extinguished. I pounded on the door.

"I know you're in there," I shouted.

It felt absurd playing diplomat to the adults. I gave the door a final furious kick and shuffled off to the camper where my father had finally raised his head enough to stay awake. I grabbed his chin to secure his attention.

"Can you walk?" I asked.

The Reverend pushed himself up from the steps, went inside

and collapsed in my bed. I wanted to move him somewhere else, but was happy enough to have him out of the elements. I pulled the boots off his feet, left the socks with holes that expose his yellowed toenails.

"You wanna explain to me what's going on between you two?" I asked.

"Put here to deceive," The Reverend said. "Ever since the garden. Don't forget, boy."

"I don't think I'll ever have to worry about it," I said.

Drool leaked across The Reverend's lips. I considered wiping it away but left it to darken the pillowcase.

"What about the one I see you with?" The Reverend asked. "The one bringing you home the last couple weeks?"

The question had loomed since the first day Angela fetched me, but with my father in such a pathetic state, I became brave.

"Just a friend," I said.

The Reverend grunted. "You don't need any whore friends."

"Sure," I said.

"You sassing me?" He grimaced as something internal protested his attempt to sit up. "I don't want the slut back here. Understand?"

I looked at the sagging waddle of neck fat, the sweat-stained armpits of The Reverend's shirt and tangled knot of his dirty hair. Even the teeth that jutted from his snarled mouth seemed worn down and loose at the roots, as if a bit of wiggling could extract them with ease. Any intimidating presence he carried had been stolen by the bottle. I felt more powerful even with my bones in decline.

"I don't give a shit what you want," I said. I leaned in to capture his eyes as they swam around the room. "You try and stop me, you try and say anything to her, and I'll make sure the whole congregation knows about you and Lady Crawford. I'll make sure they know about you hoarding the tithes."

Mentioning the money washed The Reverend sober. The fog lifted from his gaze and he lunged at me. I staggered backward, caught my feet in the rug and bowled over onto my side. I scrambled away as The Reverend tried to climb from the bed, but he got tangled in the sheets and fought the comforter for freedom before worming his way out from under the blankets. Somehow, he found steady feet and seized me by the throat. The hands felt reptilian pressing down on my Adam's apple. I closed my eyes and waited for breathing to become impossible, but The Reverend administered two slaps instead of suffocating me. I didn't have any fight left, so I curled up, prepared for boot heels and improvised bludgeons.

"Nothing but a burden," The Reverend said. His whiskey breath blew hot on my face. Underneath the sweet rot of the bourbon, I could almost taste the rage my father carried inside. I was glad to have it come to this. Better to have a real moment together than the continued lies. In a way, it was the only time he showed me the truth.

"Another mention of her and I'll bury you out in these woods," he said. "Do you understand?"

I wasn't sure which hurt more, that he wasn't just threatening or the idea that my father finally found something to love. I always knew I was never going to be that object of affection. I could accept that, but was surprised by my sudden jealousy. Even if the emotions didn't naturally meld, my swelling lips were a testament to The Reverend's affection for Lady Crawford. I wanted to feel that way about another person or, better still, have another person love me enough to utilize such violence.

"Understand?" he asked again.

I croaked out an answer. "Yes, I understand."

The Reverend took my left hand and twisted my ring finger. He moved to my pinky, grasped it tight while I begged him to stop. It wasn't the pain. I knew if he bent it all the way back, I'd never form proper chords again. I closed my eyes and felt the bone pop from the socket.

"That fixes things," he said, and shuffled back to bed. I lay looking at the bent digits. The pain must have been intense, but I can't remember feeling it. I was too busy lying in the dark for hours, trying to wiggle the unresponsive fingers. When it became hopeless, I decided to see if Lady Crawford was awake.

The church door opened before I mustered the bravery to knock. Lady Crawford wore one of the same dirty white gowns, the fabric matted tight around her waist as if she'd been sleeping in it. I couldn't imagine her ever sliding out of the gossamer sheath. In my mind, she stayed clothed until The Reverend unwrapped her.

She touched cool fingertips to the bruise smeared across my mouth while I probed at a loose canine with my tongue. The sanctuary she led me into felt like a cave, pools of darkness in the corners deep enough to sink into, light that flickered as the candle flame waned. I took a seat in one of the chairs around the altar. Lady Crawford kneeled beside me with a bowl of murky water and a dishrag. She dipped the cloth, wrung it out and patted my eyes. My cracked lips stung as she wiped the drying blood from the corner of my mouth, but I didn't protest.

"Do you want to tell me what you said?" she asked.

"No."

"Well, he didn't have to do this."

I looked at her pale arms and wondered if she hid similar wounds under the white dress. I almost asked but let her continue cleaning the cuts. Afterward, she took my fingers and popped them back into place while I bit into the cloth to keep from screaming. She fashioned me a poor splint.

"He wants us to leave," she said after I'd regained my breath. "But I can't."

"Because you don't want to take stolen money?" I asked.

Lady Crawford dunked the cloth again, pressed it to my brow. "Yes, but not just the money. I've never been anywhere else."

I knew what she meant. The mountains both isolated and secured us. Even if her reputation carried frightening infamy, it was still a reputation. Outside the valley, she'd be just another piece of country trash.

"It's not fear of the Lord," Lady Crawford said. She turned her gaze to the cross hanging over the altar. "I'm not sure I even believe anymore."

Lady Crawford set the bowl of water at her feet. The dregs were dyed dark by blood, the rag equally stained.

"Do you love him?" I asked.

"I know he loves me."

"How do you know?"

"Because I'm afraid of how he acts. Like I'm the last thing that matters."

Lady Crawford carried the bowl and rag to the altar. "You'll sleep here tonight," she said. It wasn't a request.

She prepared a pallet on the floor, sacrificing blankets from her own burrow in the corner so I wouldn't have to lie on the dirt. The fibers of the bedding smelled full of sweat from the lovers' labor. I ignored it and pulled the blanket over my chin. When I closed my eyes, the candlelight rendered the membrane of my eyelids red, veins mapped across my vision. Lady Crawford extinguished the flame and we lay down in darkness.

She began humming a soft church hymn. I recognized it from page fifty-two of our hymnal, "Leaning on the Everlasting Arms." Her voice broke on higher notes, unevenly hit the chorus where she repeated *"leaning, leaning, leaning on the everlasting arms . . ."* but something about the cracked-china quality was soothing. I drifted to sleep on the lullaby.

THE THEFT

Day Three of the Contamination

When I wake, the house is quiet as a dead planet. No clacking of computer keys or the soft patter of Rosita's feet in the hall. Sunlight pours through the windows, buttering the carpet at the foot of my bed until I stand and block the glow. I dress and wait for the chickens across the creek to bring some normalcy with their crowing. As the silence grows, I wonder if the poison ended their clucking in the night, dropping them one by one from the pole they roosted upon.

Suddenly, I know Rosita is gone. The house feels the same as when Caroline leaves. Colder somehow, the walls in the hallway tighter, like I'm exiting a womb. A look out the kitchen window confirms that the hearse is missing. The engine had been drowning and the tire flat when we coasted across the creek, but I've never known much about cars. Maybe it wasn't as bad as I thought. I sit in the kitchen and try to figure out why she wouldn't just ride back with Sheriff Saunders. Did she really need the pictures of thirsty locals at my well, or did she think a few more hours would get me to bare myself for the camera? I'll probably never know. Best to just collect my guitar and try to suss out the last of this week's songs. Music will help with the disappointment.

On my way to the music room, I notice the door is cracked. I run, clumsy feet nearly tripping over the panic that tangles around my body. All the guitars still hang on the wall and the recording equipment looks untouched, but the safe yawns open. All the disks where I've chronicled the wasteland lullabies are gone. I put my fist through the drywall. A chalk cloud erupts as I try to pull my arm from the fresh crater. I punch it again with my left hand and my fingers ache in protest. I remind myself that I can't afford to treat my hands this way and pull an acoustic into my lap to help me think. The strings are comfortably hard, biting deep into calluses that should be past pain. Every inch of me should be like those fingers, past the feelings of betrayal that are flooding inside, but I can't keep them out.

I take a minute to see what else is gone, but the playbills and pictures, even the little bit of cash stowed away in the floor of the safe, remain where I left them. Money wasn't the target. If it was, there's plenty to pillage from my walls. Someone wanted the new tracks.

For years, I've kept Angela's secrets and sent away my work. When all that remains of me are bones in the ground, people will still be listening to that music, still singing lyrics I've written, but no one will know they were mine. Nothing will rectify this. I'll just be another forgotten freak buried on the hillside. My internal conductor lets the chorus from the first wasteland lullaby slip in like blight. I close my eyes but can't shake the tune. It plays over and over till I put the guitar aside. I'm not just going to sit by while the best work of my life is stolen. No one else can have these tracks. They belong to me.

In one of the spare bedroom closets are my father's river waders. The Reverend occasionally pulled them on over his suit to help an elderly member of the congregation cross the shallows. He didn't mind getting wet but considered entering the sanctuary soggy an affront to God. I search for the better part of an hour but can't locate them. Crossing without protection would be too dangerous. Maybe I should call the sheriff, ask her to drive me downtown to look for Rosita, but she'd have questions. I'm almost ready to give answers. After the theft, all obligations feel frayed. A few more hours to stew on it might finally sever things, open my mouth to let out confessions long sealed away. There'll be lawsuits, all sorts of businesspeople squabbling, but I don't care about that. If I can't have this one thing, I'm ready to burn it all down.

A shrill crack sounds from the living room. I freeze, listen to the tinkling of glass against the hardwood and the crunch of shoes grinding it fine. I take my least favorite guitar, a weathered Ibanez too suited for metal, off the wall. Something heavy collapses onto my leather sofa. In the silence that follows, there is a quiet only possible when the exhausted are finally granted rest. I sneak into the room with the guitar held like a club.

Russell Watson sits on the couch, struggling to untie his dress shoes. He still wears the tuxedo from the concert. The jacket is soaked, the pants wet to the knees. Russell uses his teeth to remove the dress gloves. Without them, it seems he should have a better handle on the shoelaces, but it isn't much use. The knot is too tight, his fingers red and swollen until all dexterity is a memory. He grits his teeth as he works. The false fangs chew his lower lip.

I'm slipping forward to bludgeon him when I bring a foot down too hard. Russell shoots erect, his coattails flapping as he searches his pockets. I raise the guitar overhead, but Russell produces a snub-nosed revolver. He grips it with both hands as if the gun may attempt to squirm free. Even with all the tattoos, I notice the upheaval of red sores, each one's center surrounded by a school of pus-filled blisters. Blood leaks from their margins and drips down his wrist. These hands resemble the bumpy flesh of toads I used to catch down by the creek. There is barely any unblemished skin. Both of his index fingers have swelled to twice the normal size. One barely fits inside the trigger guard.

"Drop the guitar," Russell says. "Then go sit in that recliner." With the short barrel, he gestures toward my La-Z-Boy.

"How long have you had those?" I ask, pointing to the boils.

Russell looks at his hands. For a moment, I think he may cry. "Victor made me wash in our fountain."

I'm surprised to see Russell alive. I'd expected Victor to kill him and eliminate any remaining witnesses to their crimes, but this illogical act is more in line with Victor's motivations. He'd rather make Russell suffer.

Russell's face is still smeared with some of the ghoul makeup, so he's not been fully submerged during this bizarre baptism, but a few boils sprout like horns in the margins of his widow's peak. Victor must have poured water over his hair. I can't help but think it's funny that we've both been betrayed. Russell was vain enough to think his false friend wouldn't hold him accountable for his family's crimes, and I was foolish enough to think someone might finally accept me.

"I can't say you don't deserve it," I tell him.

Tears leak from Russell's eyes. "I thought he was my friend.

I tried to tell him I'd helped with Dad, but he said I was still culpable."

I take a seat and find myself surprisingly calm as Russell wipes his tears with swollen fingers. Just like that night when The Reverend beat me, I can't imagine such an infirm man being a threat. This must be how others feel about me.

Russell's eyes are raw like he's been up all night. Maybe he was watching from the brush while the rest of the town arrived with the police escort? The gun rests on his knee. This close, the man smells muddy and slick, like something just hauled from the bottom of a stagnant lake. There is a slight wheeze to his breathing, an exaggerated huff as he exhales.

"Where is Rosita?" Russell asks.

"You should know," I say. "You've been in on the whole thing." With the recordings and Caroline both gone, I suddenly don't much care what happens.

His eyes refuse to focus, so Russell blinks hard. "What are you talking about?"

"You only got close to me so that you could introduce us, right? What was the deal you made?"

Perhaps it's just the blood oozing from his palms like stigmata, but Russell looks wounded.

"I don't know what you're talking about," he says.

"I'm talking about all that fanboy bullshit you laid on me the first time you showed up."

"I *am* a fan. Fuck, man, I'm sick about how things turned out for you." He scratches his neck, and I see the splotches of red underneath the wilted collar. "Do you know how hard it is to see someone so talented get screwed out of their destiny? That music of yours is one of the only things I've ever loved, and you don't get to share it just because you're ugly. I wanted us to collaborate."

Looking at the sores marring his tattooed skin, I begin to pity him. Maybe because I am so often the recipient of this emotion, I'm always surprised by how insidious pity can be.

The way it worms in and lets us confuse it for empathy. The two emotions have no more than an atom-sized difference between them, the constant chance for one to mutate into the other. Strange that humanity's best quality is so close to its worst.

"I admire you," Russell says. "They've done all they can to beat you down and you're still here. That's how I wanted to be. That's why I always fought my father. I think that's what I liked most about Victor. He helped me feel brave."

"I want to know what happened to Caroline and I want to know what deal you made with Rosita," I tell him. "So, are you going to put the gun away and tell me, or are you gonna use it?"

"I need those pictures she took," he says. "I'm not leaving here without them."

"Well, Rosita's not here. She took your hearse and lit out this morning. Took my recordings with her."

If Rosita left in the night, I don't think Russell could've missed her. The hearse has too distinct a sound, and if he'd spent the early morning hidden in the thicket, Russell would have followed her. Maybe he's suffering from spells, falling into moments of unconsciousness. Slumped in my chair like this, he looks like a starved pilgrim. Soiled black garb and ash-white paint still on his face to appease some cruel God.

"Bullshit. You've got her hid."

"I'm being honest," I say. "She stole my new tracks and left."

Russell grins. "You're writing again?"

"Maybe," I say. He does look genuinely surprised to hear about the music. "You really didn't know what she wanted with me?"

Russell shrugs, uses the gun barrel to draw little circles in the air.

"She wanted to know all about Angela Carver, promised The Excitable Boys a write-up if we could help her score a big story. I knew you liked your privacy, but I was willing to fuck that up for some ink. I figured that's just how journalists work."

"That's all?" I ask.

"I never thought she was a thief," Russell says. "After she wrote about you and The Troubadours, it would've received global attention. I figured we'd be playing together by then."

"So, you just wanted me as a band member?"

"No, as a cowriter and collaborator. The story would've helped us get started."

Russell touches his face and smears his makeup. I see a few smaller blisters clustered around his mouth.

"You need a doctor," I say.

"Won't matter if I don't get those pictures." Russell takes both thumbs and pulls the hammer back on the revolver. It takes considerable effort, but I know pulling the trigger is easy enough. "I won't ask again, Hollis."

If I tell him the photos are already with the police, he'll probably just shoot me. There may be an opportunity for an alliance here. Neither of us can cross the creek alone. Without help getting to town, Rosita will be on the first plane home with the tracks. I can't allow that.

"Rosita has the pictures," I lie.

"You want those recordings back?" Russell asks. "You take me to her and I'll get them."

He'll probably still shoot me after we find her, but I don't see another option. "You got wheels?" I ask.

"No, I waded. Figured I was already too wet for it to matter."

"So how do you suppose we're going to get across?" I ask.

"I've got it all squared away," Russell says. "Come outside."

I hold the front door open for Russell. Outside, last night's cool air is replaced by a pitiless sun. It's not even noon, but people will need water in this heat. They'll want to sip from frosty glasses and dip their feet in cold pools. Even at a distance, the babble of the creek sounds like an invitation.

"Over here," Russell says.

I follow around the side of the house and find him standing over the discarded top from The Reverend's truck bed. This detachable shell lies upside down, the fiberglass dome meant to protect cargo wasted by age. The metal in the corners is marred with rust, the tinted glass covered in a coat of mildew too thick to scrape off. Russell steps inside the proposed raft.

"Where did you find this?" I ask.

Russell points to the storage shed at the corner of the house. The broken padlock hangs from the latch. I'm hesitant. It's not much of a raft, and I'm considering my belief that certain objects carry their owners' ghosts. If there is any truth to that superstition, we can't use this. The truck top endured years locked in the shed. All that time marinating in the same dead air will have rendered it malevolent. Nothing would be more likely to drown us.

"You want to take that thing across?" I say.

"Why not?" Russell gives it a nudge with his foot. "Good as anything else."

I touch the square front end. It won't cut smooth through the water, but the high sides might protect us from the tiny rapids.

The real concern is leaks. Each corner is full of spiderwebs, the contours so weak any strike against the river bottom might pierce the thin plastic membrane. I rub my hand over the hull. I expect it to be malleable, but the hot plastic holds firm. I remind myself that The Reverend is dead. This is just an old truck cap and nothing inanimate can harm me. Best to worry about the man with the gun.

"I guess we have to make do," I say.

Russell grabs the front of the truck-bed topper and begins to drag it closer to the bank. His tight grip causes blood to well up underneath his fingernails. His cuticles seep a clear fluid as if all moisture is being purged from each digit. He doesn't seem to notice, but I'm less concerned with the gun than his illness. I don't want to be seized by those potentially contagious hands.

"We can't shove off where the cars go in," Russell says. "Too shallow. The rocks will shred this thing. We gotta go downstream where it's deeper."

Down on the bank, Russell sits in the dirt to rest. The creek flows harder around this bend, the water a little higher so that the only exposed rocks create a downstream rapids that we'll need to avoid. The opposite shore is farther here. Almost half the length of a football field instead of the thirty feet or so at the usual crossing. If we fight the current, I think the rocks can be avoided.

Russell pushes the truck top into the shallows. It bobs in the wake while we look for leaks. I don't see it take on any water. Still, I wish we had something to bail with just in case. As Russell climbs in, the truck top sinks a little with his weight. He offers a hand, looks down at the blood dripping from the ends of his fingers and shoves them in his pocket.

"Come aboard," he says, so I climb in.

Russell breaks a nearby sapling off the bank. He goes to the squared bow and uses the crooked trunk to steer us out like the pilot of some homely gondola. The current pulls us downstream as the water presses into our side, trying to flip us. If we don't control the ride, there's a danger of beaching on the sandstone downstream.

We're halfway across when I hear a hiss like air from a pierced tire. Water seeps in through the back corner of our improvised vessel. Not a flooding breach, but enough to lap at the soles of my shoes. The false boat grows sluggish with the added weight.

"We're sinking," I say.

When Russell looks back, I see one of his fake fangs is missing. The stick he wields is slick with blood from his hemorrhaging hands, but Russell rows faster, flinging the branch from one side to the other. I widen my stance, allowing the stream of water to run between my feet. Russell drops the improvised oar, leans forward and begins to paddle. I try to stop him, but Russell spits out a frantic "Don't touch me." I think about his blood and recoil.

We hit a rock and Russell falls overboard. I grab for him, but he clings to the front of our raft. The water breaks against his chest, white froth clinging to his clothes. I wonder if it burns, if the chemicals are strong enough to eat through the fibers like acid. I should dip my hands in and help row but can't bring myself to do it after watching the blood leach from Russell. I'd never have the dexterity to play again.

A wave splashes against Russell's chin. The water washes the skin clean to reveal the stubble beneath the ghoul paint. His entire face is still a mask. The upper half ash gray, the lower covered in red dots and blisters.

Once we're closer to the bank and Russell is only waist deep, he gets behind the truck top and pushes it toward land. I step onto the soft earth entirely dry while he sloshes forward to kneel beside me. Closer, the skin on his neck looks too tight, swelling a bit as he breathes.

"You need a doctor," I say.

Russell digs the gun from his pocket and points the wet barrel at my temple. "You're still taking me to her."

I'm more worried about him suffocating than pulling the trigger.

"You can barely stand," I say.

Russell pushes himself up from the mud. Behind us, the back end of the truck topper disappears beneath the water. I could sit and watch the whole thing submerge, but Russell urges me forward by waving the gun.

"You'll never make it," I say.

He spits out the other false fang. "Gonna try."

I don't know how long we walk. My calves burn without my cane to lean on, and I keep thinking of sitting down in the weeds. The only thing that keeps me moving is Russell. If he can shamble along bleeding like a gut-shot stag, then I can't justify taking a rest. I'm surprised every time I glance over my shoulder and see he's still standing. He doesn't complain much out loud. Just winces and rubs at the burning blisters.

"I shoulda known better," he grumbles under his breath. "Shoulda known better."

I can only assume he's talking about Victor. It's the same kind of refrain men repeat whenever their hearts are broken. The Reverend warned me when I was a child that the world was full of deceit, then proved it by being equally false. Still, I let Rosita slip inside. Why is it all the hardest lessons can only be taught with pain?

Russell notices I'm watching him stagger. My face must imply some question because he shrugs his shoulders and launches into an unsolicited explanation. "It's just that no one else ever treated me equal. Everyone was always so impressed by my father and the money. I grew up with nothing but people who kissed my ass. I was just finally glad to have found a friend who didn't care about the money, who hated my father the way I did."

I want to ask him if he regrets killing the old man. There seems to be a struggle inside him, a self-inquiry into whether Victor fed the hatred into something murderous or if that was always dormant inside. I'm debating which when Russell changes the subject.

"I've been meaning to ask you something," Russell says. His tone implies he must talk to keep his mind occupied. "Why music?"

"What do you mean?"

"Well, you could have written poetry or something. Why music?"

I don't want to have this conversation but can't refuse him. Russell's hero worship has created a strange fluidity that slips my status back and forth between hostage and companion. Right now, the gun is concealed in his coat pocket. Any stranger would just see two beaten men walking, but even after him saving me on the water, I don't trust it to last. The best way to stay on the good side of the equation is to tell him whatever he wants to hear. Besides, his pain and the admissions about Victor have dredged up some sympathy.

"It's all I had access to at the time."

Without pomade to hold his hair in place, Russell keeps whipping back the damp locks. I can see he doesn't understand. How could he? Russell's been given more than any man I've ever met.

"Why do you do it?" I ask. "Shouldn't you be studying at Harvard or something? I thought rich kids had certain expectations."

Russell scoffs. "Rich country trash is still country trash. I'd never feel right with those sorts of people. Besides, I never had any book smarts. Some creativity maybe. So, when did you know songs were it? What was the first moment?"

"Who says there was one?"

"Come on," Russell says. "Certain things you just know. Like the first time you wrote something special. You sit back and go, 'That's it. That's what I been looking for.' I think all the greats have that moment."

I knew from the first time Angela and I played in the basement. Knew as soon as we struck those chords together and The Reverend came stalking by to tear me away from the guitar. I don't believe in fate or destiny, but I decided right then to spend the rest of my life making music. Of course, I'm not going to tell Russell this. That memory is just for me.

I offer a shrug. "Pretty early, I guess. What else was I going to do? There's a certain freedom that comes with no opportunities."

"For me it was when I heard 'Help Me, Rhonda' on my uncle Jack's stereo. I didn't have any real interest in music, just listened to whatever was on the radio, but something about that song got me. I actually paid attention to the lyrics."

Russell stops walking, stares up at the sun through the heavy canopy of trees. Lazy clouds drift in and the world goes darker. He smiles a little to himself. I recognize the gesture. Music from long ago is playing just for him.

"You know that song, right?" He doesn't wait for an answer. "The melody is so catchy, all sugary and sweet, but it's really just about some guy trying to get laid. It's not a love song. He doesn't give a shit about Rhonda, doesn't even pretend to, but it sounds pretty. That's when I figured out music is the only art form where you can hide."

I start to tell him that he's wrong. That when you've done it right, an impression of yourself is left inside every note, but a car interrupts my thoughts. A green Chevy pickup appears in the distance. It's moving slow, a trail of dust rising behind it. Even this far away, I see it's an older model. The tires are low, the dented hood speckled with bird shit. A long crack crosses the left side of the windshield like a scar bisecting the nose on a pugilist's face. The rest of the glass is too dirty for me to see the driver. Russell steps into the middle of the road and raises a red hand.

"Don't," I say, but he glares at me.

"I won't hurt him," Russell says and continues to wave at the driver.

The pickup slows, drops off toward the side of the road. Russell puts his hand down and walks over to the driver's door. When the window rolls down, the old man behind the wheel scans Russell with milky eyes. The driver's face contorts into concerned wrinkles. Teeth too straight and white to be anything but dentures are exposed in surprise.

"What happened to you, son?" the old man asks.

Russell points the gun at him. "Get out nice and slow," he says.

The old man stands his ground. Just grips the wheel hard with large, hairy hands and shakes his head. "Like hell," he says.

"I said get outta the car, shithead." Russell pokes the gun into the cab.

The old man climbs out. The driver's so close to Russell that for a moment I worry he might try grabbing the weapon, but the man is busy inspecting the sores.

"I hope that shit rots your face off, you little bastard," the old-timer says. "Steal a man's wheels at a time like this. I guess you expect me to walk?"

"I don't care what you do," Russell says. He waves at me to climb into the truck. "You drive."

I used to chauffeur my father some but have spent years depending on others for transportation. It's not that I can't drive, just that my back makes the position uncomfortable. The steering column always presses close to my chest and my arms bend to grip the wheel like a T. rex because extending them is impossible. I'd argue the point, but I know Russell can't manage. He's leaning against the passenger door determined to get one of his shoes off. I watch him pry the wingtip from his left foot and roll the silk sock down. Everything below the ankle is raw. The flesh patched with calico colors the same white and pink consistency as uncooked chicken. Russell takes up a handful of earth and rubs it into the arch.

"Fucker won't stop itching," he says.

I climb in behind the wheel. Russell drops his shoe and pulls the gun on me in one frantic motion.

"You wait for me," he says and reaches out to reclaim the shoe.

"Lord," the old man says. "Hijacked by a couple of circus freaks."

I put the truck in gear and circle around the man, leave him shrinking in the middle of the road, cursing our departing dust.

THE MOTEL

Day Three of the Contamination

The wooden sign hanging in the window of the Feud Country Inn greets us. It's a hillbilly caricature of a man leaning against a still, a doubled-barrel shotgun cradled in his arms. He wears overalls without a shirt and a broken brimmed farmer's hat pulled low over his dull eyes. Special attention has been paid to his bare feet, which poke from the cuffed bottoms of his pants. The splayed toes clutch the stem of a pipe that billows circles of frozen smoke. I've always despised the sign. A barefoot, buck-toothed attempt to cash in on the stereotype of our local history. The few outsiders Coopersville receives enjoy it. They like to pose beside it for pictures. Since the Feud Country Inn remains the only motel downtown, I guess they do what's necessary to keep the lights on.

"You really think she's here?" Russell asks.

Rosita told me she was staying here. Room 135, just on the far side of the complex. Still, it's hard to imagine Rosita in this fleabag. I look at the row of rooms with their weak wooden doors and decide a lone woman wouldn't risk such a lack of security. Safer to move to the Holiday Inn or the new convention center back on the interstate. Both are only fifteen miles away, but maybe Rosita wants to be surrounded by whatever life is left in Coopersville. There's opportunity for pictures here in the thick of things. Still, these are all assumptions based on what I thought I knew about her. I need to clear my mind of any expectations. I've already been wrong once.

Russell pokes the gun into my ribs to secure my attention.

"Let's go get her," he says. A wheeze follows each word. There is a fullness in Russell's throat that I assume must be a closing airway. The hand holding the gun trembles until I fear a random spasm will make him fire.

I shake my head. "You can barely stand."

Russell jabs the pistol hard into my side. That ends the debate. I climb out with him lagging a few feet behind, bleeding hands hidden in his pockets to keep from dripping past the front office. I hear the muted laughter from some sitcom through the door, but don't bother looking at the window. A warning would only get someone on desk duty shot. I should be formulating a plan, coming up with something, but I've no ideas. I just let Russell guide me toward the far side of the complex.

"There's no hearse parked in the lot," I say. "Maybe she's already on the road." I find myself hoping this is true. I want my songs back, but I don't want her hurt.

Russell blinks hard like a man fighting sleep. "Just keep walking."

When we reach the room, Russell steps to the blind side of the door and removes the pistol from his pocket.

"You don't need it," I say.

"Just knock." He levels the gun at my head.

I hesitate, and the barrel descends into my ear canal. The metal is surprisingly warm. It tickles as I rap on the door. Inside, I hear the soft sound of bare feet on carpet. The light in the peephole goes dark as Rosita steps forward.

"Who is it?" she calls.

I should scream for her to call the police. Maybe swing an elbow into Russell's mouth. "It's Hollis Bragg," I say. "Open up."

After a moment, the door chain unlatches and the deadbolt snaps back. I try to shout a warning, but Russell grabs me by the shirt and shoulders his way in with the gun held high. It's more strength than I thought he possessed. Rosita stumbles backward and her feet get tangled in the comforter at the foot of the bed. She hits the corner of the nightstand and falls to the ground. Russell pushes me to my knees. The gun goes back into my ear.

Rosita tries to rise, so Russell puts his boot heel into her stomach. The fingertips of his free hand drip blood that flowers on the motel's starched sheets.

"Where is the camera?" Russell says. "I'll only ask you once."

I scan the room for a weapon. The TV is bolted to the dresser, but the lamp next to it might make a decent bludgeon. I can't even reach for it. All the signals from my brain to my body are halted by fear.

"Where are the pictures?" Russell asks.

"With my laptop bag," Rosita says. "Over in the closet."

"Go get it," he tells me.

I crawl toward the closet on the other side of the room. I'm considering a grab for that lamp when Russell levels the gun at me. This disintegrates my plan. I open the door and find nothing in the closet but bare carpet. Russell turns to watch me rummage inside, and Rosita kicks him in the stomach. The wind flushes from his lungs, the blow knocking him backward as the revolver fires over her shoulder into the mattress. The concussion leaves me deaf, the long echo of silence ringing in the small space. Russell tries to steady himself, but the arm he throws up in defense of another strike smears blood into his eyes. He wipes at them with the corner of a damp sleeve.

"Enough of this, Goddamn it," he says, pointing the gun. "Both of you sit your asses on the bed."

Rosita perches on the corner, but I'm afraid to turn from the closet. I don't want him to see my empty hands. I'm trying to think of what to say when Rosita begins confessing.

"It's not here," she says. "I've already turned the film over to the police."

"Bullshit," Russell says.

"Call Sheriff Saunders." Rosita points to the phone. "She'll tell you."

I step away from the closet while Russell wipes his hands against the bedsheets. When he's finished, the fabric looks like a macabre finger painting.

"Are you going to shoot us?" Rosita asks.

Russell doesn't answer, so I look away. I don't want to watch the bullet bore through Rosita's brain or take the chance some magnetic pull brings the barrel to Russell's temple. The latter seems more likely. Russell looks at the gun as if it is some animal that might bite him. It's no longer a tool he wields, but a dangerous temptation. A solution to all the fears he must be feeling. After a moment, he tosses it on the bed. I expect Rosita to snatch it up, but she leaves it be while Russell hangs his head and slides down the wall to crouch on the floor. I walk across the room and pick the gun up off the bloody sheets. Russell scoots against the rattling air conditioner and lets it blow waves through his hair.

Blood wells up through the bald spot developing on his crown. It's getting worse. Soon every follicle will seep.

"What do we do with him?" I ask her. "Call the law?"

"Tie him up with something," Rosita says.

Of course, she doesn't want the police involved. Not with her own theft looming between us.

"He could die if we leave him."

"I'm not sure I give a fuck," Rosita says.

Russell digs his knuckles into his eyes but can't seem to get much relief. He gives up, closes them rather than keep blinking away whatever is blurring his vision.

"If I've got a say in this," Russell says, "I'd rather be shot than tied up. I think Victor has killed me anyway."

"What happened to him?" Rosita asks me.

"Victor dunked him in the fountain," I say. "We crossed the creek, too."

"I fell in to save you," Russell corrects me.

"After kidnapping me," I reply, only I'm not sure that's true. Something deep down tells me I could have talked my way out of things. I just wanted the recordings too much to try.

"The chemical plant is five miles from your tributary," Russell says. "Five whole miles to dilute before it reaches that stretch and just look at me."

He holds out his red hands. Even cast in the low light of the motel room, the sores look as if Russell had lain dead for days and risen like Lazarus.

"You think about that before you judge me over my father," he says.

"Where are my recordings?" I ask.

Rosita doesn't bother to lie. "Under the bed. In my camera bag."

"Did you listen to them?" I ask. It should feel trivial, but I'm more infuriated by this possibility than anything else.

"I did," she says.

When she opens her mouth to say more, I just turn to Russell. "Get the sheets and tie him." I keep the gun on him while Rosita strips the bed.

"You're just gonna leave me here?" He sounds afraid for the first time.

"Isn't that what you did with Caroline?" I say. "Just left her there with Victor?"

Rosita puts a hand on my slumped shoulder as the rage builds, but I knock it away. No one has arrived to investigate the first gunshot. I could muffle the muzzle with a pillow. Threaten Russell until he tells me everything or just shoot him down.

"Did you know your daddy was gonna end up online with a sign on him?" I ask. "That all part of your chat around the kitchen table?"

The edge in my voice is rising. I lean down, unworried about Russell's bloody face so close to mine.

"All that was Victor," Russell says. "I wasn't sure we'd go through with it. Right up until it happened, I thought we were both all talk."

It does make sense. Victor the idealist. Russell the deluded rock star. Rosita rounds the bed with a bundle of sheets to tie Russell's hands.

"I don't deserve this," he says.

I'm inclined to let him run. He won't make it far anyway, but Rosita ties his hands to the bed frame. The knots look professional. Efficient and quick, but not tight enough to cut off circulation. Not that Russell needs all his circulation. His fingertips still drip blood. After his hands are secured, Rosita opens the nightstand drawer, takes out a small pocketknife and cuts a long strip from the sheet. I watch her close while the knife is out. I don't think she'd stick me, but I've allowed infatuation to blind me once already. I've yet to harden my heart to the truth that the only woman who loved me is long gone. Even that relationship is tarnished by time.

Rosita ties Russell's feet. He doesn't protest as she checks the knots for strength. When she's finished, Rosita reaches under the bed to retrieve her equipment.

"I wanna know why," I tell her.

"Outside," she says. "I'm not talking in front of him."

"Don't leave me here," Russell says.

"Somebody heard that shot," I tell him. "Sheriff will be here any minute." I don't know if either of us believe it.

We step outside and close the door on Russell's protests. Rosita takes a soft pack of cowboy killers from her camera bag and lights up. The acrid smoke almost overpowers the smell of her unwashed body and the lingering remnants of perfume applied days ago.

"Where's the hearse?" I ask.

"I ditched it downtown. I've been trying not to draw too much attention." She scoffs and flicks ash. "You know if we call the police, he'll tell them it was us."

"I haven't done anything wrong," I say. "You'd rather let him bleed out?"

"I'd rather not be arrested." I wonder if she's pleading with me. Turning her over means I'd have to explain my songwriting. With nothing left to lose, Rosita would tell everything about my arrangement with Angela. I'm still curious how she knows, what exactly her plan was and what I should do next. None of those questions will be answered if I hand her over to the law.

"We need to get back across the creek," I say. "Considering

Victor's still out there somewhere, I think Sheriff Saunders will understand."

I'm not sure Victor will even be looking for us, but I'll exploit Rosita's fear if it helps me understand her motive. I open the door again to take a final look at Russell. Sunlight pours inside through the crack and in the new illumination, I see how rheumy his eyes look. He doesn't have much time.

"I'm not going across that creek again," she says.

"Yes, you are," I tell her. "Or else I'm calling the sheriff about your light fingers."

Rosita shakes her head, lets smoke roil out between her teeth. Now that she's caught, she seems a little embarrassed. Maybe ashamed, or maybe that's just what I want her to feel.

"Test me," I say.

Rosita bites into the filter. "This a threat? Am I being kidnapped?"

"You're being offered lodging at the only place in town with clean running water. I'd hardly call that kidnapped. Besides, there's a murderer tied up in your room. Where else you gonna stay?"

Rosita takes a contemplative drag. Even angry, I can't help noticing her beauty. Dark skin the opposite of Angela's, whose arms were nearly translucent enough to let me see the tunneling tracks of blue veins. Physically, the women are nothing alike. Angela battled pimples with layers of makeup, but Rosita's complexion is flawless. Her chest and hips are small compared to Angela's curves. Even the straight cut of her lank bob is the antithesis of Angela's curls that always seemed like coils of frozen fire. Even after all that's happened, I catch myself wondering what her hair would feel like in my hands.

THE CONFESSION

Day Three of the Contamination

We take the hijacked Chevy, only stopping once on the outskirts of Cherry Tree where Rosita calls the police from what must be one of the last pay phones on earth. The protesters are still out, shouting and stomping until she must cup her hand around the receiver to be heard. I wait in the passenger seat and scan the crowd for Victor, but he's too smart to be marching past the bars. There's no sign of the Red Cross and FEMA representatives that should be crowding the street, either. I'm not surprised by the lack of assistance. In many ways, we've always been on our own, addressed only when the rest of the country requires our resources or needs something to mock. Relief isn't coming, but that's what most of these people voted for. An old-world version of self-reliance that cuts programs of aid, environmental regulations and other safeguards against days like today. Perhaps they did it out of feelings of desperation. You could argue that the poor don't have the luxury of conservation, but I think those shortsighted notions have always been our weakness.

Rosita climbs back into the truck, drives out of town and turns down the road toward home. For the first time since my childhood, the woods look ominous. The bark on the gnarled trunks resembles scabbed skin and the thicket is shrouded before dusk. Each tree seems purposefully aligning to confuse lost travelers instead of growing by whatever natural laws plants adhere to. Harboring this idea makes me ashamed. Most country boys grow up with a penchant for totems, but I wandered the hills without a charm in my pocket to ward off spirits. Whenever remnants of my superstition manifest, I remember the night Lady Crawford anointed me with oil. Her failure provided an alternative salvation: freedom from my father's legacy of irrationality.

Rosita doesn't really know how to drive stick. She throws the truck back and forth between the lower gears, fighting the rutted road. The engine protests like an exhausted mare.

"You're killing it," I say.

"You want to drive?"

"I can."

Rosita looks ready to pull over, but the truck is making a new noise. It shudders as something inside strains, lurches with the last gasps of combustible life before it grows cold. We coast to the side of the road and stall in the ditch. Rosita slams a fist into the steering wheel.

"Stupid, broke-ass piece of hillbilly shit," she cries. After the outburst, she rubs her hands through her hair in a calming effort. It's the same gesture my father used when rallying another explosion of religious fervor. Whenever The Reverend slicked that hair back with sweat, he was preparing to testify hard. Ready to smite the congregation with his bizarre perception of the truth.

"Now what?" Rosita asks.

"We wait," I say. "Hope someone comes by to give us a ride."

"Any way to raft across?" Rosita asks.

"You saw what happened to Russell. Wanna risk it?"

"We could walk back to town?"

"Over ten miles. Not to mention how we left Russell. I'm still not sure about the legality of that."

"Obvious self-defense," Rosita says.

"I'd rather camp."

"Shit." Rosita punches the steering wheel again. The horn blurts out in the silence. "Well, I'm at least taking a look."

I follow her around the front of the truck and watch her pop the hood. She leans inside, studies the coiled hoses that connect to the giant robotic heart of the engine block.

"We could check the oil," I offer. "But that's really all I know how to do."

Rosita slams the hood, kicks the tires and sits down in the dirt.

"Why live out here?" she says. "I've been asking myself that from the first. How does a man end up out here?"

"My daddy's church," I say. I wonder why I called him that. I never use the strangely southern term of endearment. It feels foreign on my tongue.

Rosita picks up a twig and begins to sketch a steeple in the dirt. A large cross goes atop it. I sit down beside her, take the stick and mark an X through the doodle.

"Are you going to tell me what you're really doing here?" I ask. I snap the twig in half and give her a piece.

"Angela sent me. You were right about that."

I grind the stick into the mire between my shoes while Rosita gathers the words. I can't figure out why Angela would do it.

There are plenty of industry writers who could do the next album. Even if it turned out subpar, why get greedy now, when her legacy is secured? What makes my work that necessary?

"She ran into a friend of mine at a party. Now, my friend knows how much influence Angela has, so she starts talking up *The Body Book*. Angela seemed to dig it, wanted to meet me and see some pictures. So, I spent an evening showing her slides and explaining the project. Then she asked me about funding."

"And you took the money." I push the stick deeper, submerging the wood beneath the mud.

"All my travels have racked up some serious credit card debt. Angela said she wanted to support it, but that she needed a favor."

I can picture the whole scene. Angela in some bright Manhattan loft, lounging on a love seat as she sips wine from one of those stemless glasses that always let her feel less precious, closer to the unrefined roots she abandoned. Her breath would be hot with the tang of expensive grapes, mouth pouring out charm the way others tilt a bottle, touching Rosita's knee as the compliments flow. I want her back in that dugout. I want Angela with makeup running in the rain and sneakers with holes in the sides. The two of us trapped in that eternal moment, living it forever because we lost ourselves in the disappointment of the days that followed.

"Does she have copies of the tracks?" I ask.

"Maybe. I played them for her over the phone. She could've been recording."

Looking at Rosita, I can't understand how the same woman who photographs men like me is such an accomplished thief.

"How'd you know they'd be in the safe?" I ask. "How'd you know the code?"

"The four buttons on the keypad that make up the combination are worn. There's a lot of different variables, lots of combinations it could be, but they were also the four numbers that make up Angela's birthday."

I'm embarrassed she knows I've remained so sentimental. Still, I need to push through while Rosita's comfortable explaining.

"What did Angela tell you about me and the music?" I ask.

"Just that you were an old friend working on some of the tracks for the new album. She said that you were way behind deadline. That she was worried and if I'd find your new work and send it along, she'd fund *The Body Book* for the next five years. I didn't understand everything then, but I guess I do now."

"Sounds like you knew enough to know it was wrong."

Rosita hangs her head. "She said you were just helping polish the tracks and it was taking too long. I didn't know, but I guess I suspected she was lying. At least hiding some important details."

"But you do know now, so say it."

"I can tell some of it is meant for her. It has the Troubadours' style. The rest of it is something different."

"And you sent those tracks anyway. You stole them for her."

Rosita won't look up from the dirt. "I justified it to myself in a lot of ways. Told myself you'd sent her tracks before, that you weren't going to leave the woods to play them anyway, that funding *The Body Book* for half a decade was worth screwing over one person. Still, I know it's not right. I think Angela might know that, too. She's just in too deep to fix things. You're quitting and she needs to go on making records. I think she's scared to do that without you."

"She could hire someone else or tell the truth."

Rosita shakes her head. "You know it's too late for that. People would tear them apart for keeping it a secret this long."

"I have to hand it to her, a woman with a project on disabled bodies is a perfect cover," I say. "Do you even really write for *Strange Sounds*?"

Rosita nods. "I've published some articles with them."

"How did she convince you to take the risk? Aren't you afraid I'll call the police?"

Rosita smirks, but it's not meant as mockery. "That never crossed my mind once I met you. Besides, Angela told me you didn't write because you loved it. She said it was just something you had to purge. That's how she knew you'd have extra tracks laying around."

A squirrel in a nearby tree barks, angry to have intruders so close to the nest. I watch tremors of rage twitch through the animal's tail.

Rosita sighs. "You don't need to hide songs like that away."

"I wasn't going to. Or I wasn't until you stole them for Angela."

The squirrel keeps barking, so I toss a piece of the broken twig into the branches. The animal flees to a higher bough as the limb shakes. For some reason, my stomach is sick at the idea of Angela listening to my voice. I've sent written lyrics with my music sheets but haven't sung to her since the days we shared on the road.

"What did she say about the tracks?" I ask.

"You can ask her yourself. She's coming to Coopersville."

I snap the twig into thirds, fourths, so many pieces the nubs are too hard to continue fracturing.

"When?"

"Be here by tomorrow night. She and the band want to organize a benefit concert. I think she'll probably come see you."

Angela arrives in my mind again. This time, she sits in first class as young mothers carry their children past toward coach. Her ears are plugged with white earbuds as she waits for the plane to take off. The interior is the familiar cacophony of noise: giant turbines turning as the wheels begin to taxi on the runway, seat belts snapping, luggage in the overhead compartments colliding as the attendant announces rules to prepare for the miracle of flight. Only Angela won't be listening. In her ears, my gruff voice is singing about an endless world of sand. A scorched earth where only a man and boy remain and all lessons are taught by song. It isn't exactly a premonition. It's more a dream. She told me once that every dream is a private wish.

"She's gonna pay you then?" I ask. "Cash in person?"

"Yeah, she doesn't want a paper trail."

In person makes things more difficult. My palate is dry, but there's no remedy. Water would be a blessing, but all I want is a guitar. The chance to play a few chords and take my mind away from reality.

"What the fuck happened between you two?" Rosita asks.

It wasn't all bad. Our perplexing match was held together by something indefinable that normal people wouldn't understand. There is nothing more sacred than a gorgeous body coupling with a broken one. It looks like sexual charity to anyone observing the act, a sacrifice of perfection to the altar of the malformed. It probably seems pitiful unless you've ever lusted for what others thought repulsive. The truth is I depended on Angela's love to work as some sort of assurance there was decency in the world. Our relationship became more than two people trying to stay in love. Her continued acceptance of me meant broken bodies had a place, that the cruelty and indifference I feared wasn't all-consuming. I realize now how unfair a burden that was to place on a young girl, but I won't tell Rosita this. She doesn't deserve that truth anymore.

"We fucked each other up," I say. "Bled each other dry with a thousand tiny cuts."

The squirrel returns to her sentry duty, again sounding an alarm.

"Do you think we're safe?" Rosita asks. "Victor's still out there."

"We're armed at least. We can sleep in shifts if it makes you feel better."

Night comes quickly, but I don't mind much. Rosita sits in the cab with the computer on her lap, doing some work on the pictures. This new man has some of the worst facial scars I've ever seen. Under all the raised folds of tissue, his eyes look as if he's been duped, talked into believing that something extraordinary would occur if he consented to the portrait.

Rosita cycles through more pictures. Cripples in the heartland and men without lower limbs. A woman with her nose removed by what appears to be syphilis, but she was mauled by a bear. Before the next picture, Rosita warns me about the claw marks on the woman's breasts that makes it appear as if she took the beast into her bed. Some of this takes my mind off Victor, and Rosita's theft, but whenever my eyelids grow heavy and snap open there is a hazy moment when I imagine someone outside the window. I put the gun in my pocket to avoid some sleep-deprived mishap.

"My brother was a musician," Rosita says. "Did I tell you that? Not the same as you. Classical piano. He was obsessed with Schubert. He used to play things with a kind of gothic flair in the end. 'In the Hall of the Mountain King' and such."

The phrase "in the end" hangs in the air until I know she's about to offer up a sad story. Maybe this is the way she gets people to bare themselves for the camera. The flesh she exposes is only a ruse. The real undressing is this vulnerability. It's easy to show off ruined bodies next to a broken heart.

"So, he died?" I ask, but I already know the answer from that "in the end" of hers. *Died* isn't even the right word. The dead haunt us because they stay dead. The only present-tense state that's unchanging.

"He drowned on vacation, but that wasn't what stopped his music. He lost a hand in a car wreck a few years before that. He's the first entry in *The Body Book*."

"Then you should feel even worse about what you've done," I say.

The words hit harder than I anticipate. For a moment, I think she'll camp alone in the woods, but Rosita just turns to the window and drapes her jacket over herself like a blanket. I keep watch while she sleeps.

THE EMANCIPATION

The morning after I received my father's lashing, I woke to find Lady Crawford gone. I wasn't worried by her absence. The ache in my face had awoken me, and its steady spread from the margin of my eye down my neck dominated all my attention. There were no mirrors inside the church, so I couldn't view the damage without braving the camper. It would be dangerous seeing my father so soon after our fight, but I decided Lady Crawford would probably be there making amends. She'd protect me if things went bad.

I staggered outside into violent sunlight, every inch of my body a dull throb as I pissed a powerful stream near the church wall. I remember thinking The Reverend would beat me again if he caught me finding relief so close to the Lord's threshold, but I'd gone past fear.

They were both gone when I entered the camper. My father's

clothes still hung in the small closet and his Bible lay open to the book of Revelation on the kitchen table, but somehow I knew the two hadn't just decided on a stroll. I checked beneath my father's bed and found the cigar box full of money still hidden there. Seeing it calmed me a little. He wouldn't leave without the cash. I sat down at the cramped kitchen table to wait.

Night arrived and still no sign of them. I began to weigh my options. Either go searching or cross the creek for help. I could use the chicken farmer's telephone to call the police, only I'd have to explain my bruises. Instead, I settled down on the stoop and played guitar. It was difficult with the wounded fingers, but I managed a few weak chords until sleep sneaked up on me. I don't remember stirring as the hours passed. It was one of those nights where I blinked, and then someone was shaking my shoulder the next morning.

I woke with Mr. Freemont and his daughter, Annabel, kneeling over me. Once I stirred, Freemont stood back and let me wipe sleep from my eyes. The guitar lay in the mud below my feet. I picked it up and wiped the filth from its frame. It felt cruel that Freemont had to see me with it. Especially considering that I'd left his prized instrument lying in a puddle.

"We came for the service," Mr. Freemont said. "Where is your father?"

"He's gone," I said. "I don't know where."

I was a little afraid he might steal the guitar without The Reverend there to stop him, but Freemont only looked at my bruises. He touched his face as if expecting the flesh of his own jaw to be tender. Annabel wandered into the distance. She avoided looking at me, just twirled a braid of hair around her finger and dug the toe of her boot in the dirt. The long dress she wore looked uncomfortable. Several layers of fabric wrapped around her as if she were a fragile item in need of protection.

"How long has he been gone?" Mr. Freemont asked.

"Since yesterday. Lady Crawford, too."

I didn't mean to let the bit about Lady Crawford slip. With his shepherd absent, Freemont's hands shook as he knelt beside me. Seeing his fear reminded me of my own. Even though my father had beaten me hours before, I didn't know what to do if he never returned. I didn't have the skills to care for myself.

"I'm going to find The Reverend," Freemont told his daughter. "I want you to stay here."

I could see Annabel didn't want to be alone with me, but she didn't protest. Both our fathers had instructed us in the language of silence. After Mr. Freemont departed, I scooted over on the stoop to make room for her. I knew she wouldn't take the seat, but I wanted to be polite.

"Do you want me to play something?" I asked.

Annabel sat in the wet grass rather than join me on the stoop. I picked a few chords for distraction. My fingers ached, but I was beginning to acclimate to the pain.

"Why don't you put that stupid thing away?" she said.

I continued until she turned her back on me. "Is it really the guitar you have a problem with?" I asked.

"I hate being here. I hate looking at you and I hate that you want to be sweet and play me a song on your stolen guitar. It makes me want to fucking puke."

These statements meant to cut me only revealed how much we had in common. I wanted to tell her that, but I was already beginning to understand that life under my father's thumb was over. She, however, would have more years to endure before any escape could be possible. I still wonder what happened to her. Did she ever become free to live a normal life? Is normalcy even something either of us could expect after such a strange up-bringing?

"It's not my fault, you know?" I said.

"Fuck you. My father's brainwashed. That's the only reason I'm here."

I set the guitar aside and wandered across the field toward the tree line.

"Where're you going?" Annabel called, but I didn't bother answering.

Generations of brittle leaves crunched under my feet as I hiked through the woods. When I reached the creekbank, I procured a staff of ash and used it for leverage against the water colliding into my thighs as I crossed. The ground heaved up with tree roots the deeper I traveled into the woods. I became lost right away. Anger had clouded my judgment until I couldn't be sure how far I'd gone. My back ached from the hike, so I sat down on a nearby log and cried. I damned my father for leaving me. All this because someone wouldn't love him back. No one loved me and still *I* didn't shrink from my obligations. I'd even managed to keep a modicum of foolish hope, offering kindness to girls like Annabel who repaid me with rebuke. I wanted Angela's hands on me then, those calloused fingertips caressing my black eye and split lip, whispering sweet things that I could interpret as something more than comfort. Just soft words. Simple and plain.

Something swayed in the treetops, but I couldn't quite make it out. It remained obscured until I moved deeper into the maze of limbs. I noticed the shoes first. Polished wingtips hanging maybe ten feet from the ground. The pant legs above the shoes were cuffed, the white socks underneath peeking out and look-ing embarrassed compared to the rest of the formal Sunday garb. The rope had left my father's face bloated. His cheeks blackened and puffed until The Reverend's tongue poked between his lips. A cloud of swarming flies vibrated, their buzzing filling my ears. Gnats, the kind always attached to dog dicks, flew into my eyes as if to spare me vision.

I don't know how long I watched him sway. At some point, I heard the crunching footfalls of Mr. Freemont. He came carry-ing Lady Crawford through the underbrush. Her white gown was torn at the throat and breasts. Ripped pieces of the fabric trailed behind Freemont's feet like a bridal train. When he laid the body against a nearby tree, I saw the marks on her neck from the throttling. This wasn't the only wound. Lady Crawford's hair lay matted to her cheek with blood, her right temple sunken into her skull. Every exposed inch of skin was painted with dirt. I stared until Mr. Freemont moved me from underneath my fa-ther's shoes.

"I found him first, but I couldn't get him down," Freemont said. He kept apologizing for what I'd seen.

We headed back, with Freemont carrying Lady Crawford. I don't remember much about the walk other than Mr. Freemont fell twice in the creek. When we emerged on the bank, Lady Crawford had been partially washed by the spills, everything below her knees rendered their original pale.

"Go inside the church," Mr. Freemont called to Annabel as we came out of the trees. "Don't come over here." When she didn't respond, Mr. Freemont began to scream. "Go on, God-damn it."

I reached the camper first, opened the door while Freemont carried the body inside and placed it on the bed.

"I'm going for a phone," he said. "We'll get someone to help with your father."

He left me alone with her, so I stood near the bed and contemplated the body. It shared nothing with the way men talked after returning from a wake at Felt's Funeral Home. At the funeral parlor, they comforted one another with anecdotes about the deceased or complimented how lifelike the departed seemed inside the coffin. There was nothing left of Lady Crawford to compliment. In death, all humanity was absent. She might as well have been a woodchuck rotting in the sun.

Freemont eventually returned with the police. I watched out the window while Sheriff Thompson stood in the yard hollering at two deputies carrying a ladder into the woods. The sheriff looked nervous as he took Freemont's statement. He spoke softly, trepidation filling his face anytime he looked over at the camper. I suppose he was worried about having to comfort a monstrous child. Still, he maintained enough professional composure to remove his hat before entering.

"Hello, son," Sheriff Thompson said. "I'm sorry about your father. Freemont tells me she's in here. I need to come in and have a look."

I led him to the back room, where the sheriff stood over the bed clicking his tongue. A long pause permeated the air before he pulled some latex gloves from his belt and turned Lady Crawford's neck. I watched him dip a finger inside the sinkhole of her fractured skull. The sheriff was about to speak when a deputy knocked on the camper window. Sheriff Thompson slid it open with some effort and stuck his face out.

"What?" he snapped.

"We need help with the . . . some help," the deputy said.

. . .

I spent the next evening outside playing. The poor splint Lady Crawford fashioned wouldn't allow my fingers to bend, but I managed to form most chords anyway. The problem was the tremble I'd developed. I didn't know if it was only the wounds or the shock of what happened, but it was suddenly hard to press the strings. Static filled each muted note and an unharmonious twang invaded each bar. It sounded like I felt.

I'd just discovered a way to create a barre chord when Angela drove up unannounced. She gave a wave as she climbed out of the truck. Neither of us were sure what to say as she crossed the field to sit beside me on the stoop.

"What are you playing?" she asked. "Sounds funny."

She'd yet to notice my damaged hand, so I tried to conceal it behind the guitar. I thought that once she saw it, she'd decide I was useless without my one valuable resource. The fear of that rejection loomed worse than the rest of my losses.

"John Lee Hooker," I said, but it wasn't true. Just before her truck pulled up, I caught myself strumming the chords to "Hang Me, Oh Hang Me" as if it were some cruel joke.

"You got the bends down cold," Angela said about a previous awkward run down the neck. "Playing it sort of sleazy and sloppy, huh?"

"Sure," I said. The wound wasn't going away. I couldn't hide it forever, so I took my hand from behind the guitar and held it up for her to see. She didn't speak. Just took it gently in her own hands and let her fingers trace down each knotted knuckle. For the first time, her tough exterior melted away, and I could see her biting back an amalgamation of anger and sorrow.

"Who did this?" she asked.

"My father. The night before last." I felt the strange urge to defend him, to let her know it was his way of saving me from wayward girls like herself. In his mind, taking the last extraordinary thing from my body would preserve my soul. It made sense if you understood him.

"I don't know what I'm supposed to say," she said.

She would've remedied things for me if possible, but there's no balm for that sort of pain. I never expected my father's death to harm me. I'd wished The Reverend dead a thousand times, prayed for it in both sincere belief and farce until cultivating what I thought was true apathy toward the man. In the end, the childhood seed of affection I carried never left. I don't think about him often anymore, but in those early days my grief was a living thing that stalked through all silent moments.

"So, what happens now?" Angela asked.

"They've talked about foster care."

We both knew I was too hideous for safety among strangers. People taking in children want babies they can mold for adoption or quiet kids they can ignore while cashing a check. I would require banishment in some locked basement.

Angela shook her head. "No fucking way. You'll come live with me and Dad first."

"I appreciate that, but you know better. Besides, maybe they'll let me be an emancipated minor."

"Could be cool," Angela said. She took some loose cigarettes from the pocket of her jeans and lit one for us to share. "You could live in the church. I'll come help decorate. Something audacious. Maybe red walls."

I smiled. "The Hunchback of Coopersville County living in a church?"

"Didn't even cross my mind."

"Fuck these mountains," I told her. "I'm leaving."

Angela flicked ash and placed the cigarette between my swollen lips. She pressed a palm to my hot cheek while I inhaled.

"What's the escape plan?"

I felt a tingling knowing Angela's mouth had been wrapped around the cigarette moments ago. My smile was accompanied by a sore jaw.

"You think I'm a bullshitter, don't you?" I asked.

"Everyone is to some degree. I think you're stalling."

I turned the guitar's tuning pegs until the strings rattled loose. I brushed them aside, reached into the sound hole and very slowly, as if revealing something dangerous I'd captured, let Angela see the sweaty wad of cash.

"Christ," she said. "Where'd you get that?"

"Tithes from the church. I hid it as soon as the police left."

Angela plucked a bill from the guitar's hollow.

"How much do you have?"

"Enough to go wherever I like. What I need is a driver."

She was too transfixed by the cash to catch the invitation. I remember wishing I'd prepared some sort of speech. Whether it was foster care or living alone on the inherited land, I refused to remain in the mountains. I hoped Angela had the same urge to escape her father's crumbling music business. If she stayed, it would be an early marriage to whatever successful man came courting, eventually abandoning music for children and a career giving guitar lessons. Only my tongue wasn't proficient enough to express this.

"You want out of here just as bad as I do," I said.

"What about my dad?" she asked, but the question wasn't born of true concern.

"We'll head to Nashville, get a group going," I said. "I can still play decent until I heal up. You should be singing for people. Not hiding out down in that basement."

Angela handed over the money, and I stuffed the cash back inside the sound hole. She hummed an E note so I could match it while pulling the slack out of the strings.

She returned later that night, and I burned the church before we departed.

Nashville remained our intended destination, but we ended up on the outskirts of Lexington, renting three rooms above a hardware store. The bathroom sink leaked, and the sodden linoleum warped up around the base of the toilet. The carpet smelled of cat piss despite the current no-pet policy. After just two weeks, our funds were already running out. Since I'd never had money before, I was shocked at how quickly it was spent.

The apartment was in Angela's name. She'd called from a pay phone after seeing the ad and, anticipating the landlady's demeanor, went to view the place alone while I waited at the local library. After I spent a few hours being stared at by strangers, Angela picked me up. The landlady was a Jesus freak. A two-ton crucifix swung from her neck as she showed Angela the rooms and ticked off the rules. No men, no pets, only one other roommate of the same sex.

Those rules kept me living like a refugee, only sneaking out during rare opportunities for exodus. I didn't mind. The city was too crowded for my taste. I was still a spectacle on the street, but fewer people accosted me. Mostly kids or the occasional redneck who felt the need to toss ridicule from a car window. All that grew tolerable. The hard part was living with Angela.

The fantasy of playing house unraveled fast. The first night in a Kentucky motel, I lay in bed beside her with only blankets separating our clothed skin. The next morning the bed smelled of both our bodies, fire and ash. In the apartment, I slept on the couch, curled around myself like a broken-shelled crustacean. We talked less. Communion reduced to smoking the occasional joint and playing music. We built an impressive body of work, expanding the jam sessions from the basement into something more tangible. Even with a wealth of equipment smuggled from her father's studio, my guitar and her voice remained the only instruments. I remember feeling separated from my body when she sang, lifted from the broken frame until only her voice filled the dark room. My hands played along, but I wasn't present.

Like my body, I believed my feelings were something I'd never share with her. Understanding that and living with its constant reminder seemed irreconcilable. I was pondering these thoughts one evening when Angela returned drenched from rain. She looked at me huddled over my empty coffee mug, the crushed brown filters of cigarettes like small trees I'd planted in the ash-filled china. I tried to hide my frustration, but Angela was already accustomed to the mood swings.

"Any luck?" I asked.

"I put in an application at Kroger. Bagging groceries." Angela plopped down beside me. "I've got a surprise for you," she said.

Angela produced a flyer from her purse. She spread the paper across our table, scooted the cup aside and blew away the ash like a child extinguishing birthday candles. I read the block print.

REMINGTON'S LIVE MUSIC NIGHT FEATURING
COWBOY CARTER, THE TWAIN SISTERS AND
ANGELA CARVER & HOLLIS BRAGG.
TEN $ COVER CHARGE. DOORS OPEN AT SEVEN.

Some mingling of pride and regret filled me. Back then, I didn't think I could stand under the bright lights. I knew I was supposed to do it. If I contained any self-fulfilling purpose, it was the requirement of all artists. I was meant to take personal calamity and shape it into some form of truth, but that required a resolve I feared.

"No," I said and pushed the flyer away.

"Why do you think I did it this way?" she asked. "I know you, Hollis. The only option is to force you to do it."

I started to rise from the couch, but she snatched me by the wrist.

"Isn't this what we left for?"

I should have confessed that the music was always secondary. If I had, it might have saved us from what came later.

"Have you ever thought it's selfish to keep it to yourself?" she asked. "Didn't you tell me that if you have something, you're supposed to share it?"

I could've offered countless arguments about how no one wanted what I had, could've explained she was proof of that, but I knew better than to argue. I rarely told her no.

The honky-tonk we played was full of patrons in cowboy hats shelling peanuts at the mahogany bar, tossing the hulls on the floor as they washed them down with tall drafts of Lone Star or Pabst. The stage was nothing more than a small platform where a man in white jeans and a western sports coat sang "Amarillo by Morning" for divorcées in tight denim. We avoided the crowd by entering through the back door. I sat behind the drab curtain gripping the neck of my guitar while Angela paced, her boot heels clicking as she sang to herself. I tried to close my eyes and concentrate only on her voice, but the crowd on the other side of the curtain sounded agitated. Laughter exploded with the cadence of firecrackers and drunken hollering overcame the man's serenade. He finished his set to anesthetized applause.

There are gaps. Moments of lost memory like scenes cut from a film. I can only recall certain things. The scent of cigar smoke. A cold glass of water perspiring in my hand. Angela running up and down her vocal range. Somewhere in this blur, a man announced us over the PA. Angela wrapped her hands around my shoulders and gave a squeeze of encouragement.

When I'd fantasize about these moments, the applause always halted, the spectators silenced by the sight of my body until I played. Slowly, as if chiseling away at their shock, my guitar made them take notice. Sometimes the daydreams failed midway through, stalled by someone jeering from the back row. As private wish turned to nightmare, an audience member inevitably threw something.

No bottles sailed past my head that night, but the silence was palpable. Angela gave a brief introduction while I waited for an outburst of protest. I noticed a group of women seated at a table in the far corner. Even today, I can recall the expression present on one woman's face, the way her breath seemed caught in her throat and her red nails trembled as she touched her lower lip. It didn't hit until Angela and I reached the final chorus of "Fare Thee Well, Miss Carousel," but I recognized it as pity. The absolute rawness of the woman's pity for the body I must live in. It was more painful than any other barb. I played the last song poorly, but Angela left the stage ecstatic. She took me behind the curtain, clutched me tight and raked her fingers through my hair.

"Thank you," she said.

I didn't even feel her body. All I could concentrate on was the tender way that woman in the audience dabbed her eyes with a cocktail napkin.

Angela and I shared the bed that night. It began as platonically as any other evening. Angela still drunk off the audience's admiration, singing all the way home, dancing about the kitchen while I pretended to be equally impressed. There was no way to duplicate her energy as she sashayed from the fridge with a beer in each hand. We crashed on the couch together, and I listened to her go on about the crowd.

"I mean, we had them captivated," she said. "Absolutely captivated."

"I botched that last one."

"No way," she said. "You were great."

"Thanks." I swigged beer for a distraction.

"Don't give me that. You were great. I want you to quit being so hard on yourself. You need to acknowledge it."

"Sure, I did great," I said.

"Sometimes I don't get you. I mean, what's it gonna take to show you how much they liked it?"

"They liked you," I said.

I don't think she ever understood what I meant. I knew my performance was decent, knew that even with the poor timing and missed chord on the final song I didn't play a shitty set. The audience might have responded to my skill, but they stayed to see a beautiful woman accompanied by such a man. For a moment, I considered telling her about the woman in the crowd but decided it would only deflate her.

"They liked you, Hollis," Angela said. "You're just never going to believe it, are you?"

"Maybe not."

She placed a hand on each of my cheeks. "I mean it," she said, cradling my skull in the gentle vise of her palms. "Somehow I'm gonna get through to you."

One moment I was listening, watching her mouth move as she formed words meant for a dimwitted child, then she was kissing me. I'm still not sure where our bravery came from. There's never been a more awkward first kiss. Our teeth cracked together, my tongue tentative to emerge, then buried deep and unskillfully prodding her molars. Any witness would've attested to the ugliness of the act. I felt Angela's hands move up and down my body, canvassing the unnatural curves of my sternum. With every advance I made or new area she explored, I expected it to stop. I became the aggressor, but now I understand she relinquished the dominant role, acted as the silent guide for the unskilled virgin.

We didn't stay on the couch. Once we'd shed our clothing, Angela took my hand and led me to the bedroom. I thought things would stop, that the slight interlude to change location lacked the inertia necessary for us to go through with it. Too much time for her to see all of me. She pulled me close to the bed. When she sat on the edge, I took the opportunity to look at her. Nothing about Angela ever felt average, but I was struck by the almost holy qualities of the common body's perfection. Tracing my hands over her hips, my eyes over her breasts and shoulders, the natural form stunned me.

On the bed, she straddled my lap and guided me inside. I caught a glimpse of us in the mirror over her shoulder. A beautiful woman riding atop a twisted little man. I wish I could say we looked elegant moving together, but I wouldn't find anything pleasing about my crooked body melding into hers until much later. That night, I watched our reflection and decided the seduction was just another form of pity. I knew it was an offense to believe this, that to think her capable of that was to view her the same as the crying woman in the bar or worse. She wasn't the sort unable to see me as a person, but once the thought infected the moment, I never fully dispelled it.

My erection began to weaken. Angela climbed off, and I started apologizing. She put a finger to my lips while stroking me.

Afterward, we lay atop the sheets. I tried to pull the coverlet over my chest, but Angela threw it back. She lay nude, resting on an elbow.

"I want to see you, Hollis."

I knew she'd seen me before. Moments of walking in while I changed my shirt, but this was different. Even after what we'd just finished, I felt exposed, stripped and presented for inspection.

"I just wish it mattered as little to you as it does to me," she said and put a hand on my chest.

The body must matter, I thought. *The body is all there is.*

THE WARNING

Day Four of the Contamination

Taps against the window wake me. At first, I think it's something natural I can dream my way past. Maybe rain filtered through the canopy of trees, but the metronome precision continues until I rub sleep from my eyes. Sheriff Saunders pecks on the window with a fingernail. She's traded the Jeep for a larger Ford Explorer whose chassis is jacked up high to accommodate heavy underbrush, the wheels outfitted in mud tires with thick rubber studs.

I roll the window down. Sheriff Saunders doesn't lean in. Instead, she rocks back just enough to let me see her hand hovering near the gun holster. I've never been arrested before, but I open the door prepared to feel the bracelets biting my wrists.

"I came by to see if you're ready for those tankers," she says. Her look tells me she knows this truck isn't ours. "You two have car trouble?"

I shake Rosita, who just slaps at my hand before jerking

awake. After a wide-eyed moment, she pulls her jacket on, becoming immediately alert and prepared for this meeting.

"Tankers?" I say. Some vague recollection of the sheriff mentioning these drifts through my head, but I can't grasp it.

"Trucks to siphon water from your well. So, do we still have our agreement?"

Even though the conversation was only two days ago, it sounds like something that happened to an ancestor.

"Sure," I say. "Whatever helps."

My guard is still up. I don't bother asking for the real details. If she's going to take us across the creek, I expect to hear the rest on the ride.

"Good, I didn't want to break out my bargaining chips," Sheriff Saunders says. She adjusts the wide-brimmed hat on her head and points to the Explorer. "You two climb in back. I'll take you across."

A reinforced glass divider separates us from the driver's seat. The airless confines have trapped the scent of all the other bodies that previously rode inside. It looks clean, the floorboards recently vacuumed, but there is a deep stain under my left foot I'm sure must be blood. Rosita tosses me a look out the corner of her eye. There is a pleading quality in the wide stare that's hoping for subliminal communication. Maybe she thinks I'll start blabbing about the stolen tracks. It hasn't crossed my mind until this instant. Now that we're in the backseat, I'm not sure either of us will emerge with our freedom.

As we cross the creek, I scan the bank for the remains of the truck top. The first tanker truck follows behind, its diesel engine making a low, rumbling growl. It's a behemoth with an empty reservoir rigged on top, anaconda-length hoses wrapped around the side and secured high so that they won't touch the tainted water. Another comes into view, and I'm surprised the sheriff could procure two of them. Those elephant snouts will suck the ground dry. If we aren't in jail when this is over, I'll have to petition the county to sink a new well.

The sheriff parks close to my front porch. She climbs out, and for a panicked minute I think she will simply leave us locked in the backseat ready to be read our rights. Instead, she opens Rosita's door.

Up at the house, the guitar I'd planned to bash Russell with still lies on the living room floor. I pick it up and return to the porch where the others wait. I hunker down on the steps and strum a nearly silent song. I can't be sure if the sheriff or Rosita hears. It doesn't matter. The music is full in my mind.

"You two want to start explaining?" Sheriff Saunders asks as she looms in my open doorway. "Or do I have to prompt you?"

Rosita turns toward me, absolving herself of the decision. I don't know what to say. Sheriff Saunders waits as if the passage of time only ages others. Finally, she removes her hat and wipes the sweat from her forehead.

"Russell Watson is dead. Passed in considerable pain on the way to the hospital after we got an anonymous call."

Heavy tears are ready to leak from the corners of Rosita's eyes. They are something she's biting back, perhaps out of pride, perhaps afraid they will only incriminate us further. Either way, she loses the fight. My mind won't stop pumping the music into my ears long enough for me to comprehend the gravity of what's being said. Even with my fingers still, a hidden vibration pulses through the strings, urging me to continue playing.

"He admitted to murdering his father and taking Hollis hostage. I can't say I blame you two for the way you left him. We don't exactly have normal circumstances here."

Sheriff Saunders turns toward the hillside as the tankers enter the field and make their way to my well.

"One of you assholes better say something," she says.

"I didn't know what else to do with him," I say. "We were afraid to stick around."

There is a moment where I expect the sheriff to either knock the guitar from my lap or to sit down on the steps in exhaustion. I can read her indecision, watch as some internal court tries to decide what is right. In the end, she just straightens her gun belt. Out in the yard, the first tanker truck backs up, lights flashing as it emits a loud series of shrill beeps.

"I'm inclined to let it stand as a pretty unconventional type of self-defense. Particularly since I have another murderer on the loose."

"You haven't found out anything new about Victor?" Rosita asks.

"No, we haven't, which is even more troublesome because we're national news."

Sheriff Saunders removes an iPhone from her pocket and brings up a video. It's the images from days before, in downtown Cherry Tree. The last known sighting of Victor. In the video, he holds his Stetson hat over his heart as if marching in a funeral procession with the protesters. Something about his rawboned, skinny appearance, the western-style shirt two sizes too large and his ass sagging in the Wranglers, makes him look as if he's been exhumed from one of the outlaw graves on the hill.

"Goddamned freak show," the sheriff says.

"We saw a quick soundbite the other day," Rosita tells her.

"The video already has a few million hits and is getting re-played over and over on all the major networks. My department looks like a bunch of fools."

The tanker trucks idle in the yard. One of the drivers shouts out his window to a man on the ground who's busy unlatching the hoses. Two men in overalls shellacked by mud stand beside the well. One gestures instructions to the man in the truck's cab, so he can be understood despite the loud suction of the vacuum pump. The rhythmic rattling of the motors sets my foot to tapping.

"I need you to look at something else," Sheriff Saunders says. "It's unpleasant."

On the phone screen, Caroline lies framed from the shoulders up. The metal of a morgue drawer is visible beneath her hair, but I don't need to see it to understand. I'm struck by the realization that bodies don't look like people. Something during the process of expiring makes all flesh as lifeless and nondescript as meat in a supermarket. Nothing left reminds me of the woman I knew. Boils stand out on her shoulders, neck and face. Cheeks puffy and bruised in deep shades of purple and black around eyes that have swelled shut. Her lips are split, a single chipped incisor poking out between the engorged skin.

"We found her this morning in a stream not far from here."

"But why?" Rosita asks. "Why kill her when he already knows about the pictures?"

I know the answer. I'm afraid it was retaliation against me.

My fingers no longer feel the vibrations hidden in the strings, and the thumping motors of the tankers have become nothing but noise. I shouldn't have left her behind, should have stayed even if it meant we both ended up sunk in the river. Rosita wraps an arm across my shoulders, but she's sobbing too hard to be a comfort. What I need is the music, only now the music is silent.

"I'm going to station a deputy here with you tonight, Mr.

Bragg," Sheriff Saunders says. "I think it's clear Victor is looking to eliminate all witnesses."

"I don't need it and you can't spare one," I say. I run a minor pentatonic scale and throw in a few improvised blues licks, but it's like trying to start a fire with damp kindling.

"Listen, I've got more dead bodies in the last two days than this county's seen in years," Sheriff Saunders says. She knows I'm acting petulant but displays real patience. "It's happening."

I drop the guitar on the wood planks. Rosita's back straightens as the instrument clamors down the porch steps. It bangs out of tune, the whammy bar on the front bending and the pickups rattling in the frame.

"I don't need your Goddamned deputy. I need you to get out there and find that son of a bitch."

Rosita rubs the slope of my back. I shake her hand off.

"I'll station him on the other side of the creek if you're adamant, but we're not leaving you unprotected," Sheriff Saunders says. "I'm not losing anyone else." She turns to Rosita. "You need a ride anywhere?"

"I'm going to stay," Rosita says. Afterward, she looks to see if I'll allow it. Our talk last night has nearly convinced me that she's sorry about the theft. I know she just wanted to preserve her art. Since I'd considered betraying Angela to help promote the wasteland lullabies, it seems hypocritical to judge someone who almost committed the same crime. The Reverend has made me hate hypocrites, but I may just be gullible.

"Suit yourself." Sheriff Saunders descends the steps. She never looks back, crosses the yard to the Explorer and drives off, leaving the men to tap the well.

. . .

I leave Rosita to her computer and go mourn alone in the music room. There is a change happening. Any bad memories of Caroline are being replaced by some more forgiving version of the truth. I've always despised the idea of elegy and the unfair way trauma works on the mind. It's happened before. As soon as Angela and I were finished, she became a saint. An almost mythical woman with no human failings or idiosyncratic flaws that troubled me. I've wondered if I became the same thing to her. Probably not. I'm the one who took on all the blame.

Loss isn't the same for disabled men. Every time something good appeared in my life, I needed to observe all the angles. Scrutinize it until nothing felt genuine or I became convinced it was a sort of cosmic trap. A ploy by the universe to expose me as a rube weak-minded enough to believe the impossible. How many times have I lost a good thing because I couldn't trust? It might be more prudent to ask how many times I've never even noticed the opportunities because I was too busy protecting myself from the coming failure.

Most men think their last woman is the only woman who could still love them. In that aspect, I'm not so different from everyone else. Men, at least where the capacity to love is concerned, have regenerative powers. Same as the old blue-tailed lizards that used to sun on the church walls and slink off into a crack whenever I tried to seize them. Grab a tail and they'll leave the severed appendage bleeding between your fingers. Eventually this will grow back, the same as a man's belief in love, but the act can only be performed so often. Too many close calls and things harden, refuse to grow back. Maybe men like myself only get to perform this once.

. . .

By now, Angela's plane will have touched down at Yeager Airport. The band will have already navigated the small hive of the terminal. Other airports are a blend of accents and styles, individuals from all over the globe moving fast to catch their flight or sitting in stasis at their gate, but not Yeager. She'll recognize the people waiting. The West Virginians grouped tight, their clothing emblazoned with WVU's Mountaineer Mascot or some sort of camouflage. Sometimes a mixture of both. They'll stand uneasy, shift in their seats and watch the Arrivals screen for returning relatives. Most will have been waiting for hours, a punctual group annoyed with the excess of the airport. Children cling to their mothers, no doubt warned that in the city kids go missing daily and are never recovered. Grandmothers read from paperbacks or Bibles with the graph of a family tree inscribed on the title page. All births and deaths get inked in here. These elderly women smell of a distant kitchen, like powdered sugar even in the sanitized air.

Will Angela still feel any kinship? Looking out the window of the plane, watching the small humps below change to mountains, does she feel the familiar pull, I wonder? Here, where civilization remains in constant danger from flash floods, landslides or simply from the vegetation growing back down through the asphalt into the usurped soil. Can a person ever escape the imprint of a place that still feels like pioneer life? Men blazing out a homestead by blasting the tops off mountains. Burning combustible stone for power like some antiquated alchemy. Does she miss it?

I decide to quit stalling and find out.

I sneak into the bedroom while Rosita makes alterations to

the photo of a woman with no arms. I take Angela's picture off the wall, open the frame and retrieve the small business card hidden inside. I remember the mailing address by heart but have purposefully expunged her cell number from my mind.

The phone rings three times before she answers.

"Hello." The voice is the same. A mixture of husk and smooth enunciation that a younger Angela cultivated. I've been trying to dodge it despite her popularity, avoid hearing it utter anything that might share a syllable from my name. The sound drapes old memories over me.

"Angela," I manage. "This is Hollis."

Something catches in her throat. She swallows it down with a little sound over the line. "Hollis, oh my God. This is a surprise." There's a falseness in her voice I've never heard before. It makes me wonder how much the money has changed things.

"I know you've heard the new tapes." Not how I wanted to open the conversation, but the words just spill out.

"They're brilliant, Hollis. Some great stuff. I'm not so sure if concept albums are selling, so I'll have to speak to marketing about the overall arrangement. They may want a few changes, but it's such impressive stuff. Really relevant to now, you know?"

"I'm glad you like it," I say. I can't understand how she glides into business so quickly. Speaking directly should cause her at least a momentary pause. It makes me feel insignificant.

"I think we might need to do something about the tone," Angela continues. "Eight tracks and it's all acoustic. We need something a little more energetic on there. I think we can keep at least four, fill the rest in with some electric and save the other ballads for the next release."

This just shows how little she understands the idea. I'm thankful the work isn't hers to butcher.

"You can't have it, Angela. Doesn't matter who you sent to steal them."

A long silence from her end of the line. I can feel her groping for a lie.

"We've all been worried about you after months with no word. Now, I'm even more concerned."

"I didn't release them. They aren't yours, Angela. I'll write you something else, but these songs are mine."

"Hollis, I really don't know what you're talking about."

Anger swells inside until I'm gripping the phone tight enough to make the plastic crack.

"Can't we talk this through? I mean, the band really loves these tracks. I love them. It's an honor to sing them."

"I've owed you, but not that much," I say.

"Listen, we'll be at the Mountaineer Hotel the day after to-morrow. Why don't we talk in person? I'll send a car to pick you up?"

A change comes over the line. A hardening that Angela must carry into the board meetings, the strategy sessions with the publicist and record executives. Anything human is severed. From this point on, I'll likely be negotiating with the lawyers.

"It won't change my mind," I say.

"You'd be surprised," Angela says. "Things change whether you want them to or not. You know that."

The line goes dead.

III

IF YOU HAVE GHOSTS, YOU HAVE EVERYTHING

THE MEETING

Day Five of the Contamination

I t's been a morning of folk songs, sitting alone in the music room singing forgotten hymns. After the sun rose, I checked to see if Rosita was awake. She lay underneath the sheets in the shadows of the guest room. Aside from her breath moving fallen hair across the pillow, she remained still as a heart between beats. I didn't want to wake her. Didn't want to explain where I was going or have her try to follow. I closed the door and started for the creek.

That was ten minutes ago. Now I stand in the yard, the words of those dead songwriters still echoing in my head. The notes feel so precise and urgent, like the last argument against the slow erosion of everything we make. Proof that something does in fact survive the undefeated encroachment of time. I hum the melody. My joints feel fused this morning, less mobile than only a day before. At the edge of the woods, I select a walking stick from the bramble to lean on. A solid piece of hickory the length of my stunted legs. It eases my stride, but there is no question who is winning the contest between myself and time.

A deputy is stationed on the opposite bank. The windows of the SUV are rolled down, the brim of his hat pulled over his eyes like a field hand resting after a long day's labor. A paper cup, no doubt filled with the dregs of cold coffee, sits on the dash. I stand close by the water, but he doesn't notice me.

"Hey there," I shout.

The deputy pulls the hat from his eyes. He blinks while considering my shape. These looks are so familiar I can almost read a stranger's thoughts by the furrow of a brow, the way an eye widens as if to accommodate the scope of such a sight. This used to stir feelings of anger. Now, I'm just annoyed by lost time. The deputy wipes a trickle of drool from his mouth and leans out the window.

"Mr. Bragg?" he says. "Everything all right?"

"I need a ride."

No doubt he's frustrated enough with the strange guard duty. Nobody told him he'd be expected to operate as a taxi service as well. He seems reluctant but puts the Explorer in gear and drives across the creek to collect me. I have considerable trouble climbing up into the cab.

"Where to?" the deputy asks.

"Just head toward town," I say. "I'll point out the way."

I'm a day early for my meeting, but surprise is the point. I want to catch Angela off guard and not come like a dog when called. The power dynamic has always been in her favor. Arriving to confront her in a police car might remedy some of that. My escort isn't very cooperative as I give directions. He sulks behind the wheel as we turn onto the interstate, grumbles about how he'll be nearly out of his jurisdiction by the time we reach the convention center where Angela is staying. The road winds through hewed-back mountains, town nothing but a memory as we move farther into the brush. We take an exit off the road and begin to ascend a hill.

"I didn't sign on to be a shuttle service," the officer tells me.

"I thought your assignment was to protect your witness?" I say. "Or would you rather I came alone?"

We both know I couldn't have made it alone, but he doesn't bother arguing. Just clenches the wheel and drives on.

"At least tell me what we're doing out here."

"She'll be there," I say.

"She" makes him sigh. He casts a weary look out the passenger window, and we drive the rest of the way with the radio crackling as garbled voices speak over the police frequency.

The Mountaineer Hotel and Convention Center isn't like anything an outsider might picture. The name alone is deceiving. It's just a decent hotel with two large conference rooms where state employees can hold their meetings all day, then raid the little restaurant and bar before sneaking off to each other's suites for discreet infidelities. The log cabin exterior attempts a rustic tone that doesn't match the inside's decor. The interior has a penchant for parquet floors, and inauspicious prints hang on the walls. It's as if the decorator wanted to defy the hillbilly sensibilities on the outside. I've only been here once before but admired the stone hearth of the bar's fireplace. The Troubadours chose it because it's separated from the current chaos of Coopersville and the closest thing we have that approaches fancy.

My driver parks by the front entrance. The rest of the lot is empty aside from two black Mercedes sedans and an old Buick Regal sitting alone in the far corner. Through the glass doors, I see the faux marble of the entryway. A small woman in a tight business suit stands behind the high front desk, playing on her phone.

"You mind waiting just a minute?" I ask the officer.

"Don't look like I've got much of a choice." He scans the empty lot. "What could you possibly have going on here?"

"If you wait, I'll fill you in when I'm back," I say.

The officer nods. "Whatever. Just be fast." He leans back in the seat, readying for a long spell.

The woman behind the desk drops her iPhone as I enter. It slides between her feet where she snatches it up, inspects the screen with relief that it isn't cracked and tries to recover.

"I'm sorry, sir, but we aren't accepting any occupants at this time."

Then what are you doing on duty? I think. Instead, I just smile and rest my elbows on the oak desktop.

"I'm here to see Angela Carver," I say. "My name is Hollis Bragg and I have an appointment."

"I'm sorry, sir. We don't have any residents."

"Call her," I say.

The woman peers out the window and sees the cop car waiting. I smile until she cradles the phone between her neck and ear, whispers into the mouthpiece with her head tilted away as if afraid I can read lips.

"Someone will be right down, Mr. Bragg," she says.

I sit in one of the leather chairs near the entryway. The straight back isn't comfortable, but I can endure it until Angela arrives. I remind myself that "someone" doesn't necessarily mean Angela, but my heart beats hard in anticipation. Even my hands tremble. With no guitar to calm my nerves, I look out the window. A few turkey vultures circle in the distance, triangulating the location of some carrion. At this elevation, the mountains look smoky, sections enveloped in a fog that hangs heavy over the valleys. Groundhogs making coffee, my father used to say when he'd look out on similar misty mornings.

Nature can't keep my attention. I'm wondering about that Buick in the lot. The Mercedes sedans belong to Angela's crew, and the receptionist's suit looks too expensive for someone driving such a broken-down ride. I'm trying to reconcile this when I hear shoes clicking across the floor.

A man in a three-piece suit approaches. The garment is tighter than men wear in the mountains, the jacket shorter and lapels slimmed in the more fashionable style of a man from the city. He removes his glasses from his face and cleans them with his silk pocket square. Its purple shade matches the fat Windsor knot of his tie.

"Mr. Bragg, I'm Walter Quinn. I represent Miss Carver."

I'm not surprised she sic'd the lawyer on me. Still, I'm angry to be met by some emissary. My belief that the past meant something is starting to slip.

"Where's Angela?" I ask.

"Miss Carver isn't here right now. You weren't expected until tomorrow."

"I'm not very patient," I say. "When will she be back?"

"I'm not certain. Would you like to join me for a drink? I think there's a few matters we could discuss."

I could keep my seat and just wait, but there wouldn't be much point in that. The chair is killing my back and if the suit is willing to talk, I might as well hear him out until Angela arrives.

"Lead the way."

I follow across the main hall and down a tight alcove. Closer, I smell the spice of his cologne, hear the crisp rippling of his creased pants as we walk. His polished wingtips look more expensive than anything in my wardrobe, but nothing about the attire can compete with his looks. Cleft jaw, expensive haircut with sparse gray strands that shimmer under the low lights. A calculated stubble on his cheeks. For the second time this week, I'm surrounded by wealth beyond anything I've considered. Once the shock wears off, a pattern emerges. The material possessions are imposing, but it's the owners, the privilege of the bodies they inhabit and the erasure of men like me that stands out. It seems like one of the qualifications for success is a wholesome physicality. When you're surrounded by beautiful things, you can't have the tone muddied by unattractive people.

Walter leads me to the fireplace adjacent to the bar. The wing-backed chairs have been dragged away from the hearth and a small table set out for our meeting. A crystal decanter sits atop the linen tablecloth. A tall carafe of ice water rests in the center, flanked by two glasses. Walter takes a seat. I watch the condensation sweating on the outside of the glass, the way the ice bobs when my hip brushes the table as I sit. Walter pours two glasses and slides one my way.

"Ice is a rare commodity right now," he says.

I hold it up to my nose, pleased to inhale something neutral after days of the licorice scent.

"How much bottled water do you have on hand?" I ask.

Walter takes a sip. "We brought a trunk full, but the hotel has a reserve."

He isn't gloating. It's just never occurred to him that I'm unwashed, or that this could be my first drink in days that wasn't warm Coca-Cola. Men like Walter don't consider that they could've brought more supplies for the locals. His concern is the benefit concert. The Facebook hits, retweets and media storm that will accompany Angela's return home. Even the charity is a public relations stunt.

"Do you think much about commodities, Hollis?" he asks.

"Can't say I do."

Walter smiles. "I have to think about them. That's my job. I procure things for The Troubadours. Anytime I get them a hotel or a new contract, well, those are commodities. After a while, I started to realize that time itself is a commodity. I've only got so much of it, and I'm selling it away bit by bit to be comfortable in what free time I have left. I didn't like that thought."

"I can see why," I say.

"It's disconcerting to think of yourself that way, but then I started to consider The Troubadours' music. Those songs, well, they're just commodities, too. Don't you agree?"

"Maybe I'd prefer to think of it as art."

Walter nods and takes another sip of water. "It feels purer that way. Your songs are impressive. They feel like art, but I think art belongs to future generations. Maybe, if you and Angela are lucky enough, one song gets saved that way. Immortalized. But for now, with the songs filling arenas full of fans, that's not art."

"An awful cynical way to look at it," I say. My throat feels dry. I need a drink, but don't want to sip from the offered glass. I push it away like a poisoned chalice.

"Trust me, it's not cynical. It's realistic. You've always known that. It's why you sold the very first song to her. You knew that it mattered who sang it. Because people don't want to buy it from men like you. Or from men like me. Angela gets to be that. But she's just a commodity, too. Once you accept that, you'll realize what I realized."

Walter takes a manila envelope from the corner of the table.

223

He opens it, pulls out a fat packet of paper and a few index cards. He sets the contract aside, removes an ebony fountain pen from his jacket pocket and writes on the back of an index card.

"This number isn't negotiable, Hollis. I think you'll find it fair."

Nothing has been fair about our conversation, but the amount is certainly generous. It's more money than I could've imagined. Walter pushes the pen toward me, sinks into his chair and waits for me to take the bait. There is truth to what he preaches. The world has moved past the innocence of art for the sake of truth. We have packaged every aspect of the human spirit, leaving nothing but amalgamation and capital. Not even the water in my glass is a right anymore. If I had any sense, I'd drink deep. Instead, I wad up the paper and stuff it into my water glass.

"If she plays one of these songs, I'll do everything I can to take the legacy apart. I'll tell the same to Angela when I see her."

Walter shakes his head. Even I know this isn't a pure act of defiance. I don't expect to change anything or be a martyr for some cause. It's only vanity, but I've never had the chance to be prideful about anything other than music. It feels good to be allowed a moment of ego.

I've purposely avoided the music store, but know it still stands despite being vacant for years. I suspect Angela had something to do with that. Probably bought the building as soon as the band started making money and preserved the structure even if she couldn't save her father's declining business. I look at the display window, the glass covered by reams of white paper, the panes on the end busted out and fortified by sheets of plywood. The bricks are weathered and smeared with black soot as if some miner's coal-dusted hands have beaten against them until the stains became part of the mortar. The marquee sign overhead is devoid of letters. The deputy gives it all a hard stare.

"Are you sure about this?" he asks.

I check the parking lot next door. No cars, but I'm sure this is where Angela will be. She always felt best working on new material down in the basement. There is power inside those rooms and if she's this close, I'm sure it's called her back.

I nod. "You wait here on me?"

He doesn't bother to answer. The radio squawks to life as I climb out and walk around to the side door that Angela led me through all those years ago. It's unlocked, and I hear the murmur of music even before I descend the dark stairs. A voice sings the lyrics I've written. Not one of the new songs, an old one sold for a pittance. As I hit the bottom step, I promise it's the last one they will have.

"You need to focus," a male voice says. "You're a bit flat."

I don't wait to hear Angela's response. I knock on the door, stand back as the couple inside murmurs about the intrusion. A long-haired man opens the door and tries to block the entryway with his frame. I don't recognize him. Probably one of the newer members, a replacement in the cyclic iterations the band went through after I left. He's handsome, a strong jaw jutting forward from a face framed by curtains of blond hair. He looks like some studio head's suggestion. A companion who would look appropriate alongside Angela onstage. The man grips a guitar by its rosewood neck.

"What are you doing?" he asks. "Get outta here."

"Who is it?" Angela calls.

I reach for the door and the man recoils from the possibility of my touch.

"Look, this is private property."

I shoulder past while he holds the guitar up like a shield. The room is more spacious than I remembered, the antiquated recording equipment replaced by a small couch and a large mirrored vanity someone probably installed in anticipation of the band's arrival. Angela sits in front of the mirror trying to attach her false eyelashes. The left lash is already applied. It flutters like a butterfly wing as she blinks. The right one is missing and allows me to see her iris unobscured by any adornment. I still prefer her eyes drawn in the feline arch of poorly applied black shadow, but some stylist has scrubbed the runaway ecstatic out of her.

"It's okay, Felix," she says. "This is Hollis Bragg."

When she says my name, her voice takes on the same tone she often whispered into my ear after a night of standing beside the amplifiers. Her legs look longer with the tall heels she wears, and when she stands, Angela clacks forward with grace she never carried before. She takes my hand. Her palms are cold, fingers tacky with the adhesive from the eyelashes. She's aged, but the makeup hides most of it aside from laugh lines that become genuine and deep as she smiles.

"I figured you'd be down here," I say.

"Nobody wanted us to come downtown," she replies. "They act like its Baghdad or something. I have to admit, it's worse than I remembered. All the empty shops."

"You've been gone a long time."

A slight coo comes from the far side of the room. A bassinet rests in the corner with a small child swaddled inside. Mittens cover its tiny hands and a knit cap gives it the sexless look of all infants. Felix sets the guitar down and goes to the baby, picks it up and rocks it slow in his arms. The gesture is too natural for him not to be the father. Still, Felix rocks too fast and the baby begins to fuss. Angela takes it from him, hefts the child and pats its back.

"I didn't think you'd even remember this place," she says.

"How could I forget it?" I don't want this small talk, but it's a performance I'll have to endure. "What did you name him?"

"This is Aaron," she says. "That's Felix."

"Pleased to meet you," Felix says. He shares the same blue eyes as his son. "That's some amazing material you've sent us."

My stomach is sour. I don't know if it's seeing Angela with the child, or if it's left over from my meeting with the lawyer, but all the pleasantry is sapped from me. Spite roils in my gut. I resist the urge to snatch the guitar and shatter it against the wall for daring to play my songs. I'm more upset by what's coming. Outside, I'll have to face the knowledge that a life like this could have been mine. That could be our son Angela sings to sleep at night, my wife's lullabies serenading us, but I drowned any chances of that future under a tide of fear.

"I didn't write them for you," I tell Felix. "She stole them from me."

"That's not fair, Hollis," Angela says. "Look, I met Rosita and thought her project might be something you would benefit from. You're so hidden out here. I've been worried about you."

"You've been worried because I cut off the supply," I say. "You can't have these songs. I'll turn in my work for the album, but not these tracks."

"You've been selling work for a decade," Felix says. "And just decided you were a rock star all of a sudden?"

"Felix," Angela says, but the baby's cries cause her to go quiet. She bounces and shushes him.

"What would you do with it?" Felix continues. "You're a good songwriter, so why not stay in your lane."

"I'm going to play them," I say.

Felix smirks. "For who? Drunks and unemployed coal miners?"

"Felix!" Angela snaps again. "You're right, Hollis. How about we give you full writing credit and double the commission? The lawyers can work out royalties."

It's the best opportunity to get the music out of barrooms and open mic nights where the audience will only come for the freak show, but my pride still won't allow it. Angela could have ghost-writing from the best in the world; whole teams of musicians working just for her. If she wants my songs this bad, I know I truly have something.

"I've already turned your lawyer down."

Angela turns away, and I get a closer look at the baby's fat cheeks, the bewildered eyes that are seeing everything for the first time. What would it be like to see that way again? For every mundane image to be rendered a miracle? Closer, the child almost exclusively resembles Angela, but a small mixture of Felix's genes certainly blended into the boy. Already the tiny jaw juts in a way that seems ridiculous on an infant, but he'll grow into it, make women want to nuzzle against the growth sprouting on that cleft. Locks of wavy hair like his father's fall out of the boy's cap. It's not the sort of child we would have produced, but I can't help pretending for a moment. My son perfect and whole despite the legacy of illness that should've condemned him. Saved by luck or love or sheer will.

"Look, we've still got time to negotiate something fair. Will you be at the concert?" Angela asks.

"I don't think so."

"Don't be like that, Hollis. We can work this out. You could even come into the studio and play on the tracks."

I shake my head.

"I don't understand," Angela tells me. "I thought it was all about the writing. You told me that it was something you just had to get out."

"A lot of it was about writing with you, or about how it made you think of me."

I can tell Felix doesn't like this talk. He's about to interject when the baby reaches up, grasps a strand of Angela's hair and gives a tug.

"This one's about to pull me bald-headed." Her accent slips in here. Felix looks shocked to hear his woman's true voice. "Look, if you feel that strong about it just keep whatever songs you want. As for the ones you've already agreed to sell us, I'll have the contract ready," she says. "Full writing credits this time."

I don't really believe this last bit will happen. The lawyers will fight her. They can't risk the myth they've built, can't accept the possibility that the songs written by an unknown hunchback might have too much of the flavor of past hits. Once what's false is rendered truth, it becomes vital to protect the lie. It's not something I'm interested in, anyway.

Angela passes the baby to Felix, who lays him in the bassinet and comes to wrap his arm around her. It's a chaste but territorial gesture, something he can do to fight the silent signals both Angela's and my body are remembering. I've never made any man insecure before, much less a man like Felix. I ascend the stairs feeling proud.

THE RETURN

Day Five of the Contamination

O ut on the street, I smell something bitter on the wind. The Explorer is still parked alongside the building, but the driver's-side window is busted out. Tiny pellets of glass litter the ground and the deputy slumps in his seat. I know he's dead even before I see the stain cascading down the front of his uniform. I turn to run, but it's more an awkward waddle than a sprint. Boot heels slap the asphalt behind me. The sudden cold from a blade flicks against my earlobe. When the sharp tip presses into my neck, I stop.

Victor grasps a handful of my hair. I wait for my chin to be pried back, for the blade to bite deep toward my spine, but Victor just spins me around. I see him in blurred periphery as I twirl, his expression as hard to decipher as an old brand scarred into animal hide.

"Hold still," Victor says. The makeup is gone from his face. Just a bit of corpse-fleshed gray remains in the creases of his neck. "I don't want to cut you."

The knife rests against my throat, but he eases back on the blade's pressure.

"You gonna run?" he asks. "Or can we have a conversation?"

"I won't run," I say. "Don't wanna look more foolish."

Victor nods. "A man's gotta keep his dignity. What little he's allowed to keep anyway."

The Colt rests in the holster slung low on his hip. I understand the smell in the air now. Gunpowder and cordite. Even with downtown deserted, somebody must have heard the shots. If I can stay alive a little longer, backup will be on the way.

"You understand what I mean about dignity, Hollis? When even the water is poison, a man doesn't have any dignity left if he doesn't do something about that. You agree?"

"I heard enough of this in the kitchen the other night."

"I think you know I'm past talking."

Then what's with this monologue, I think. I nod toward the dead officer, making the blade prick my throat. "I suppose he was part of the problem?"

"He should have been looking for a way to put men like Watson in prison. Instead, he's busy cracking heads at the protest downtown."

The blade slides into the hollow of my clavicle. Did he see me coming out of the basement? I can't let him go down there. Not with Angela and the baby below. Before that happens, I'll pull the blade from my neck and thrust it into Victor's eye.

"I'm pretty proud of that work," Victor says. "How many YouTube hits now? Now how many people are following what's happening here?"

"Who gives a fuck?" I say. It's the wrong answer. The blade plunges a little deeper, releasing a welling of blood.

"You should," Victor says. "Think about all those fucks who

called you too ugly to contribute. Don't you want to see something balance the books?"

I scan the street for help, but all I see is the Buick from the convention center. He must have been following me all along. No one is coming. If Angela could sneak in without being noticed, nobody will arrive in time to save me.

"Do it if you're gonna," I say.

"I ain't gonna hurt you, Hollis."

I should let him rant. Just nod while he burns through all this rhetoric, only I can't leave it be. Regardless of how foolish it is, I feel the words forming, ready to expel as involuntarily as vomit. I've never shrunk from bullies. Not after that final night with The Reverend.

"A murderer isn't the kind of spokesman we need."

"People are watching because of what I did. Next time will bring even more attention," Victor says. "Don't you ever wanna get even? Wouldn't you like some payback on that bitch who climbed out over your back, like all you hicks were just crabs in a Goddamned bucket?"

I don't speak. I feel the blood seeping from my cut. Victor releases my hair and the knife disappears into his coat pocket. He turns, walks down the street and leaves me beside the cruiser. The radio is crackling with the dispatcher's voice. I don't know how to work the receiver, but I pick it up, press buttons and shout for help.

Sheriff Saunders arrives to canvass the scene. She's accompanied by two squad cars, precious resources in this time of crisis, but no officer is going to argue about being redirected when one of their own is down. There are no paramedics to spare, so the officers photograph the car before laying the dead man in the backseat of another cruiser. They cover his body with a plastic raincoat while Sheriff Saunders treats my neck with the first aid kit from her trunk. I can tell she's done this before. Her movements are efficient yet tender as she wraps the gauze around my throat.

"You wanna tell me what you two were doing out here?"

There is anger in her voice, but I welcome it. Someone is dead because of me, and Victor is still free. If she wasn't pissed, I might lose respect for her.

"I asked him to bring me here to meet Angela."

The sheriff's hands stop working. "Angela Carver? Where is she? Did she see it?"

When I try to shake my head, the gauze tightens until I gag. It's a relatively small nick, but the throb worries me. I was never blessed with a beautiful voice. Still, if the wound interferes with singing, it'll rob me of one of the few tools my body has left.

"I don't think so. I kept his attention."

"Did he mention specific targets?" Sheriff Saunders asks.

"No."

"So, Angela, is she still here?"

"I guess so." The pain increases as my adrenaline plummets. I doubt I'll be able to swallow in a few hours.

"I need you to make an introduction," Sheriff Saunders says.

I don't want to see Angela's child again. I just want to be back across the creek, lying in bed with a guitar across my stomach, fingers forming familiar chords and strumming patterns that don't require thought.

Sheriff Saunders takes me under the arm. "Ready? One, two . . ." She heaves, lets my full weight rest against her while a young officer fetches me a borrowed cane.

I lead the sheriff around the building to the side door. It's still unlocked and as soon as she opens it, I hear a Troubadours' classic wafting up from downstairs. I doubt Angela heard any of the sirens from inside this soundproof cocoon. Sheriff Saunders takes my arm so I don't stumble on the stairs. Something gentle in her touch lets me know this isn't my fault. It's as close as a woman like her can come to saying sorry. All her anger is transferred into a hard knock on the studio door. It sounds like we're serving a warrant. Felix answers with the Gibson strapped low across his waist.

"Angela Carver?" Sheriff Saunders says, looking past him. "We need to speak with you."

The sheriff lays it all out. She talks about the threats Victor made, explains how all the people in attendance and the media coverage make the concert an enticing target. It's a convincing case for shutting things down, but Angela sits defiant, arms crossed and mind made up that she's going onstage. Added security or whatever the sheriff wants will be tolerated, but she won't cancel.

Felix looks less certain. He sits in the corner rocking the child as Angela's protests stir it from sleep. The pillowy white bandage on my neck has developed an insatiable itch. The more I scratch, the more I believe the itch would remain even if I scraped the skin off. When I pick at the dressing, Angela and the sheriff stop debating long enough to scold me.

"I can't recommend this, Miss Carver," Sheriff Saunders says. "But if I can't stop you, I'm going to assign you and the rest of your group an escort. I'm also going to call in some state troopers for the concert."

"I appreciate that," Angela says. I know she isn't scared, just making concessions so they get to perform. The resolve makes me proud of her, and I wonder why I still feel anything for a woman who hasn't been a part of my life in a decade. Perhaps it's only my imagination, but if anything scares Angela, it's my continued presence. Is she wondering about how well I know the sheriff? Wondering if I'll turn her in for stealing my songs? Maybe a little bit of bluff is a good thing. I decide to let her mind wonder.

After the negotiations, Sheriff Saunders dons her hat and ascends the stairs. Before I can begin the climb, Angela takes me by the sleeve.

"Hollis, I'm glad you're okay." Her hand rises to touch the bandages.

"Of course," I say. "Couldn't lose your writer."

I don't know why I said it. Something deep inside just feels the need to lash out.

"That's not fair, Hollis."

Fair. I never want to hear the word uttered again.

THE INTERVIEW

Day Five of the Contamination

Sheriff Saunders gives me another ride across the creek. The whole time we're surging through the cresting swells, she insists I should be going to the hospital. I tell her to just drive. As we pull up to the house, Rosita comes out onto the porch. She's barefoot, her black jeans and tank top a dark blot among the chipped paint of the pergola.

"What's the story with you two?" the sheriff asks.

I don't have a satisfactory answer, but I know what I'd like it to be. Despite the theft and dishonesty, I can't help feeling a connection between us. Something that goes beyond my need to avoid being alone or her search for more fractured men to add to *The Body Book*. When she came clean about the theft, I justified it by considering the lengths I'd go to preserve my own art. I almost betrayed Angela for Russell's money, and that made me feel too hypocritical to judge. Now, I'm wondering if I've deluded myself into believing Rosita might eventually care for me. I know I still want her. This realization scares me.

"She came to interview me."

"That was days ago," Sheriff Saunders says. "You don't have to tell me the truth, but don't lie."

It's a fair compromise, so I nod in agreement. As Rosita paces back and forth across the porch, I hear the soft notes for the chorus of another song.

"Jesus," Rosita says as I climb down from the cab. "What happened?" She covers her neck as if guarding against a similar wound.

"Let the sheriff fill you in," I say. Luminous music swirls inside my head until all of creation is smothered by song. The notes reach a crescendo as I climb the porch steps, echoing in such a cacophony it makes me teeter. Rosita helps me inside. The sheriff follows without invitation. We've gone past pretenses anyway.

"Where are we going?" Rosita asks.

"The bedroom," I say. "I need a guitar."

In my mind, the troubadour is dying. Some injury he's hidden from the boy for days is festering. A putrid smell emits from his flesh and breath. I've discovered the man used to be an astronomer and views his coming demise as the natural order of creation. He knows the atoms in his playing hand are filled with the particles from exploded stars. This cosmic dust is also in the boy. Because of this, he knows the boy will understand the songs. The man takes the guitar and strums slow. Lets the boy see the way his fingers change position on the chipped neck. When he hands it over and the boy plays, the rough notes become a symphony in the darkness of their camp.

Back in reality, Rosita chastises me with each step down the hall, asking why I left without her, if I met Angela and what was said. This might just be self-preservation, but underneath that cynicism, I believe she's concerned about me. It's been so long since a woman inquired with worry in her voice, I can't help but smile as Rosita helps me sit on the edge of the bed.

"Bring me a guitar," I say.

"Why did you go without me?"

"I had to do it alone." The music is fading. It's a labor to keep hearing the notes. "A guitar!" I say.

Rosita exits and returns with the acoustic. She lays it in the empty spot on my bed a lover might occupy. I pick it up and my hands become possessed. I'm a part of the old traditions of creation. Muses singing through my digits to play the dying troubadour's last song. Rosita listens for a minute before the sheriff calls for her. I can tell she wants to linger, but Sheriff Saunders calls again.

The women begin a conversation in the hall. Their whispers rise, occasionally punctuated by Rosita's sharp swearing. I hope she isn't confessing her theft. If she is, there's nothing I can do. My hands won't cease composing.

Once Sheriff Saunders has gone, I sit on the couch and transcribe the work into a notebook while Rosita changes the dressing on my neck. The room is basted with the stink of our unwashed bodies. The windows in the kitchen stay open but have little effect against the days of our accumulated sweat. The last of the food in the fridge is gone, so we sustain on canned fruit from the cupboard. Rosita drinks a warm Coca-Cola. I forgot to refrigerate the bottles and we've eaten all the ice.

The television segues into another update about the police

officer's murder and how the manhunt for Victor Lawton has intensified. A member of the Watchmen environmentalist group is being interviewed. The man's identity stays hidden by the triangle of a red bandana tied over his face, a ball cap and sunglasses concealing the rest of his features. He says Victor was a member of their organization, but maintains they are peaceful whistle-blowers. Victor was excommunicated for plotting terrorist acts against polluters. Watson Chemical was a name he frequently mentioned.

The reporter grills the man. She wants to know why he didn't come to the press or police sooner. He stutters through excuses as Rosita peels the bandage off my neck.

"How bad?" I ask.

"You'll have a scar. I really think you need some antibiotics."

I should be on guard after the stolen tracks, but I remain softened by her company. Just watching her descend the stairs the other morning, the way she stretched and scratched bed-tussled hair felt like a gift. This companionship is the normalcy better-made men get to experience. The beginning of each day punctuated with a sleep-tinted kiss and a groggy smile. This is what I used to have and lost.

Rosita turns the TV off. "Asshole could have killed you."

The pessimist inside tries to dismiss the concern in her voice. I can't let myself believe she could desire me. Not after the theft. Perhaps *The Body Book* has made her more comfortable with the misshapen, but she still wouldn't want to roll over in the night and see me sharing the bed. Just like my theory regarding the blue-tailed lizards, she'll leave and take something with her.

"Do you wanna talk about it?" Rosita asks.

"I can tell you do."

She pulls at one of her toes until it pops. It's a nervous fidget

I've noticed. As she hangs her head low, fallen bangs cut across her eyes. Perhaps she doesn't want to look at me while saying whatever comes next.

"I've told you I'm sorry more than once," she says.

"I forgive you," I say. "But it doesn't keep Angela from having heard." It also doesn't mend my feelings, but I don't see the need in telling her that.

Rosita nods. "What did you two decide?"

"I told her these songs were mine and promised to fill my quota with the tracks I originally wrote for her. I'm not sure that will keep her from playing whatever she wants. The only way to be sure is to go public with what I've already written."

"Maybe you should," she says. "I think you underestimate your audience. There are plenty of shallow people out there, but that's not everyone."

She dabs the crusted wound with a damp cotton swab, applies some ointment and wraps the new bandage around my neck. It stings, so I wince and knock the guitar off the end of the couch. Rosita rests it against the plush cushions.

"What would you know about most people?" I chuckle. "You take naked pictures of freaks."

"They're not freaks. Anyway, I believed in it enough to steal your music."

I believe in it, too. I keep thinking about one man she interviewed in Denver with tumors growing on his face. Each mass looked like ripe fruit ready to drop. There is a single picture toward the end of the session where the man grins. Some of his teeth are obscured by a bulbous growth dangling from his upper lip, but the smile is still more genuine than any I've cracked in years.

"The people you interviewed?" I ask. "Did it help them afterward?"

"You wanna talk about it now?"

"Yeah, if you don't care."

She lights a cigarette. "I just want you to make up your mind."

"Does it help them?" I ask again.

"I started it hoping so. Now, I'm not sure I'm qualified to answer."

"Let's just hear your opinion."

Rosita inhales her cigarette. "Some of them. It might help break them out of the cycle of self-loathing, all those feelings of self-hate, but they'll slide right back down if they let themselves. I can try and show them their worth, but they are the ones who need to believe it. That's hard to admit, but I think that's the truth."

"I've been thinking some of the questions might help me."

Rosita shakes her head. "I don't want you making rash decisions. Not while you're fucked up."

"I'm no more fucked up than usual."

Part of it may be an olive branch, but it's also a hope for something I can't quite articulate. A last chance to revise how I see myself. Rosita's poker face is solid, but the opportunist rises inside her. My exposed body is the logical progression from the photos she's already taken. We both know it's a necessary addition to the book. Not just stationary nude spreads, but my body engaged in the acts she's already documented. Without both, the project is incomplete.

"If you feel different later, we trash the photos. Deal?"

"Deal."

Rosita leaves to gather her equipment. I watch the trail of cigarette smoke disappear in her wake and run a hand over my lower back trying to feel the first spot where the vertebrae went awry, snaked out on an alternate course.

Rosita comes back to position me on the couch. She sits in the chair across from me, readying her cameras. Aside from her Nikon, there is a camcorder to record the session.

"Any questions before we start?"

"No."

"Okay," she says, raising the camera. "Tell me your name."

"My name is Hollis Bragg."

"Where are you from?"

"Coopersville, West Virginia."

"Why did you agree to this interview?"

Rosita pulls off her T-shirt, exposing the sweat stains on her bra and the stubble under her arms. I'm struggling to get my own shirt off. If I think too much, I won't continue. I manage to pull the fabric over the great hump of my back and wiggle like a snake shedding its skin. Now, all my most malformed parts are naked. Back forever crooked forward, forcing my stomach into permanent lines, flesh left sagging from being unable to perform even modest exercise. Caroline is the last woman to have seen me like this, and while we developed a familiarity, I never gained true confidence. Her touch moved over these hidden places, but never healed as they lingered.

Rosita begins to work on the clasp of her bra, but I raise a hand to stop her.

"I agreed because I wanted people to see me," I say.

Rosita looks uneasy. Maybe I'm the first to stop her. She seems to be waiting for something profound to follow. Should I rise and close the distance, wrap my arms around her and pull her close? Is she wondering what it would feel like to grasp shoulders so sloping, to find a man perpetually bent bending lower to meld into her? Would she feel more whole against me? All are questions I'd ask if I lived in a body like hers. I already know the other side of the equation. Every wholesome body I've touched has only made me feel more twisted. That's the true pain of my relationship with Angela that I never wanted to acknowledge. As much as her body pleased me and offered me pleasure, I was both lustful and envious of it. I desired to be as complete as her as much as I desired to touch her. It's one of my most shameful secrets. One I know I can't repeat if I'm lucky enough to have the next woman.

"I wanted people to see even if they don't want to look. Even if they don't want to consider the possibility of it. I've done things. I made music. I was loved by a woman."

I slide my pants down. My legs are thick from the work of carrying the rest of me, covered in so much hair I look caught in transformation into some beast. They're the furry legs of a satyr.

Rosita raises the camera to snap a few pictures. Her hands are trembling.

"Do you hate your body, Hollis?" she asks.

"I think people made me hate it."

"Has anyone ever loved it?"

"Yes, but I didn't believe them. Not until they left."

"Do you love it now?"

"No, but only because it's the reason I've rejected most things."

There might be more, but that confession is the extent of the poetry in me. Rosita takes a few more pictures.

After my clothes are back on, we sit in the kitchen booth and burn Rosita's cigarettes. I'm getting hooked after the chain-smoking sessions these last few days but assure Rosita I'm the sort who can always buy a pack, smoke a few and toss them without much thought. Rosita warns me she used to say the same thing.

Outside, a few crows cackle from the bare limbs of the oaks.

"I haven't heard the chickens in a while," I say.

"What chickens?" she asks.

I tell her about the fighting cocks and my suspicion of their death, either dehydrated or poisoned from drinking the water before people were warned. I think about all those dead birds. The field full of dirty white feathers, wings spread wide like fallen angels as the farmer walks across his property picking them up with a gloved hand and shoving them inside a Hefty bag.

"I don't know anything about chickens," Rosita says. "Were they white?"

"Some of them," I say. "He raised all types. Rhode Island Reds, Plymouth Rocks, even a big rooster so dark his eyes were black."

I stare outside as if expecting the birds to come scratching in the dust of the yard.

"I'm going to see her concert," I say.

"What are you gonna tell her?"

"I have no idea. Before it's over, I'll probably have fucked things up for you. The money, I mean. I can't help that."

Rosita nods. If she's bothered, it's well hidden.

"Will you go with me?" I ask.

"To the concert?"

"I'll need some moral support being out in public."

"Sure, I can do that."

"Thank you. I owe you a lot for this time."

Rosita shakes her head. "You're the one with all the hospitality. I know that wasn't easy after what I did."

A splatter hits the roof before I can reply. I cock my head and place a finger to my lips. "Listen."

Outside, a soft pattering begins. A crack of thunder follows and we both turn to the window. It's raining. Not a hard downpour, still more mist than precipitation, but I lurch toward the door.

"Get a bucket or something," I say.

The door swings wide, slams into the side of the house as I trip and fall down the few porch steps. I sprawl on the grass, eyes wide open to the sky. I'm not injured, but Rosita comes out to help me stand. Clods of grass and dirt stick against my back as if growing from a small mountain, then wash away as the rain increases. I turn my face up toward the sky and laugh.

Rosita makes two more trips inside for a total of seven receptacles. I never leave the yard. Just stand looking up into the rain with my shirt off until Rosita goes inside a final time and returns with a camera. Some of the last frames of her time in Coopersville are these images. Photos of me shirtless, hands held out to catch the drops, skin slick as the rain runs off the waterfall of my back.

THE LOVERS

Angela and I didn't speak about our night together for days. I noticed the occasional glance, moments heavy with unstated tension, but was too fearful to be the first to engage. The act had altered me so completely that I couldn't understand why she wasn't equally changed. I tried to tell myself only physical connections were made, but knew it was something deeper. My body no longer felt like my own after her touch. The old perception of inhabiting a damaged vessel faded into moments of uncommon pride. I still loathed my physique but took solace in the idea that she'd found pleasure there. Before that night with Angela, love was an abstract concept. At best, I thought the world gave you a few animal instincts and you tried to satisfy them. She tested that belief.

Playing the show also reinvigorated our creative ability. We devoted several hours a day to writing new material. A week into this regimen, Angela began to suggest a full band. I was skeptical and, deep down, knew I harbored a jealous need to keep her to myself, but Angela persisted. She spread the word in bars until we found another guitar player and drummer.

Since our apartment wasn't large enough to accommodate everyone and the noise would be an issue with neighbors, Angela arranged for us all to meet at the new guitarist's home. He owned a small plot of land ten miles outside of Lexington, with an old tobacco barn on the property. Even arriving at dusk, I could see that the barn looked ready to collapse. The wood was a feast for generations of termites and paint flecked off the walls until the weathered red resembled peeling scabs. Starlight leaked inside through small holes in the roof. I imagined colonies of bugs hidden in the leafy folds of tobacco hanging from the ceiling. It felt a wrong place to make art, but we'd learned to make do with what we had.

The new boys offered greetings too formal not to be rehearsed. One of them even called me "sir." I smiled and let them ramble, but it made me wonder why my body left mundane moments impossible. Why doesn't the shock wear off within an hour or so? In ways, they reminded me of the congregation from The Reverend's church. The same stark eyes of men who've known too much poverty. Scars hidden in subtle places from childhood labor.

The drummer's name was Lester, a rotund man with a nose like a hawkbill knife, who spent all practice cursing and sweating. Deep pools stained his shirt until it looked like a spigot leaked underneath. His lank hair dripped on the drums, splashing as he beat them with his chipped sticks. Gary, the guitar player, had long swizzle-stick legs. He chewed Beech-Nut tobacco, which discolored the corners of his blond whiskers, and spit between his shoes regardless of where he stood. The giant wad kept his left cheek perpetually packed like a squirrel's.

We played well together, but I spent the session watching for some flirtation. For Angela to touch one of the men in a familiar way or laugh a bit too hard at one of Gary's jokes. The fucker was always joking, breaking out little pieces of colloquial wit like "If I say a mouse can pull a house, hitch the little bastard up" and "If I tell you a rooster dips snuff, lift his Goddamned wing." Lester didn't concern me. Too shy and awkward. Gary, however, seemed to have a certain charm. I reminded myself that if Angela could find something worthy in me, perhaps any normal man could steal her away.

I hated coveting her like some possession, but no amount of self-disgust changed these feelings. I wanted some commitment between us even if all I could claim was a single night. There had been sweet words, but since she'd made no more advances, I thought it better to bury those urges deep in memory. Let it become a fragile thing for rare occasions alone.

We played for several hours before the new boys stepped into the field to share a joint. I watched them pass the glowing ember in the distance and wondered if they discussed ways to exclude me. Trusting them felt impossible.

"What's the matter?" Angela asked. The heat in the barn made her sweat. The perspiration left wet curls in the curtains of her hair. "Didn't you think we sounded good?"

"Yeah," I said. "Gary's pretty solid."

"You're better," she said. "But he can hold his own."

I didn't understand it at the time, but my negativity was driving her away. There was a distance between us more than physical, a need for me to say something to make her understand how much I appreciated her, appreciated the way she'd uprooted to try to facilitate a dream with me. I felt these things intensely, just didn't have the words to say them. I'd been trying to articulate my feelings through musical notes, but songs are too passive and open to interpretation. She might have been more apt to accept me sooner if I'd just seemed like less work. Eventually, the well of her understanding would run dry. A person can only cultivate patience so long.

Angela squeezed my hand.

"I don't just want it for myself," she said. "I want it for you, too. I want people to see what I see."

She gave me a kiss that felt almost apologetic until I returned it. I closed my eyes, tried to transport us away from the barn to that day in the dugout with the rain pounding on the tin roof, but the smells of the field, the marijuana wafting on the air and the heat of the barn wouldn't allow escape. Angela put hands on me. That was enough.

We toured all the nearby cities. Knoxville, Louisville, Columbus. Gary bought a 1984 Ford Econoline. The door had to be slammed repeatedly to stay shut and the interior smelled of vomit and stale cigarettes. I slept in the back while Gary and Lester took turns driving. Angela stayed in the rear with me, singing and guarding the Folgers can where we hid the band fund. All expenses were paid with its contents. We boys stayed road weary, but Angela maintained her radiance. The travel added blush to her cheeks and her conversations focused on our future. She felt certain we were one exceptional show away from stardom. All it takes is the right ear, she'd say. We had the talent, all we lacked was some luck.

I remained the pessimist. The venues were all late-night jukes where the alcoholic clientele appeared capable of sucking spilled drinks from the rag used to mop up the bar. We won the crowd over each night, but I still worried half of the audience only watched me. It was never as apparent as the woman crying during our first show. Still, I noticed certain glances, remarks whispered into ears obscured by cupped palms. I feared being a spectacle that would always mute the songs.

The band defended me on the few occasions where things went bad. A heckler in Bowling Green, Kentucky, stood by the stage, pantomiming my hunched posture and unsteady walk. As soon as he got within range, Gary mule-kicked him, busting the man's nose flat across his right check. We had to eat our portion of profits from the door that evening. Another night, Angela made the bartender eject a man yelling from the back corner.

Men remained the only aggressors. Women seemed either completely heartbroken, looked on my body as if it were a walking expression of universal cruelty or watched me as though I were a wounded animal that needed protection, their pity so apparent it removed any shred of masculinity I'd been able to secure. If there was one positive in seeing this, it's that I realized how singular a person Angela was. I knew she viewed me as an equal.

One night outside of Knoxville, Angela insisted we get our own room. I expected some argument from the others. It seemed an abuse of the band fund, only no one protested. That night in the motel transformed things. We didn't officially cement our relationship status, but we emerged a couple in practice if not in name. We no longer slept apart, even shared a bed while Gary and Lester bunked on the floor when funds wouldn't permit privacy. I spent the months waiting for things to implode. Whether by fate or self-fulfilling prophecy, it all came to a head over a year later in Memphis.

Gary and Lester left the motel intent on visiting Graceland.

Angela and I used the time to be alone, lying in bed wrapped in the tangle of each other's arms. I wanted her, but was too shy to make an advance. We'd been together at least a hundred times by then, but the old fear of rejection stayed with me. It was always her touch that started things. I never considered that perhaps she wanted to feel my hands on her first.

Her body felt stiffer in my arms that night. When she wouldn't rest her head in the great dip of my chest, I knew something was wrong. Angela always found that disfigurement an inviting hollow. It let her listen to my heart.

"We gotta talk," she said.

"Okay." I expected it to be the end, but she didn't have the sadness of separation in her voice.

"I've been late all month."

It seemed impossible. Not only because we'd been careful, always sheathing me, but because I'd never considered the possibilities of fatherhood. It seemed a horror too unbelievable to face. What did I know about parenting? My own father could only provide a negative example. The practical things about childcare didn't worry me. Diapers, bedtime and bottles I could learn, but the genetic inheritance I'd likely pass on remained outside my control. How do you protect someone from what you are?

When I didn't respond, Angela slid away from me.

"Are you mad?" she asked.

I was angry at myself. I should've taken the precautions to keep another life like mine from the world.

"What are we going to do?" I asked. The wrong words.

"What do you want to do?" she asked.

There were multiple arguments I could've given, speeches both altruistic and selfish. I could've told her that we didn't have money for a child or that any chance at making our music career flourish would be over. The baggage of motherhood would push her from the stage. She'd never sing again aside from lullabies. The truth was I feared my contributions. Even if I possessed a strong mind, the form we mutually constructed would bare all my flaws. Willing it into existence out of my own need to love something entirely my own was a sin I couldn't commit. Sometimes when I look back on that night, I miss that chance to be a father, but this never lasts long.

"We can't," I said.

Tears tumbled from her eyes. "How can you say that? We made it, Hollis."

"I can't make anything good, Angela. I'm not capable."

I expected protest. For her to offer another declaration of my worth, but we didn't talk any more that night. I sat outside on the hotel balcony, looking down on a pool filled with children. They splashed waves onto the concrete deck, ran screaming in circles around the edge regardless of their mother's half-hearted warnings. Angela never joined me. I smoked cigarettes stolen from her purse until she fell asleep, then slipped back inside to draft my note on cheap hotel stationery.

I read it twice. Whatever poetry I can create with strings was absent in those words. I folded the letter lengthwise and laid it on the nightstand. I didn't stay to watch her sleep. At the van, I found the Folgers can hidden under some blankets in the back. I took fifty dollars, a minuscule amount of my percentage, and locked the van doors. I hid the keys atop a back tire. Not the best place for them, but I couldn't face Gary or Lester.

I walked down random streets. The lights of Memphis shone bright, intruding in a way I've never acclimated to after so much time in the dark provinces of the hills. I remember wishing I'd given her hair a final caress and stolen a cigarette for the road. The sky pissed rain. The drizzle turned to stinging diagonal showers as I put out a thumb. Eventually, a blue Corolla slowed. A man with road-raw eyes rolled down the window. He was a bit drunk, his suit coat emitting the stench of gin and sweet vermouth. His breath reeked of alcohol-infused olives.

"Where you headed?" he asked.

"Coopersville, West Virginia."

"Never heard of it," the drunk said, scratching his beard. "I'm heading to Ashland. Take you that far."

I climbed in realizing I'd forgotten my guitar. The man drove fast as if daring the rain to wreck us, outlaw country playing as he offered sips from a bottle stowed in the floorboards of the passenger seat. As soon as the city was behind us, the man quit watching me in the rearview and spoke up.

"Look," he said. "I might be outta line here, but I just gotta know. What the hell happened?"

I didn't know where to begin.

Returning home was like walking barefoot into Hell. Since I'd no one to say good-bye to when I left, there was no one to greet me on my return. I found the camper the way I'd left it, aside from a few broken windows. Rocks that had sailed through the panes still lay on the floor when I entered. I sat on the bed and held them, wondered what sort of heathens had thrown them and what spooky stories they'd told about the twisted man who'd lived here with his murderous father. I've heard incarcerated men say how the first night is the hardest. That eventually, you grow accustomed to the bars, constant sounds and smells of a jailhouse. It wasn't like that for me. The first night, I bedded down in total relaxation, not comfortable but accepting the familiar defeat of my home. I only felt the haunt of my father the next morning when I went to walk among the burned planks of the church.

And that's how it went for a few months. I made infrequent trips to town, walking to the store to spend what little money I'd squirreled away on canned food I hauled back across the creek. I lived the life of a mountain hermit, spent nights sitting in the absolute dark of the camper, wondering if something would ever intervene on the slow, boring decay I'd decided upon.

The guitar arrived a few weeks later. A nervous UPS man delivered it in the early morning. He stood on my camper's small porch looking perplexed, uncertain anyone could be inside the little hovel. I came out of the shadowed bedroom to accept the package, and he left without bothering to wait for my signature. I'm sure he still tells the story. There was a small letter explaining that it wasn't my guitar, just a replacement since mine had been pawned for band funds. That was something Angela would apologize for years later. At the time, I was less excited about the old acoustic Fender with its tobacco sunburst than knowing that the band had settled somewhere in Nashville. I could picture Angela sitting in the cafés, writing music out as she sipped café au lait. I took the letter and tacked it to the bedroom wall.

The guitar opened a floodgate of song. I spent days composing new pieces, writing some of the music on the tiny bathroom wall. When the first songs were finished, I traveled to town, bought a small tape recorder and made a cassette of the material. I dropped it in the mailbox with a note that I wanted the band to have them, a personal thank you and apology for leaving in the night. I warned myself that it would probably come back "Return to Sender." Instead, I received a note from Angela, an eight-hundred-dollar check and a request for more. That was the start of our new relationship.

THE CONCERT

End of the Contamination

The day of the concert, the governor holds a press conference to let the people of Coopersville and the surrounding counties know their water is safe. He stands behind an impromptu podium someone packed out onto the steps of the capitol building, looking slick in a pinstripe three-piece suit, his red politician's tie woven into a fat knot. Under the camera's scrutiny, he congratulates the people of West Virginia for their perseverance.

I watch the entire conference. The reporters ask safe questions, supplicate themselves in appreciation for being granted an audience with the man and an event that will push slack ratings a bit higher. I wait to see if the governor will take a big drink from the nearest tap. Better yet, I want to see the man remove his suit jacket, roll up his pant legs and wade deep into the river like he's being baptized. After that, I'll be convinced.

Loneliness is making me bitter. Rosita left two days ago. I

tried to talk her into staying, but she wanted to go back to the hotel and take some more photos downtown before the concert. I was concerned about Victor, but Rosita seemed certain she'd be safe on her own. Maybe she's right, or maybe she just didn't want to stay with me. When the solitude gets the best of me, I'm sure it's the latter.

Since she departed, I'm agitated by nearly anything. A broken guitar string is apocalyptic, the sound of squirrels cutting acorns in the trees deafening until I can't enjoy a midday nap. The only solace comes from playing. Even then, I fight the urge to think about Angela and Felix practicing one of my wasteland lullabies.

Sheriff Saunders showed yesterday with some supplies and a letter from Angela. Nothing personal, just a Hallmark thank-you card stuffed with two VIP tickets. She also brought Angela's signed guitar back from the office. I set it in the bedroom without opening the case. I didn't want to see the handwriting. The sheriff asked if she and Rosita could come fetch me Sunday evening for the concert. I told her I appreciated the generosity, but that wouldn't be necessary. After I thanked her for the note, Sheriff Saunders revealed one last surprise. A parcel wrapped in green and red Christmas paper, a few reindeer with glitter encrusted hoofs prancing across the snowy rooftops on the package. The glitter flaked off as I tore the wrapping and found a gray chambray shirt inside. The buttons were white pearl snaps that shone as Sheriff Saunders held it up to my body. She proclaimed it a good fit without forcing me to try it on.

The shirt hangs from my bedroom doorknob. I've paired it with some jeans Sheriff Saunders insisted on ironing before she left. All these strangers fussing over me seems like the final reason needed to tear up the tickets, but I'm afraid to even crease the paper. Before our reunion, I would have preferred crucifixion to seeing Angela again. Now, I need to be sitting in that first row, a reminder of whose songs she's been playing.

I dress in front of the dirty bathroom mirror and slick my hair back with bottled water. The greasy layers are too long. Several unruly strands drape down onto my collar in curls that refuse to be tamed by a comb. Outside, tires roll over the gravel in the driveway. I swallow a pill for fortification. When I step out, Rosita is waiting on the porch. She's wearing her uniform of dark jeans and a band T-shirt, her tan leather jacket clinging tight around her. A camera bag is slung over her shoulder. The weathered strap dangles down to her thigh.

"Looking sharp," she says.

Compliments, even if they are honestly intended, only make me feel like a shy child who requires the praise. Rosita slips a hand into her coat pocket.

"I got you a gift," she says, revealing a bolo tie with a turquoise centerpiece. "I know it's a tacky sort of thing." She dangles it from the string, the turquoise swinging back and forth as if trying to hypnotize me. "But I thought it was very cool in an outlaw country way. I can't help that I've got bad taste."

"It's lovely," I say and mean it. I can't recall the last time I received so many gifts.

"Bend," she says.

I lean forward while she slides the tie over my head and pulls it tight.

"There," she says, giving my collar a final smoothing. "You look very dapper."

"Never been accused of that," I say.

"It's okay to be afraid," Rosita tells me. "That's only natural." She takes my hand and helps me into the back of the sheriff's SUV.

. . .

The Coalfield Cinema was the last of the grand Fifties movie palaces. In its prime, gold scrollwork adorned the vaulted ceilings in the two-hundred-seat auditorium, and balconies were positioned around a chandelier dangling like a uvula in the room's center. Wood carvings of Greek myths flanked the staircases: Poseidon rising from the depths and Zeus standing behind two heavenly ascending columns. The architect decided that all carpeting should be scarlet to match the velvet curtain on the stage and the upholstery on the seats.

After it closed in 1972, the structure fell into disrepair. A small fire in one of the balconies and the destruction of some of the statuary in the lobby prompted a campaign to declare it a historical landmark. Everyone from Chuck Berry to Merle Haggard played it in the Sixties after its stage was converted into a concert hall. So, after years of sitting vacant, a wealthy benefactor had the place refurbished right down to the brass doorknobs. If I had to guess, I'd bet Angela slowly rebuilt it for a return home.

Concertgoers trail through the venue's main doors. Wives hold the arms of husbands who've donned their only suit. Groups of single women huddle in tight clusters, looking at the couples with either relief or envy depending on their current tolerance for loneliness. As the crowd slips inside, ushers in red blazers rip tickets and guide patrons to their seats. Sheriff Saunders's work-release boys have polished every fixture inside until it glows, shampooed and spot-cleaned the plush carpet until it looks dyed with their own blood. Even new wallpaper, a similar golden shade as before, has been hung.

Rosita squeezes my hand. She offers a tight-lipped smile that keeps the hot taste of bile from creeping farther up my throat. I'm just about to thank her again when a man in a black suit steps toward us through the crowd. His hair is reminiscent of a samurai topknot, his goatee trimmed down to neat stubble. The man extends a hand, and I can't help but notice the ostentatious gold watch around his wrist.

"Mr. Bragg," he says. "Ms. Carver has asked me to take your party to your seats."

The man leads us through the sea of people. If all the eyes weren't on me before, they are now. I'm afraid we'll become separated in this swarm, but our escort is patient with my slow stride. He makes his long legs take baby steps while I follow. Our seats are in the front row. I sit down expecting questions about the premium accommodations, but Rosita just gives my arm a pat. She folds her leather jacket in her lap.

The Troubadours come onstage to deafening applause. I hardly listen to Angela's introduction, a soliloquy about how much Coopersville means to her and what incredible people are hidden in the hills. It's genuine, but I can't focus. I'm imagining the younger version I loved swelling in the early months of pregnancy, the motel fight resolved with the slow admission that our van life must be traded for another shithole apartment with broken appliances. Maybe in this alternative reality we crawl back home to live in a trailer, occasionally travel to town where I must suffer the stares and whispers every time we need supplies. At least in that version of the story, I wouldn't be alone. Would life have been better that way? If so, why did I do so much to resist it?

Onstage, the band transitions from solo-filled blues to a soft ballad. Angela straps on a twelve-string guitar. The notes rise in harmony as a second guitarist enters to accompany her. The A-minor chord he plays reverberates through the audience.

"This song was written by my good friend, Hollis Bragg," Angela says.

The first track of the wasteland lullabies begins. The song moves like an electric current, surging from man to woman until every foot taps the solemn rhythm. The words cut deep as a scythe. Even with such undeniable power, the arrangement feels wrong. The twelve-string too full, the music too complete and lacking the fractured quality of the song's reality. The man in my story wouldn't have all the precision instruments to fill in the silences. In that world, there isn't a scrap of metal left as perfectly formed as a cymbal. The man would only have the pad of his thumb striking the strings and the wind outside smacking the thin fabric of his makeshift shelter. A bitter breeze might seep in through the holes, the desert night so cold his guitar struggles to stay in tune as the wood warps. The landscape outside would be his orchestra. Something he couldn't control that would bleed overtop him, create its own violent harmony whenever his instrument faltered. Angela has replaced this anarchy with violin strings.

This isn't personal tragedy distilled into song. This is a false attempt at completion, a refusal to admit that nothing is ever whole and that the best we can hope for are moments of grace in the great spans of dissonance. I should be angry at how she's butchered it, but my mind breaks the notes apart, rearranges them until I hear the places where the guitar should alter tone. I erase the other instruments until it is only a parched voice, raw and without the beauty of Angela's dulcet vocals. The straining guitar in my mind is absent a required string and attempting the melody regardless. I need a pen. I need to transcribe this before it leaves.

. . .

"I'll be right back," I say. Rosita snatches at my shirttail, mutters something about it being my masterpiece, but I climb the stairs, desperate to hit the ticket booth, where they must have some writing materials.

Upstairs, the ushers stand with their faces pressed to the glass doors, whispering to one another. The manager of the group, a tall mustached man in shirtsleeves and a red vest, gestures them away from the door in exasperation. I start to ask him for a pen, but the blue-and-red flash of police lights scan across the front of the venue. The walls are cast in the glow of these primary colors for a moment. Outside, I see the cause of it all.

Victor stands with one arm handcuffed to a parking meter and several jugs of water arranged near his feet. Another gallon jug swings from his free hand. I can't hear his voice over the crowd gathering, but the force of his words makes him tremble until the water splashes into a pool between his shoes. Police keep their distance, lurking with guns drawn outside the zone of a potential soaking. Only the news cameras seem anxious to move closer. Were they not hindered by the officers' perimeter, some reporter would stick a microphone in Victor's face.

I step outside, where I can hear Victor shouting against the wind. His voice cracks as he tries to raise it above the sirens. Across the street, the rubberneckers shiver and breathe into cupped hands. The night is cold for spring, but none will risk missing the climax to go fetch a coat.

"It's only water, boys," Victor says in full provocateur mode. His voice sounds like a carnival barker's braying. "If anyone of you will take a drink, I'll go to jail no questions asked. I got it from the tap this morning. Don't you trust your governor?"

The fuse is burning. In a few moments, Victor will douse the closest cop. It could all be an elaborate hoax. Just bottled water or piss or something from the tap this morning that truly is safe. It could also have been collected days ago for this occasion. I smell licorice, but it might be fear playing on my imagination.

As I wade through the crowd, I notice most of them holding up cell phones. A thousand little replicas of the moment play on their screens.

"What's going on?" I ask the nearest cop.

"Sir, I need you to step back," the officer says. He barely glances at me, too concerned to offer a double take.

"Let me talk to him," I say. "He's a friend of mine."

The cop finally gets a good look at me and the wind goes out of him. It's too bizarre to absorb so much in one night. The officer opens his mouth to argue, but Victor spots me.

"Hollis Bragg," he screams and gestures with the overflowing jug.

"Hello, Victor," I call. "What's this then?"

"Like I told you, Hollis. Gotta make an impression to get people's attention." He jabs the bottle toward the cameras. The jug spits a small fountain that splashes near my feet.

"I'm not sure this is the way."

Victor shakes his head. "Only way when nobody gives a shit. They want a scene, so someone needs to get thirsty." He goes back to addressing the crowd. "Come on, you hicks. Just a sip!"

Behind us, more patrons have slipped out of the concert. They stand along the sidewalk, watching while the police herd others out of the street. Rosita is among the new batch of onlookers. Her camera is out, the lens focused on Victor.

"You could take a drink," Victor tells me. "That would show

them, wouldn't it? The freak they all took advantage of was the only one with any balls."

"Will that satisfy you?" I ask.

"I'd rather your old girlfriend came out to have a taste. Is she playing your songs in there?"

"Yeah, she is, but I don't care anymore." I don't bother to tell him she's given me credit this time. I'm not sure it matters.

"You should. You trusted it would be different this time, but it's never going to be. I wish there was some way I could teach all of you that."

Victor holds his arm high until the streetlights overhead cast their shine through the jug. The shadow of a small wave appears on the sidewalk.

"You trust this water?" Victor asks.

"I don't guess I do."

"Then take a drink. Die with some purpose instead of wasting away on the mountain."

Rosita shouts something from the sidelines, but I let my ears go deaf. Her voice sinks into the crowd's white noise.

"The cameramen must be pitching tents in their pants," I say. "If a terrorist rock star wasn't enough to draw some coverage, the local recluse playing martyr should have the video on constant rotation."

"Exactly," Victor says.

I could just walk away. Victor doesn't have any leverage, no real threats or ability to bargain. Eventually, the cops will just incapacitate him with some nonlethal means or a deputy will find an excuse to put a hollow point through his cranium. Either outcome sounds fine to me. Only, then no one will know about the water. The cycle will continue. Angela will keep playing my music. She might give me the credit as the writer, but I'll return to being alone on the mountain, too afraid to perform the work I create.

"Give me the jug," I say.

Victor hands it over. The officers move forward to stop me. If I'm going to drink, it'll have to be fast, but I've enough time to consider whether this is the end. So many nights I've pulled the jigsaw pieces of my father's final hours out and turned them every which way trying to decide what made him choose the rope. Was it the woman? Something as familiar as lost love, or something harder like acknowledging he'd spent his life as a counterfeit prophet, taking from those who already had next to nothing? In the end, it doesn't matter much. Same result. This moment probably should have come for me earlier, so if Victor wants to murder me in front of these cameras, maybe at least it brings about some change. Besides, does anybody care about songs anymore?

The jug is surprisingly light. I'm certain about smelling licorice now. This sets my hands shaking, but I steady, close my eyes and try to fill my mind with a glorious final image. All I can see is Angela, young and wrapped in the sheets from our bed. I tip the jug back.

The water tastes clear. The night air has left it cold. I open my eyes and see Victor smiling. I'm still waiting for the burn. Waiting for my throat to swell and tongue to bloat, for air to be sealed off until I drown on land. Victor bends at the knees to retrieve another jug. I swat at him but slip on the wet asphalt and collapse to a knee. As soon as Victor uncaps this new gallon, I know it's the real thing.

"Don't want any of this on you," he tells me.

Victor drinks deep, starts to raise the receptacle again for another sip and gags. He drops to his knees, clawing his neck as if some invisible hand strangles him. The water spills out as the police move in. One officer fumbles with a handcuff key, trying to get Victor unchained from the parking meter as he shakes. Vomit splatters between Victor's shoes. His face turns red, lips swelling until the membrane of skin looks ready to split. The cop finally unshackles him as Victor collapses on the sidewalk.

Just outside the orbit of this chaos, Rosita steps forward, raises her camera and snaps some quick photos.

EPILOGUE

All I need is a bridge. The E, A, B arrangement came easy, the following chorus erupting as if always hidden inside. What I can't seem to find is a set of chords that brings these two sections together. It could be my environment. Rosita's apartment is spacious but feels unoccupied. The living room is nearly empty. Just a couch where I've been sleeping and a coffee table that's weathered a lot of take-out dinners. In the bedroom, her mattress serves as a workstation. The body-shaped space on the bed is surrounded by books, laptop cords and photo equipment. The desk in the corner remains unused.

I've been a guest for two weeks. After Victor's death, Sheriff Saunders questioned both Rosita and me about our involvement. Once convinced we didn't know anything more about the strange suicidal spectacle, the sheriff dropped Rosita at the first hotel outside the county line and gave her the mountain tradition of a polite warning not to come back. That first night alone after

Victor's death was hard. I haunted the kitchen, unable to face either a guitar or the picture of Angela in my bedroom. Eventually, I took the frame down and sat up all night with a forgotten pack of Rosita's Camels and my acoustic. I wrote the first of six new songs before daylight. Later, the lawyer Rosita helped me find mailed these tracks to Angela with a notice of the suit we'd filed over the wasteland lullabies. She paid for the new tracks without comment. I cashed the check.

It was Rosita that suggested I fly out to New York. Our story was major news after the video of Victor's death went viral. The combination of my lawsuit against Angela for writing credits and the recordings of Victor's death heightened enthusiasm for a possible album. The Troubadours settled out of court and added my name to the writing credits on all re-releases of the previous albums. Even with the exorbitant payment, Rosita still offered to buy my ticket. I think it was her final apology.

She's tried to convince me to rent a place near her, but Brooklyn doesn't appeal to me. No silence, no creeks running behind the house and no chickens to roust you from sleep. Nothing but a constant human noise that drones on even at night. In the end, I've not spent much cash. I might have purchased new shoes but found my father's maroon wingtips in the back of the closet, hidden beneath the dead man's biblical paraphernalia. We buried him in the black patent-leather ones I watched swinging in the trees, but I have some memory of these maroon counterparts. I'm wearing them now. The creased leather radiates warmth as if alive and the heel is equipped with a hidden platform that offers perhaps two extra inches of height. They describe the old man perfectly, false and vain.

What isn't false is the work. Since I watched Victor strangle, I understand how limited time is and what I'm supposed to be doing with mine. In my imperfect, yet temporary mistake of a body, I have a rare perspective. I understand now that all bodies are glorious mistakes.

Only now, the song's bridge still eludes me. I've searched all over the fretboard, down and up octaves, even tried to lower the tuning in the hope of discovering where it's hidden. The melody was so alive in an earlier dream, but the notes evaporated as soon as consciousness hit. In the old days, I'd chase the muse until the idea was treed like a hounded squirrel. Now, I know that even with time always leaking away, it's best to wait. Men like myself are better suited to the slow advance than sprinting after what we want.

And if this song eludes forever, that's fine too. That night at the concert, picking Angela's notes apart provided a sort of epiphany. Broken men are bluesmen by circumstance, forced to mold the catastrophe of their bodies into something artful. It's the dissonance that matters in our lives, the jazz-like improvisation because plans will always crumble. Now, the music doesn't always come easy, but what I finally seize is real.

Rosita returns from her showing before I find the bridge. Stills from *The Body Book* and other photos from Coopersville have been gathering a crowd. The gallery isn't in Manhattan, but it's still a spacious loft tucked into a trendy corner of Brooklyn where most of the uptown wives won't mind traveling. Rosita smiles at me, stands by the bed and removes her earrings. She seems in a hurry to change, the dress purchased for the evening worn like uncomfortable armor. Her legs rub pleasurably together as she strides across the mahogany floor and the satin garment threatens to slide off the single shoulder that holds it across her breasts.

I imagine she's never been more out of her element, but mingled with a smile, shaking the hands of men and women whose approval could change her life. In ways, our lives have already changed.

"How was it?" I ask. I suspect she's disappointed I didn't go, but I was frightened of the art crowd. I didn't want to draw their eyes away from her work. I'm already displayed enough in the photos.

She tells me about the people sipping champagne and pointing out the children photographed next to my well. Just a few states away, but they treat the images as if they've been imported from some distant, war-torn shore. A few took the time to seek out the photo of me on the stoop, or the one where I stand shirtless in the rain. Even I must admit the raw beauty in those prints. Somehow the camera captured the individual drops of rain, the resolution so high that if one observes closely, they can see the precipitation as it collided with my skin the moment the shutter clicked. A barrage explodes across my uneven chest as the water slides down the arch of my back. It follows my crooked lines to the ground as if needing to touch every inch of me before returning to the mud.

"They all asked about it," Rosita says. "I told them that right after I took it, I knew. 'Here is what was always missing,' I told them. Not the body forced to withstand the gaze, but the body in communion with life itself. After that picture, my old canvases might as well be used for kindling."

"Such flattery," I say.

"Don't be too cocky," she said. "There was a man who didn't know you."

"I'm glad." It's been hard being robbed of anonymity.

To still be unaware of my story is difficult. Video of Victor's death received over twelve million hits on YouTube and was replayed by all the major networks. She's a little ashamed by it, but Rosita collects the memes and comments by Internet trolls. One of the most striking she showed me represents the final image of Victor gasping on the wet concrete. This is juxtaposed with a monk participating in self-immolation. Underneath it reads THAT'S HOW YOU FUCKING PROTEST. A different version we saw days ago reads, THAT'S HOW YOU FUCKING PARTY. She said it made her sad to see everything reduced to a punch line. I think Coopersville probably does owe the man for the recent inquiries into the safety of their drinking water.

"All night people came up and congratulated me as if I was an explorer from antiquity," she says and sits on the bed beside me. "Like I survived an isolated winter in the Arctic instead of heading a few states south."

She reaches out and silences my strumming hand.

"I kept pointing to the picture of you on the porch steps."

I hate that photo. Sitting clothed in shadows, cane resting by my knee like a sorcerer's wand whose magic has been extinguished.

"I'd tell them, 'These are the ones worth buying,'" she says.

I can't tell her about my fear of being a spectacle, so I bend the strings into an exaggerated whine.

Rosita grins, steps into the bathroom where I hear her changing clothes. She leaves the door open. I realize it could be perceived as an invitation. There have been other less ambiguous moments between us since I arrived. I'm not ready yet, but she's been patient about my fear. We just need a little more time. I can't treat her the way I did Angela. She needs to be an equal partner. Not a conduit for my salvation or the only thing that gives me worth. That wouldn't be fair to either of us. I play until she emerges dressed similar to the day I met her. Black jeans and a Black Flag T-shirt. Rosita grabs her folded leather jacket from the chair in the corner.

"What do you say we go for a stroll?" she asks.

The sound of the city is immense. A blur of conversation and machinery that never stops running whether it's the cars idling at the intersection or the trains rolling underneath our feet. Rosita tells me it's impossible, but I claim to feel the vibrations in my bones. It's as present as the coal trains back home that shook nearby trees, their whistle breaking the silence of country night.

We grab coffee in a diner a block from her apartment. The patrons quiet down for just a moment as we take a booth by the window. A young man nearby is boasting. He stands beside the table to better illustrate his story for a cackling couple and the single girl whose hoop earrings flash as she shakes her head at him.

The coffee is dark and strong. I taste something metallic in the consistency, but not a single drink has tasted right since Victor's death.

"Are you nervous about the show tonight?" Rosita asks.

Three hours from now, I'll play in a bar for maybe a hundred people. I shrug and stir cream into my coffee, intent on making it taste like dessert. All this time hoping to make it this far and I still feel unsatisfied. I thought some critical success would carve out the doubts. Now, I don't know what it would take to satisfy me, but maybe that hunger is the point. Maybe satisfaction is just stasis.

"It'll be okay," I say.

I take Rosita's hand. I haven't said it all. Perhaps whatever it is can't be said, but I can live with that. Accepting that is what's important. Sporadic moments of grace rather than completion.

"Do you wanna stay a while longer?" Rosita asks. "Maybe you shouldn't travel until this new song is finished?"

It's Thursday. We both know I have nowhere else to go.

"Yeah, I'd like that."

Across the street, a young girl with a violin stands on the corner, the case open at her feet as she lays the bow on the strings. I expect something classical, a sonata or piece from a symphony. Instead, the girl fires into lively fiddle work that comes out high and lonesome. The strings whine in glorious agony as her fingers tear up them. Her boot heel stomps out the rhythm. She sways with the music, bends a little curtsy at a couple passing by who drop some money in her case.

"Listen to that," Rosita says. She rubs small circles in the palm of my hand, her nails dragging across the lines where some other woman might be able to read my fate.

I'm listening. The music is speaking directly to me, whispering through the pane glass as if she plays just for us, reminding me of each individual's duty to contribute a verse.

ACKNOWLEDGMENTS

While a writer's work begins in solitude, the process of bringing a book into the world takes the combined effort of many people. The following is a list of those who helped make this book a reality.

First, many thanks to the teachers, mentors and fellow writers I've been fortunate enough to have support my work over the years: Jonis Agee, Joy Castro, Sean Doolittle, Smith Henderson, Ted Kooser, John Van Kirk, Rachel and Joel Peckham, Ron Rash, Timothy Schaffert, Bradford Tatum, Anthony Viola and Stacey Waite. Your support let me keep hopeful in dark times.

Thank you to my fabulous editor, Sara Minnich, for her belief in the book and sharing a vision for the story. My gratitude to her, Patricja Okuniewska and everyone else at G. P. Putnam's Sons and Penguin Random House.

I'd like to thank my agent, Noah Ballard, who is the best advocate, reader and friend someone in this business could have.

ACKNOWLEDGMENTS

He and everyone at Curtis Brown, Ltd., have made me feel like family.

Thank you to those writer friends who've been early readers or workshop companions in the past such as: Belinda Acosta, Megan Gannon, Gabriel Houck, Bernice Olivas, Raul Palma, Casey Pycior, Christine Harding Thornton and Nick White.

For my family and friends, I can't thank you enough for the endless love and dedication. Often, I believed because you kept believing in me. I'll keep trying to live up to the important responsibility of making you proud.